# SUPREME JUSTICE

# SUPREME JUSTICE

A THRILLER BY

## MAX ALLAN COLLINS

THOMAS & MERCER

Text copyright © 2014 Max Allan Collins
All rights reserved.

Published by Thomas & Mercer, Seattle

www.apub.com

ISBN-13: 9781612185309
ISBN-10: 1612185304

Cover design by Jason Gurley

Library of Congress Control Number: 2013920856

Printed in the United States of America

I wish to acknowledge my frequent collaborator,
**Matthew V. Clemens,**
for coplotting,
forensics (and other) research,
and the preparation of a story treatment
from which I could develop this novel.

—M. A. C.

*For Jacque—*
*always on the author's team*

# SUPREME JUSTICE

"Presidents come and go,
but the Supreme Court goes on forever."

*William Howard Taft,*
*Twenty-Seventh President of the United States of America,*
*Tenth Chief Justice of the Supreme Court.*
*Section 30, Grave S-14, Grid Y/Z-39/40,*
*Arlington National Cemetery.*

# ONE

In less than an hour, Nicholas Blount would be staring into the infinite blackness of a Glock barrel.

But right now, at the end of another typically long and tedious day as a Supreme Court law clerk, Nicky seemed almost to bounce across the well-appointed outer office of Associate Justice Henry Venter.

If you didn't have endless energy, best not to clerk at the top court in the country—especially if you were working for this notoriously conservative, famously hardworking African American justice.

Six foot two, with a bland blond handsomeness counteracted by piercing hazel eyes, the youngest son of Senator Wilson Blount of Tennessee was well aware he'd not risen to this elevated position due to personal achievement, though on paper he was as qualified as anyone here. Nonetheless, his posting was strictly a matter of privilege, nothing more, nothing less—the Blounts had been wealthy, and politically connected, since before the Civil War.

Then why, to the rednecks back home, did the Blount men maintain their good-ol'-boy standing? Simple—the Senator talked only about guns, God, and America. Like the two Blount senators before him.

Granted, the Democrats had won the last presidential election, but after twelve years of having things their own way, the Republicans knew a pendulum swing would come, and now that it had, the idea was to swing that sucker back as soon as possible. Thanks to two-term neocon President Gregory Watson Bennett, the GOP still controlled the Supreme Court. But then the sure-thing next prez— Vice President Michael Hasten—had been upset by the African American Democrat Devlin Harrison, and all bets were off.

Harrison had been a hell of a campaigner—with a name that close to *devil*, he'd had to be. On the other hand, a guy with the middle name *Hussein* had managed it, not that long ago . . .

Another black man in the White House was not enough to take the grin off Nicky Blount's well-tanned face. The conservative Supreme Court had already made numerous inroads, not the least of which was finally overturning that disastrous Roe v. Wade decision. The next election would surely see the Grand Old Party taking back political control of the other two branches of government.

Nicky's older brother, Governor Nathaniel Blount of Mississippi, was odds-on favorite for top of the ticket next time. They would wangle a moderate, Gilson of Indiana or maybe Kelly from Pennsylvania, to appeal to northerners. Then, once Nathaniel was elected, Nicky would move in next to him, as attorney general.

What the hell—it had worked for those damn Kennedys.

Some in the GOP thought the Blount boys too inexperienced for high national office, but Nathaniel was only the fourth Republican governor in Mississippi since 1876, a feat not easily shrugged off by the old guard of the party. Nathaniel would be forty-three, the same age as JFK, when he got elected two years from now. Nicky would be thirty-six (about the same age as Bobby K. had been), and as for experience—wasn't he clerking for Associate Justice Venter?

Nicky glanced into the AJ's office. There sat the man himself, leaned over in his tufted-back chair, tiny reading glasses perched on his nose, a green-shaded banker's lamp on the corner of the massive mahogany desk providing just enough light to view the brief before him. Bull-necked with graying hair, Venter had played football at the University of Missouri, though keeping in shape had never been a priority. Still, soft around the middle though he might be, Venter was fairly fit for seventy.

"Mr. Blount," came the resonant rumble from within the office, "you're hovering again." The man hadn't as much as glanced up.

*How did he do that?*

Nicky froze.

And the deep voice continued: "Is there something I can do for you, Mr. Blount?"

"Uh, no, sir," Nicky said, flushing. Why did he always feel that Venter considered him an idiot? "It was just the opposite."

Now Venter looked up, a crease between his brows. "Oh?"

"I mean, I was just wondering if *you* needed anything."

Venter took off his glasses and rotated his neck. "I'm fine," the Justice said. "I think it's about time we called it a day."

*About time is right,* Nicky thought.

The AJ might have been past the average man's retirement age, but his work ethic showed no sign of flagging. The judge was still the first one in and, generally, the last one out. At just after seven, stopping now would make a twelve-hour day, but Nicky knew all too well that Venter routinely worked an hour or two—or more—beyond that.

"Should I call Hudson?" Nicky asked, referring to the Justice's driver, a retired bailiff.

Venter rested his glasses on the desk, then wiped two meaty paws over his face before answering. The man sighed. Actually sighed. "Do you have time for a drink, Mr. Blount?"

*Was that a trick question?*

The AJ had never shared a coffee with Nicky much less a meal during the six months that Nicky had been here—six months during which Nicky had never felt more than a glorified gopher.

"Of course, sir," Nicky managed.

"Call Hudson. Tell him we'll be down in ten minutes."

"Yes, sir."

Within half an hour, Nicky was sitting across from Venter at a table in the bar of the Verdict Chophouse, a restaurant frequented by the judiciary and its top staffers. Nicky was used to being in the same room with the most powerful men in the country—after all, his father was a senator and his brother a governor—but the patrons of this restaurant were enough to give a cable news anchor whiplash. One former Cabinet member, a former Supreme Court Justice, the current Director of the CIA, and two CEOs of major financial institutions . . . and that was just one table.

The bar was all dark wood and linen tablecloths (meals could be ordered here), with a formal service staff as alert as first responders. Tradition oozed from the walls of the Verdict, which had served its first customer during the administration of Teddy Roosevelt and had been a DC staple ever since. Oil paintings of past justices were spotted around with tiny gold identifying plaques. Venter and his aide were seated at a table for four off to the side, near a fire exit.

Justice Venter had ordered a Scotch on the rocks, and Nicky was allowing himself a martini, but only one.

"You have been chafing, Mr. Blount," his boss said, the man's voice hushed, his tone friendly, but resonant enough that Nicky did not feel relaxed—all the martinis in DC couldn't have done that.

"I'm not sure I follow, sir."

"You feel underutilized in your position."

It was not a question, yet Nicky wondered if he should answer as if it were. The statement rang true, of course. Of the four clerks working for Justice Venter, Nicky came from the most politically powerful family, had the best scholastic record, and had outshone the others at every opportunity. Yet Venter had always seemed to favor them over him.

Against his better judgment, Nicky said, "I guess I do, sir. Feel underutilized."

"I don't think there's any guesswork involved." Venter gave him a rare hint of a smile. "You're under the misapprehension that I dislike you."

Emboldened by this honest exchange, Nicky said, "That's a little strong, sir. I would say . . . I suspect you don't particularly care for me."

"I'm sure that's an accurate assessment of your own feelings, Mr. Blount." He shrugged the big shoulders. "But I assure you it's a misrepresentation of *mine.*"

"How so, sir?"

The hint of a smile blossomed into a grin—a goddamned grin. But was it friendly? Or sinister?

The Justice said, "Clerks at the Court come and go, Mr. Blount. Some will go on to great things—most will not."

"Yes, sir."

"You, Mr. Blount—you, I believe, can do great things."

Nicky frowned, not sure he'd heard right. The AJ might have slapped him. "Thank you, sir . . . ?"

A cough of a laugh seemed prompted by the unsureness of Nicky's response.

"You're welcome, Mr. Blount. Perhaps now you'll understand why I've assigned my other clerks to write up the summaries of the certiorari petitions thus far."

But Nicky didn't understand. If he was the best of the clerks, why were the others getting the summaries?

The certiorari petitions were the documents filed to request that the Court review a case. A well-written summary of the cert was often the first step in getting the case before the Court. Likewise, a poorly written one, even on what could be a major issue, could mean certain death for said petition.

Reading Nicky's confusion, Venter smiled again, and this time there was no way to read it as anything but sincere. "I've been saving you, Mr. Blount. To use a sports analogy . . . you are going to be my cleanup hitter."

"Sir, I . . ."

"Just listen. There is a certiorari petition coming in on a case I want to make sure the Court hears. Your summary, Mr. Blount, will be the first volley. Now do you understand?"

"Yes, sir, thank you, sir," Nicky said. He sat forward. "If I might ask, what is the case?"

"Illinois v. Meachem—you know it?"

Nodding, Nicky said, "Yes, sir."

"Do you mind *demonstrating* that you know it?"

"Yes. That is, no. The State of Illinois arrested Laverne Meachem under the state's eavesdropping statute because he used a cell phone to take footage of three officers who were beating up his brother."

"Yes," Venter said. "Thoughts?"

Two ski-masked men in black burst past the maître d' and into the bar. The smaller of the two brandished a 9-millimeter pistol while the bigger one clutched an AK-47.

Both Nicky's and Venter's mouths hung open in interrupted conversation turned to shock.

The larger of the intruders shouted, *"Ladies and gentlemen, this is a robbery! Hands where we can see them! Get frisky and die— understood?"*

No one answered, but most hands went up or at least rested on tables as the 9-millimeter-wielding, smaller figure moved deeper into the room, withdrawing with his free hand a plastic garbage bag from somewhere and shaking it open.

In a harsh, high voice, he yelled, *"Wallets, jewelry, and cell phones!"* He began at the bar, with the patron nearest him.

Fear spread through Nicky's body like sudden flu, and just as abruptly his bladder seemed at bursting. Until those men exploded into the bar, he hadn't even known he had to go. Now the discomfort was unimaginable.

The man with the pistol moved around the horseshoe-shaped counter collecting wallets and other valuables from customers. His partner's eyes roamed the room, searching for any hero who might try to break up the robbery or call 911 before a cell had been confiscated.

Nicky's own cell felt like a brick clipped on his belt. He would not be the hero. He would not die in some stupid damn bar robbery and never be attorney general, never follow his brother into even higher office. He resolved right then, for the good of the nation, he would not do anything stupid.

Under his breath, Venter said, "Now is not the time to do anything rash, Mr. Blount."

*No shit,* he thought, but did not share this response with this Associate Justice of the Supreme Court. He merely nodded, which was all he could manage, busy as he was doing battle with his bladder.

The holdup man with the garbage bag and the big pistol now moved closer to Nicky and Justice Venter, collecting more items as he hopped from table to table.

Nicky risked a look at the bigger man, whose eyes slow-scanned the room like a prison tower guard, ready to use the AK-47 he held at port arms.

When Nicky turned back, the shorter one stood before him, as if he'd materialized, and Nicky found himself staring down the barrel of the Glock into that endless black hole. Again, his bladder screamed.

"Stop stalling, haircut," the holdup man said, the barrel of the Glock inching toward Nicky's face.

"I . . . I . . ." was all Nicky got out.

*"Do it!"*

Nicky reached slowly to his belt to remove his cell phone, fumbling a little. From the corner of an eye, he saw Venter start to rise.

*What was Venter doing? Trying to stop this?*

Nicky wanted to shout "No!" but the word caught in his throat. The Glock swung away from Nicky's face, toward Venter, who was on his feet now. The gun barrel belched flame, and its explosion brought Nicky momentary deafness followed by intense ringing.

A pink mist lingered between him and the falling Associate Justice, and blood and brain matter splattered the nearby fire exit. Several patrons were screaming, a woman and a man or two, in terrible nonharmony that got cut off by an automatic burst from the AK— into the ceiling, not the patrons.

The weapon's owner yelled to his partner, "*Let's book!*"

The shorter holdup man glared at Nicky, who knew, if he survived this, he would never forget the ice-blue eyes behind the ski mask. Then the barrel of the Glock filled his field of vision again.

The young man with the assured political future prepared himself to die, saying a silent prayer, but the shot didn't come.

The holdup man said, "The nigger didn't have to die. You *hesitated*, asshole. It's on *you!*"

Then the holdup man hit Nicky across the face with the pistol, the gunsight tearing his cheek, his bladder releasing, even as his vision was filled with a mini Fourth of July sky works accompanied by shooting pain that seemed to engage every nerve ending in his body.

Chairs tipped over and patrons yelped as the thieves ran like hell out the front.

Nicky lay there, breathing hard, the warmth where he'd pissed himself strangely comforting. But he had to turn away from the vacant-eyed stare of Associate Justice Henry Venter, who had, before getting shot in the forehead, finally acknowledged his aide's potential.

"I always turn to the sports page first,
which records people's accomplishments.
The front page has nothing but man's failures."

*Earl Warren,*
*Thirtieth Governor of the State of California,*
*Fourteenth Chief Justice of the Supreme Court.*
*Section 21, Lot S-32, Grid M-20.5,*
*Arlington National Cemetery.*

# TWO

Though patient by nature, Joseph Reeder only truly found peace in one place: Arlington National Cemetery. Strolling those gently rolling grounds, among heroes and patriots, he found a tranquility unavailable to him anywhere else on the planet. Of course, the serenity provided by the endless white markers would be eclipsed in another hour or so—at 8:00 a.m., the cemetery opened to visitors.

Reeder was a member of a very exclusive club: a Secret Service agent—in Reeder's case, *former* agent—who had taken a bullet for a president of the United States. This granted him, and others like him, special dispensation to wander the grounds at any time that suited him. Those times were mostly very early in the morning, well before others were allowed in.

A shade over six foot tall, five years north of forty, Reeder still had the anonymous look of a Secret Service agent: fit, with regular features that split the difference between rugged and handsome, his dark brown eyes behind sunglasses on this already bright morning.

His most distinctive feature was his short-cropped white hair, which included his eyebrows; he'd gone white before his thirtieth birthday, a family trait, and had colored it during his agent days, not out of vanity but to blend in better. No need for that now.

The quiet, the calm, wasn't Reeder's only motivation to visit Arlington. These early mornings also helped him work off the extra ten pounds he carried now that fieldwork was behind him. Or at least that was the idea.

Wearing jeans and a red Washington Nationals windbreaker, cell phone clipped to his belt, Reeder might have been any other tourist. Of course, there were no tourists here yet, and he might have been a ghost haunting the place. Maybe he was. Maybe that was why he felt so much at home here.

As he ambled through ANC, he seemed to sense the souls of the dead walking with him. Fellow ghosts, perhaps. Anyway, they sure as hell didn't haunt him. They only added to the serenity. Around him, at rest, were men and women who had made a difference— many had given their lives simply in defense of a vague ideal, while others had a more solid intellectual grasp on what had led them into government service. Either way, Reeder appreciated every one of them and relished their company.

As he often did, Reeder—on this brisk April morning, the sun slowly climbing in an almost painfully blue sky—found himself in front of the grave of John F. Kennedy. Not a perfect man, but a great one nonetheless, and a hero.

Most visitors had been taught in school about that day in Dallas. They rightly thought of the assassination as a tragedy, the day America lost its innocence, sixty-some years ago. Although Reeder shared those feelings, the tragedy for him involved Clint Hill as well, the Secret Service agent who ran from the limo behind Kennedy's to jump aboard the President's vehicle and help reel Jackie back into the car when she crawled onto the trunk lid to retrieve a piece of her husband's skull.

Hill, a decorated agent who finally retired in 1975 (a decade before Reeder's birth), had always been haunted by not making it to Kennedy's car in time to take the third shot himself.

When his turn to take a shot came, Reeder was there, saving President Gregory Bennett, but he well understood Hill's frustration.

President Bennett had been shaking hands, pressing the flesh, in the town of Burke, Virginia, on a day not unlike this one, when Reeder saw something. To this day, he didn't know for sure exactly what tipped him: a narrowing of the eyes perhaps, a subtle shift in body language—*something*—but a millisecond before he saw the shooter raise his pistol, Reeder moved. The only reaction he had time for was to dive in front of the President, taking the bullet. It clipped his Kevlar vest, burrowed into his shoulder, shattered his collarbone, ricocheted, and tore through his rotator cuff.

Two agents took down the shooter before he could fire again, while others hustled President Bennett into his bulletproof limousine and to the safety of the White House.

Reeder ended up at Inova Fairfax Hospital, where surgeons did their utmost to repair the mess that was his shoulder. Weeks of recuperation and physical therapy followed. By leaving him in the hospital, the Service's hope had been to somewhat derail the media frenzy, at least.

It hadn't worked.

So many reporters were on hand when he was released, the hospital nearly had to shut down.

Looking at President Kennedy's grave, Reeder knew that *without question* had he acted a nanosecond later, he would have entered the same living hell as Clint Hill. Instead, Reeder had saved a president.

As it happened, a president he despised, a leader of the Free World who stood against everything that Reeder believed in. That had meant a different sort of hell for him than Hill's, but like Hill he had done his best. Even been decorated for it.

Like everybody else here in Arlington, though, medals didn't mean shit to Joe Reeder. Particularly *that* medal . . .

What had he gotten out of it, really? The satisfaction of doing his job? A shoulder that predicted precipitation better than the Weather Channel? The reality that the near martyr President Bennett had been sent swaggering into a second term?

Besides serving as his personal weather vane, that balky shoulder had relegated Reeder to a desk job. This he tolerated for only a month before putting his papers in and retiring on disability. Or anyway, that had been the official reason.

For almost four years, liberal-minded Reeder had stood in the background like any good agent, watching mutely as Bennett and his neocon cronies subverted, and sometimes just flat-out ignored, the Constitution of the United States.

Reeder did not hate Republicans. His father had been a Republican, and a conservative in the best sense of the word. He and his dad would argue themselves blue in the face, but it was always good-natured and he could see where his dad was coming from. Small government, states' rights, balanced budget.

But he knew deep in his DNA that his fair-minded pop would have hated these excuses for real Republicans.

Even though policy dictated that Secret Service agents be apolitical, Reeder finally could not stomach it anymore, and he had quit. His wound, and the desk job, had simply provided a convenient cover. Still, his resignation had been step one in his becoming a pariah among most federal law enforcement personnel.

Though a hero—and a hero who had saved the President of the United States at that—Reeder had broken the unwritten rule. He had unwisely shared his real reason for leaving with several fellow agents, including his immediate superior. The political basis for Reeder quitting spread like a cancer throughout the Service and eventually all of federal law enforcement.

Finally, the *Washington Post* had written a story for which he had declined to comment—in the eyes of many, an admission of guilt . . .

If there were a Hall of Fame for the Secret Service, Joe Reeder would forever be its Pete Rose—he had accomplished great things, but would spend eternity on the outside.

The cell on his belt vibrated, and forced by some inner sense of courtesy, he turned away and withdrew a few steps from Kennedy's grave before answering.

"Reeder," he said, keeping his voice low.

"Peep. Glad I caught you." The familiar voice belonged to Carl Bishop, a DC homicide detective Reeder had known for the better part of two decades.

The nickname *Peep* had been bestowed on him by his fellow Secret Service agents for his storied ability to read people. The more Reeder discouraged its use, the more it had kept up, until the appellation stuck. Now it seemed everyone called him Peep except his eighteen-year-old daughter, Amy. And his ex-wife, Melanie, when she called him anything at all.

"What's up?" Reeder asked.

"Seen the morning papers?"

"Not yet. Besides, you know all I read is the sports."

Without preamble, Bishop said, "Henry Venter was shot and killed last night."

"Jesus. Where?"

"Verdict Chophouse."

Reeder took a few more steps from Kennedy's grave as he tried to process the detective's news. He stopped before a Japanese flowering crabapple tree surrounded by an army of pink tulips and pale yellow daffodils. A more peaceful setting would be hard to imagine, but right now Reeder's serenity was as shot to hell as his shoulder.

"Venter murdered," Reeder muttered. Then, strong: "Do we know why? Who?"

"Hell," Bishop said. "I forgot. You *knew* the man, didn't you?"

"I knew him."

"Oh, shit, Peep, I'm sorry to blindside you like that."

"Forget it, Bish. We weren't pals."

For all his liberal leanings, Reeder considered himself a middle-of-the-road Democrat. The ultraconservative Venter, he considered a borderline fascist. Venter had voted to uphold laws that expanded the Patriot Act and gave law enforcement a no-knock policy so lenient that it allowed the government, from the local police on up, to enter any citizen's dwelling at any time.

Venter also voted to uphold laws that allowed religious relics on public grounds, sanctioned prayer in school, and advocated the teaching of creationism. He even authored the majority opinion when the Court upheld new legislation resurrecting the Sedition Act of 1798. Congress's intention had been to make a law banning flag burning. What they ended up with was a law that made it legal to arrest anyone for speaking, writing, or publishing anything against the government of the United States.

Venter's kind of despotic conservatism would have disgusted Reeder's late father, who bragged that his first vote for president had been Ronald Reagan.

"How did it go down?" Reeder asked. "Shot going in or coming out, I'd guess."

"You'd guess wrong. Right at his table, having a drink with one of his clerks—Senator Wilson Blount's son Nicholas."

*A callow waste of skin*, Reeder thought.

"Two armed holdup men came in and terrorized the place," Bishop was saying, "and evidently Venter went after one of them. Got shot to death for his trouble. TV news crews are proclaiming Venter a hero. He'll be James Bond by the end of the news cycle."

Reeder knew how the media worked and that his friend was right—Venter would wind up canonized. "So why call me about it?"

"ABC handles security for the Verdict, right?"

ABC Security was Reeder's company. The ABC didn't stand for anything, other than "easy as."

"Yeah, they're a client," Reeder said with a shrug in his voice.

"Well, you got eyes that see shit other people's eyes don't, or can't. Help out a poor DC homicide cop, why don't you, and take a look at your own security video."

Reeder's Secret Service–schooled ability to read people, as well as his expertise in the field of kinesics—the science of facial expressions and body language—was well known. It made a major selling point for his firm—a good deal of his income came from consulting with law enforcement agencies nationwide.

Reeder sighed. "Where is it?"

"I'm sending a copy to your e-mail."

"Why isn't the FBI handling this?"

He could almost hear Bishop grimace.

"They are, or will be," the cop said. "But right now DC Homicide has it. Joint task force is coming together, or will be before the end of the day."

"Lucky you."

"Peep, I just want to get out ahead of this while we're still in charge. By lunch, hell, by nine-*thirty*, we'll be warming the bench in this game. The Feds'll march in here, tell us they're going to cooperate, then I won't see any of them until the press conference where they announce they caught the killers. I'd like to for once have half a shot at beating them to the punch. You going to help me out or not? I still have pics of you drunk at our Christmas party three years ago, y'know."

Smirking to himself, Reeder considered the request. Normally, he would gladly help his friend, but knowing that the FBI, and every other agency in the federal alphabet soup, would be on this made him hesitate. Nobody in that world had anything to say to him, except maybe "Who farted?" when he entered the room.

If he was going to assist Bishop, Reeder needed to get right on it.

"Okay, Bish. I'll get to the office as soon as I can, then I'll give you a call."

"You are a god among men," Bishop said.

"That's what my mother always said."

"I would never contradict a man's mother."

Quick good-byes, and they clicked off.

Reeder made the short commute from Arlington to his company's headquarters in Georgetown in under half an hour. His casual attire surprised no one, since he avoided suit-and-tie unless he had business appointments. He grabbed a cup of coffee from the break room, spoke briefly with Janine (his assistant), then shut himself in his private office.

For the CEO of a high-profile security company, Reeder boasted a surprisingly modest work space. His oak desk sat toward the back, two client chairs in front of it, a large window behind it. One wall was consumed by bookshelves filled with everything from manuals to studies to paperback novels, with trophy-style awards serving as decorative bookends.

The opposite wall held a fifty-inch video monitor, currently off, bordered by citations and plaques ABC had earned for helping law enforcement in communities all around the US, but chiefly on the East Coast.

Conspicuous in their absence were any signs of Reeder's Secret Service career, with the exception of a single framed *Time* magazine cover with the famous photograph of the agent taking a bullet for the president he despised. Reeder had been pressured to display it because prospective clients needed the reminder of just whose services they were enlisting. He had positioned it on the wall where he couldn't see the goddamn thing from his desk.

Sunlight flooded through the window, and he hit a wall switch, activating a motorized curtain that slowly drew the room to darkness. Muted overhead lights came on as Reeder dropped into his oversize tufted-leather desk chair, the one real indulgence he allowed himself at work.

He booted his computer, then opened his e-mail and loaded the video Bishop had sent. Pushing a button, he got the image up on the wall monitor. He watched the holdup men enter and go into their routine; he fast-forwarded until he saw Venter fall. Then he backed up the footage to watch from a couple minutes before the perps entered.

The view from the rear faced the bar. Venter and his clerk, Blount, were at the far left of the frame, other tables of customers nearby. He couldn't zoom in to get a better view of the pair, but even from this wide perspective, it was clear that, despite the social setting, the Associate Justice and his clerk were having a serious if cordial talk.

Paying no attention to the others in the room, Reeder concentrated on the two men. Venter reacted first, eyes widening to look toward the bar, followed by his clerk's head turning—the younger man sitting with his back nearly to the intruders.

Though concentrating on Venter and Blount, Reeder remained aware that the other diners were reacting, as well. One nearby customer stood, then—on what was probably an order from one of the robbers—sat immediately back down.

Despite the lack of sound, Reeder could tell exactly what was going on. The thieves were doing all the talking, the gist of what they were saying easily discerned.

Slowly, the holdup man with the pistol made his way around the bar collecting valuables from the customers, working inexorably toward Venter and Blount.

As the holdup man approached, Blount was looking back at the other perp. When the kid turned, the pistol was aimed between his eyes, the young clerk's terror obvious. As Blount fumbled for his wallet or maybe his cell, Venter rose, but before the judge got fully to his feet, the gunman swiveled, set his feet, and fired. Justice Venter went down, the room erupted in panic, and the shooter paused to pistol-whip Blount, knocking the clerk to the floor. Then the two gunmen exited the way they'd come in.

Bishop had tagged footage from an outside camera onto the tail of the clip, showing the ski-masked intruders sprint out and climb into a black SUV parked at the curb, front and back seat. The driver could not be seen, the SUV's windows tinted. Then the vehicle eased away as nonchalantly as if those within had just enjoyed a good meal at the famed Verdict. No view of the license plates.

Reeder watched the security footage at regular speed several more times. Then he slowed it down, going frame by frame, starting from Blount seeing the pistol in his face through where Venter rose. Venter's hips were turning slightly to the left, toward the fire door, *not* the gunman.

*The Associate Justice was rising not to attack, but to make a break for it.*

Reeder stopped the video, reran it, then watched the Justice again. Based on Venter's expression, his overall body language, Reeder had no doubt: *Venter was trying to save his ass, not his clerk.*

The judge had panicked, and was going for that fire exit.

The next time he watched, Reeder concentrated on the shooter. As the man turned and blasted Venter, he was calm, not panicky, and took time to set his feet and aim. Hell, the shooter even slowly exhaled before he fired. This wasn't a stickup artist reacting to movement, freaking, and shooting.

No.

Reeder knew with deadly certainty that he wasn't watching a robbery at all; he was witnessing a cold-blooded execution. He shook his head in disbelief.

The urge was to call Bishop right away, but he made himself take a step or two back. He watched three more times, and the longer he studied the video, the more he realized that he'd been right from the start.

Last night, at the Verdict Chophouse, a sitting Supreme Court justice had been assassinated.

"There is no friend like an old friend,
who has shared your morning days,
no greeting like his welcome,
no homage like his praise."

*Oliver Wendell Holmes,*
*Associate Justice of the Supreme Court.*
*Section 5, Grave 7004,*
*Arlington National Cemetery.*

# THREE

When he called Bishop's cell, Reeder got relegated to the homicide detective's voice mail. No way he was leaving this kind of message. He phoned the precinct, was told Bishop was unavailable, and left word for the detective to call him ASAP.

But as the time neared to meet his daughter for dinner, Reeder had still heard nothing from the DC cop.

When caller ID finally flashed Bishop's number, Reeder jumped on it.

"Where the hell have you been?" Reeder asked.

"Serving and protecting," Bishop said, with barely any sarcasm.

"Don't give me a high-priority errand and then go out of pocket."

"You are such a pleasure to know, Peep. Look, the Feds are here, and they've already 'cooperated' our asses into following them around like beaten puppies."

Not quite under his breath, Reeder said, "Shit."

"Shit indeed. Do you have something that could get me back in the game?"

Obviously he did, but should he share his take on Venter in the security footage now that the FBI would be on the receiving end? Anybody from the Bureau who knew him from White House days still viewed him as a selfish prick, even a traitor. And many agents considered kinesics smoke-and-mirrors bullshit.

But he knew he was right, and if he didn't share that knowledge, the FBI would come out of the gate on the wrong track—searching for armed robbers was a far different task than searching for professional assassins.

"You still there?" Bishop asked, at last.

"Oh yeah," Reeder said.

"Okay, then, Mr. Hot to Fuckin' Trot. What did you see on that security video that mere humans might miss?"

". . . You may not want to mention where you got this."

"Got *what*?"

"It wasn't a robbery."

"How could it *not* be a robbery?" Bishop demanded. "Nearly everyone in the place got cleaned out. That is by *definition*—"

"It wasn't *just* a robbery. I think the holdup was a blind."

"For what?"

Nothing to do but to dive right in. "Henry Venter," Reeder said, "was the target."

"Of the robbery?"

"Of an assassination."

Phone-static silence separated them like an electrified fence.

Finally, Bishop managed, "You mean . . . they took the place down just to get to Venter. To make a hit seem like collateral damage."

"Why aren't you chief, with a mind like that?"

"Screw you, Peep. Can you prove this?"

"It's an opinion."

"An informed opinion. An educated goddamn opinion from an expert who—"

"Who nobody in federal law enforcement would piss on if he were on fire."

The electricity-charged silence was back.

"But you are an expert in the field," Bishop granted, "and former Secret Service. Is what you saw enough for me to kick this to the Special Agent in Charge?"

"It's a risk. If your SAIC is somebody who has me on his shit list, my opinion may send him in the robbery direction out of sheer spite."

"Well, maybe we drew a lucky card this time. The SAIC is Gabe Sloan. Don't you two go back a ways?"

That they did. In fact, if Reeder had one friend in the FBI, it was Gabriel Sloan.

A relieved Reeder said, "Better lucky than smart. Absolutely you can tell Gabe. He believes in me, and he believes in kinesics."

"And fairies and Santa Claus?"

"What great man was it who said, 'Screw you, buddy, and the horse you rode in on'?"

Bishop laughed. "Seriously, Peep, I appreciate this."

They said good-bye and clicked off.

Checking his watch, Reeder realized he had just enough time to make his dinner with Amy.

Wedged between a tiny dress shop and a BB&T Bank branch, DC Subs on Wisconsin Avenue Northwest was bigger than Reeder's office, but not by much. Standing just outside the restaurant, waiting for his daughter, Reeder reflected on Amy's birthday in a few days, and he still had no damn idea what to get her.

He spotted her not quite a block away, coming from the direction of Georgetown University, where she was a freshman. Amy might as well have been her mother, a million years ago. Same brown hair, worn long like Melanie's when she and Reeder first met. His nineteen-year-old daughter had her mom's tall, slender frame, as well, wrapped up in a navy Georgetown sweatshirt with bulldog mascot, jeans, and running shoes.

On her arm, goddamnit, was Bobby Landon.

Reeder made his grimace turn into a smile as the couple approached.

A twenty-year-old sophomore with dark hair nearly as long as Amy's, Landon had been dating her since last October. He wore jeans, sneakers, and a T-shirt for some apparent band under an unzipped hoodie with the Georgetown seal.

Like most kids that age, Landon knew everything already. His save-the-world, far-left brand of progressive liberalism was already creeping into Amy's conversations with her dad. Several past conversations with Amy and her boyfriend had devolved into near shouting matches.

In Landon's eyes, Reeder was the worst kind of liberal—a middle-of-the-road Clinton type. And in Reeder's eyes, Landon was a naive joke. This kid thought that by taking all the guns and dumping them in the Grand Canyon or something, you could end gun violence. Sure, and if you just buried all nuclear weapons at the bottom of the ocean, the threat of nuclear war would disappear, right?

Never mind that the technology was, hell, everywhere. Any asshole with a Wi-Fi connection could learn how to make a plastic gun, a dirty bomb—anything a twisted brain could come up with. Recent history was pockmarked with the reality of that.

Shaking away such thoughts, Reeder kept smiling, nodding as they neared.

Breaking away from her date, Amy came up, gave her dad a hug, and planted a tiny kiss on his cheek. "Dad, you don't mind Bobby tagging along . . . ?"

He minded, all right, but said, "Not at all. A pleasure."

Reeder nodded toward the young man, who managed a nod and a "Hey, Mr. Reeder" in return.

The sub shop was, as usual, crowded, but they soon had their sandwiches, Reeder paying the bill—you'd think Landon could have at least offered, but then far lefties never paid for anything, did they? Then they managed to find a table in a corner.

Reeder asked his daughter how her classes were going.

Landon was absorbed in his veggie sandwich, aware that the father-daughter conversation didn't include him.

Amy shrugged. "Not bad. Okay."

"How long till finals?"

"Started yesterday."

"Ready for 'em?"

She just looked at him.

Amy had been a straight-A student since birth. Such scholastic-oriented questions Reeder needed never to ask. But he was her father, and always did.

With school matters covered, Reeder had no idea what to say to his only child. The apartment he'd set her up in near campus was not a good point of conversation. She had rather blatantly manipulated him into pressuring her mother to let her live off campus, alone.

If only. Che Guevara here was probably sleeping over most nights, something Reeder didn't want to think about, much less inquire over, and every time he brought up the apartment, Amy thought he was trying to control her with it, since Daddy paid the rent.

Anyway, that's how she'd reacted when he'd moved to George-town, to be closer to her, the result of which was that he saw her even less frequently now.

"How's your mom doing?"

"Fine," Amy said, giving him a noncommittal smile.

"You have a birthday coming up."

"I do."

"So what can I get you? You don't want to leave it to me, do you?"

She glanced at Landon, who had abandoned his sandwich at midpoint and was surfing the Net on his phone. The kid gave Amy a look that had a shrug in it.

"I'd kind of like to get away for a few days," she said. "We have a break coming up."

*What, with this fuckwad?*

"What do you have in mind, hon?"

"Cabo San Lucas maybe. Puerto Vallarta is nice."

"Why, have you been there?"

"No, but I'd like to."

"Just get away. By yourself?"

"No. I, uh . . . might go with a friend."

"Well, I might finance a getaway for you, sweetheart. But your friend? *She* would have to pay her own way."

Landon smirked to himself, eyes on his cell.

Amy nodded. "Let's talk about it later, okay?"

"Okay."

They finished their sandwiches in silence.

Conversations between Reeder and his daughter were rarely much longer. Not since the divorce, anyway, four years ago. Reeder had gone along with Amy living with her mother, though he and his ex-wife shared custody. His and Melanie's relationship had gone wrong, but Mel was always the right kind of mother.

Then two years ago, Mel remarried. Reeder's replacement was Donald Graham, a political lobbyist who at least was a liberal. Reeder liked Graham just a little less than he did Bobby Landon. Wasn't that Graham was a bad guy, really, just that Reeder disliked lobbyists on general principle.

He also disliked men sleeping with his ex-wife on irrational principle.

But at least Graham had supported the notion that Amy get her own place, citing the need for her independence. Of course, Reeder figured Graham realized his own seas would be calmer without Amy around.

Reeder's cell chirped. He snatched it off his belt, checked caller ID: *Gabriel Sloan.*

To Amy, he said, "I better take this."

"Sure," she said, long since used to that.

"Where are you?" Sloan asked, an edge in the familiar mellow baritone.

"Dinner with Ames and Bobby," Reeder said. Years ago, he and Sloan, her godfather, had started referring to Amy as "Ames," like her high school girlfriends. Amy disliked the nickname now, and Reeder rarely let it slip out anymore except to Sloan.

"Tell her I said hey," Sloan said.

"Gabe says hey," Reeder said.

That got a smile from Amy, and she held out a hand. "Can I talk to him?"

Reeder shook his head. "Business."

"Hi, Gabe!" Amy shouted, and several other patrons were startled into glancing their way. "Call me!"

Even Reeder had to smile.

"Tell her I will," Sloan said.

"She probably just wants to remind you her birthday's coming." Amy threw a wadded napkin at her father, but she was smiling.

Sloan asked, "Is the dipstick boyfriend along?"

"Oh yeah."

"So they'll be ditching you soon."

"You always were a detective. You want to get together, right? The FBI needs my help? I thought this day would never come."

"Go to hell. But I need you to go over what you told Bishop. Who knows? Might be something to it."

"No 'might' about it. If you trusty G-men can spare a moment from running off in the wrong direction, I'll be glad to straighten you out."

"When? Where?"

"My place, an hour. I'll have the Nationals game on—you bring the beer."

"See you then," Sloan said.

Soon Reeder was walking Amy and Bobby back to the street. He gave his daughter a peck on the cheek and shook her boyfriend's damp hand. The couple strolled off, arm in arm again. He supposed he should cut Landon a break—at least the kid hadn't spouted any Marxist nonsense tonight. Amy must have put him on his good behavior.

Darkness was settling in, and a distinct chill sent Reeder's hands into his pants pockets as he took the short walk to Thirty-Fourth Street Northwest and the million-dollar town house he called home. Selling a 49 percent interest in ABC to investors had, to say the least, left him better off than staying in government service, and best of all, he still maintained control of the company.

The two-story white-brick building was finally starting to feel like home to Reeder. Built in 1900, the town house appealed to his sense of history, but had been renovated to meet his twenty-first-century needs. He stopped, got his mail, then unlocked the red door and was greeted by the annoying beep of the alarm timer. He punched in the seven-digit PIN.

A pleasant female voice said, "Disarmed, ready to arm."

"Thanks, Rosie," he said to the alarm voice, which he'd named after the robot maid from a cartoon show his father had watched as a small boy.

From the entryway Reeder took a left into a white-walled living room, footsteps echoing off hardwood as he moved through the dining room, dropping the mail off on the table before entering the galley kitchen. He opened the stainless steel refrigerator, grabbed a Heineken, twisted off the cap, took a long damn pull.

Reeder was not a heavy drinker, not anymore, but he lived for a beer at the end of the day the way he once had the after-dinner cigarette that had stopped almost twenty years ago—when Melanie found out she was pregnant, Reeder quit cold.

He rarely watched TV in his living room, but since he was expecting Sloan, he dropped into one of the easy chairs, grabbed the remote, then turned on the large screen over a fireplace whose mantel was arrayed with framed pictures of Amy at various ages. Soon he was watching the Washington Nationals game. Pittsburgh was in town, and wily veteran Stephen Strasburg was on the mound for the Nats.

Raising his bottle to the TV, Reeder said, "Never fear, Stephen. Experience and cunning can beat youth and skill anytime."

The game was in the top of the first, no one on, two outs, and a two-two count on the third hitter in the Pirates' lineup. Confirming

Reeder's salute, Strasburg threw a changeup to the hitter, who was so far off balance he almost fell to a knee trying to hold up his swing.

By the top of the fourth, Reeder had taken his empty bottle to the kitchen and wondered if he shouldn't just go on upstairs. He had all but given up on Sloan—the FBI agent said an hour, and it'd been almost two.

Reeder was reaching for the remote when the doorbell chimed.

There, on Reeder's doorstep, was Gabriel Sloan holding up a six-pack of Guinness dark. Wearing half a grin, he said, "So I'm late. Peace offering."

"You're *fucking* late. Peace offering accepted."

Reeder stepped aside, and Sloan strode straight through into the living room, set the beer on the floor in front of the coffee table, yanked a bottle out, and plopped into the chair next to Reeder's. The only light in the room was the screen and bleed-in from the dining room.

Several inches shorter than Reeder, Sloan wore a charcoal pin-stripe Brooks Brothers suit he usually reserved for federal court appearances.

"You must've announced the task force to the media," Reeder said casually, grabbing a bottle from the six-pack before slipping into his chair. He muted the TV.

Sloan nodded, his side-parted blond hair a shade that hid any encroaching gray. Though they were about the same age, the white-haired Reeder had always looked older, until a family tragedy had taken a toll on Sloan.

While they were on opposite sides of the political spectrum, the two had been close since before their girls were born, having met on a joint Secret Service–FBI job. Their two families had spent much time together, and when Sloan's daughter, Kathy, died, Amy—who'd viewed Kath as a sort of big sister—took it hard.

Kathy Sloan had found herself pregnant, and—hoping her conservative parents would never know—had gone sub rosa to a "doctor" who turned out to be a flunked-out med student who left her with an infection that turned septic. Gabe Sloan had never really recovered from the loss of his child, and he'd wound up losing his marriage as well.

Reeder found it frustrating that his friend remained such a hardline conservative after so obvious an indictment of the radical right's antiabortion stand. But this was too touchy an area to explore, even with so close a friend. Or was that *because* Gabe was so close a friend?

"Yeah, we made the announcement this morning," the FBI agent said. "Since when do you watch the news?"

"You're wearing your 'testifying' suit."

After loosening his silver-striped navy tie, Sloan undid his collar button. He had lively blue eyes and an easy smile that showed lots of white teeth. Well, not as easy as it had once been.

Sloan said, "You don't miss a damn thing, do you, Peep?"

"Trained professional. Don't try this at home, kids."

"So how's my goddaughter doing?"

"She's trying to talk me into funding a getaway for her and that commie boyfriend of hers."

Sloan snorted a laugh that sent beer out his nose. "You're starting to sound like me! . . . How're the Nats doing tonight?"

"Two to nothing, bad guys."

"Strasburg still in?"

"Yeah," Reeder said. "He's only given up three hits and a walk . . . but one of the hits was a homer."

Sloan took another swig of beer, turned away from the ball game. "So what's this crazy shit you foisted on Bishop about Venter trying to run? A hit on the *judge*? Are you kidding? Looking to embarrass us federal boys?"

"If I wanted to do that," Reeder said, "I'd have kept my mouth shut."

Sloan waved a hand in the air, swallowed some more beer. "So let's say Venter tried to run. That's a good motive for a panicky stickup guy to blast him, am I right?"

"You are right as far as it goes, Gabe. But this was an assassination, no doubt about it. Did you look at the footage?"

"Yeah!"

"And what did you see?"

"I saw a robber pointing a gun at Nicky Blount, and I saw Justice Venter getting up—to intervene, looks like. Then the robber shot the Justice."

"Which is exactly," Reeder replied calmly, "what somebody wanted you to see."

Sloan blew a Bronx cheer. "Peep, stop spotting a conspiracy behind every tree, already. How did you dream up this half-assed crapola, anyway?"

"By watching the footage."

"Same as me."

"No. You saw it, buddy, but you didn't *watch* it." Reeder sat up, turned away from the screen. "Ever hear of cognitive dissonance?"

"I had Psych 101, thank you," Sloan said, a little testy.

"Prove it."

"It's when you hold on to a belief when all the facts say the opposite."

"A-plus, Mr. Sloan," Reeder said. "Outside the classroom, the practical application is simpler—it's called overlooking the obvious . . . Come upstairs."

Moments later, in his home office, Reeder used the already booted computer at his desk to load the e-mail and run the video on his wall-mounted forty-six-inch monitor between bookcases.

The second time they went through the video, Reeder froze it as Venter made his first movement to rise. "What do you see?"

Sloan studied the frame for several seconds. "The Blount kid has a gun in his face. The robber is threatening him . . . and Justice Venter is getting up to try to stop the guy from shooting his clerk."

"Okay, here's what I see," Reeder said, approaching the screen. "Let's start with Venter. He's rising, with a clear path to the holdup man, right?"

Sloan said, "Yeah—a straight shot. So to speak."

"Then why is the judge's left foot cocked away from the holdup guy?"

The FBI agent stepped closer, squinting at the screen.

Reeder pressed: "Justice Venter played football, right?"

Sloan nodded, straightened. "Yeah, in college, if I remember."

"So, he could just drop his shoulder, charge ahead, tackle the guy. Take him down."

"I suppose."

"Yet his left foot is angled away—toward the door, wouldn't you say?"

"Could be . . ."

"And his left shoulder?"

Sloan, studying the screen, said nothing.

Reeder said, "It should be *lowered*, right? But it's *not*—it's open, his arm flung to his left, like his foot . . . toward the fire exit."

The FBI agent said nothing.

Reeder put a hand on his friend's shoulder. "Venter wasn't going to play hero, Gabe. He saw an opening and was going to take it, to try to save his ass."

"Maybe. But even so, how does that change anything? Or maybe you'd just like to see a conservative icon painted a coward."

"Gabe, Venter getting wrongly tagged a hero is hardly the biggest issue here."

Back at his desk, Reeder started the video in slow motion. "Watch how your 'robber' takes his time. This isn't a panicked reaction to an unruly stickup victim. The killer abandons his attention on Blount. The kid, had he wanted to, could have picked up something off the table, a knife, a fork, hell, his glass, *anything*, and attacked the killer at this point . . . but the shooter doesn't give Blount a second thought. He turns, sets his feet, takes his time, then . . ."

They both watched as the pistol fired in slow motion, Venter engulfed in a pink cloud and going down.

". . . and then," Sloan said in a hushed voice that implied he could hardly believe he was saying it, "executes Judge Henry Venter."

Reeder nodded. "*Now* you've 'watched' the video, Gabe. Now you're *not* overlooking the obvious."

Sloan turned to his host. "Are you, Peep?"

"You mean that, for the first time in American history somebody has assassinated a Supreme Court justice? No, Gabe. No, I noticed that, all right."

"If Columbus had an advisory committee,
he would probably still be at the dock."

*Arthur J. Goldberg,*
*Associate Justice of the Supreme Court, 1962–1965,*
*United States Secretary of Labor,*
*United States Ambassador to the United Nations.*
*Section 21, Lot S-35, Grid M-20.5,*
*Arlington National Cemetery.*

# FOUR

Every flag in DC was flying at half-mast this morning, and the one outside the trapezoidal building with its severe lines and many windows was no exception—the J. Edgar Hoover Building, headquarters of the Federal Bureau of Investigation.

In his lightweight light gray suit with a powder-blue dress shirt and a dark blue tie, Reeder might have been just another agent reporting in. But this was reluctant duty: Only after Gabe Sloan had done much arm-twisting last night had Reeder agreed to meet with him now, for a session with the Bureau's Assistant Director, Margery Fisk.

Meeting Sloan just inside, Reeder accepted the visitor's badge from his friend, clipped it on his breast pocket, and said, "If you think the FBI is gonna add me to this task force, you're ready for premature retirement."

Sloan waved that off. He was in the Brooks Brothers pinstripe again—or maybe he was *still* in it. "Just tag along and behave yourself, Peep. I'll take the lead."

They walked toward the security station.

Reeder said, "I'm only putting up with this because you're Amy's godfather."

"Here I thought it was because you're a patriot. Did you catch the President's speech this morning?"

"Heard it on the car radio."

Sloan grunted a laugh. "You'd think Venter was his goddamn daddy."

Reeder grunted one back. "And you'd also think Venter was the greatest American hero since John Wayne played Davy Crockett. Busy morning so far?"

As they went through security, Sloan said, "You have no idea."

"I'd bet your buddies on the Bureau just can't wait to see me come around."

"Well, Patti might."

"Who's Patti?"

"My partner. You remember. I told you about her."

"Oh yeah . . . the kid."

"She's thirty-five, Peep."

"Yeah, well, *we* aren't."

They entered an elevator.

Sloan said, "I've talked you up around her, gramps. She thinks *you're* John Wayne."

"Please."

On the top floor, Reeder followed Sloan down a typically anonymous corridor. At the AD's office, they entered a reception area larger than Reeder's office.

A redhead in wire-framed glasses and a dark gray suit said to Sloan, "Go right in, Agent Sloan—the Assistant Director is expecting you." Despite her businesslike appearance, she looked barely older than Amy. She did not acknowledge Reeder in any way.

Sloan went in first, pausing to close the door behind them. The office was spacious, dark-paneled, wall-to-wall-carpeted, with a mini conference area and framed wall hangings ranging from diplomas and citations to photos of the last several presidents, including the one whose life Reeder had saved.

Assistant Director Margery Fisk rose from behind her aircraft carrier of a desk but did not come around to greet them; she just gestured toward waiting chairs and offered a slice of a smile before returning to her swivel chair. Tall, slender, in a navy business suit, her dark straight hair a lacquered helmet, Fisk had the high cheekbones of a model and the hard dark eyes of a cheetah about to spring.

Reeder had never met Fisk, who'd been AD for less than a year, but he knew her by reputation, all right. She was tough and smart and, it was said, a little bit ruthless. Cross her and she would smile and nod even as she began to plot your career's demise.

"Mr. Reeder," she said, extending her hand and requiring him to lean in over her work-stacked desk to accept, "I've heard so much about you."

He retrieved his hand, smiled at the ambiguity of that, and took his chair—Sloan already had taken his. "I've heard enough about you, Director Fisk, to know not to rise to that bait."

She seemed to like the sound of that—an unintimidated response but not a disrespectful one.

In an alto with no music in it, Fisk said, "Special Agent Sloan has already made a case for putting you on this task force. Part of that was showing me—and walking me through—the security footage . . . with your kinesics read on Justice Venter's behavior." She gestured to the monitor of the computer that was to her left on the endless desktop. She had no framed family photos on display, Reeder noted.

He said, "Kinesics is as much an art as a science. What it comes down to, Director, is my opinion."

"Understood. And I respect that opinion. But you've been a player in the DC game long enough to know that there's no way I can put a private citizen on an FBI task force, regardless of his background."

"I do," Reeder said. "And I agree with you. Anyway, the ill will toward me could hamper the investigation. I've given you a nudge in the right direction, and I'm sure the Bureau can run with it."

He gave her another smile and a respectful nod and was getting up when she raised a hand that was halfway between traffic cop and pope.

Reeder sat back down.

"Joe," she began, then politely, pleasantly asked, "May I call you Joe?"

"Certainly, Director." He wasn't about to ask if he could call her Margery.

"I agree," she said, "that you're on to something here. And I'm not inclined to send a first-team player back to the bench who may have turned this investigation around before it even began. You're not just a citizen with impressive credentials in federal law enforcement. You're head of a prestigious and well-respected security company."

"Well . . . thank you."

"So . . . what I can offer you is an advisory position. Given that you've provided advice to us already, I need hardly justify to anyone adding you to the task force as a consultant."

Reeder glanced at Sloan, who gave him nothing.

She was saying, "You'll have no real authority, which is the bad news. The good news, however, is that you will only have to answer to Special Agent Sloan . . . and to me."

"Director Fisk," Reeder said, "a lot of people are going to be unhappy with you."

She shrugged. "Only behind my back."

That got a grin out of Reeder. "It would be a pleasure working for you, Director Fisk. An honor."

"Good. As you may know, SAIC Sloan is heading up the task force."

Sloan said to Reeder, "Every agency in DC wants a piece of this—a chance to grab the credit for bringing in this killer."

Fisk said, "The FBI—thanks to you, Joe—is at the top of this particular food chain, having been in on the investigation at the start."

*Actually,* he thought, *by that logic,* DC Homicide *would be at the top of the food chain. Not damn likely.*

She was saying, "Homeland Security, your old colleagues at Secret Service, the Supreme Court Police, DC Homicide . . ."

She'd finally gotten to them.

"Why, by the end of the week, I wouldn't be surprised if we didn't have NCIS and Coast Guard representation."

Sloan laughed at that—more than it deserved, but she *was* the boss.

The SAIC said, "Director Fisk, the first question that comes to mind is the one any homicide investigator would ask in this situation: Who might want this victim dead?"

She folded her hands as if about to say grace. "Joe—what's your response to that?"

Reeder shrugged. "How about white supremacists? Killing an African American justice wins their cockeyed cause a hell of a lot of attention."

With a glance at the Director, Sloan said, "Including unwanted attention from us."

"Well worth the hassle," Reeder countered, "because others with the same racist outlook will see the murder as a victory."

"All right," Fisk said. The fingers of one hand drummed quietly. "Who else?"

Reeder opened his hands. "How about far-leftists fed up with Venter's extreme right-wing stance?"

She nodded.

He pressed on: "Or antigovernment terrorists? And God only knows what there might be in Venter's personal life."

"You might have something there," Fisk said with a finely arched eyebrow. "Inappropriate behavior with female office clerks was an issue in Justice Venter's confirmation hearings."

"Not the makings of a murder motive, though," Reeder said. "Not the way this one went down, anyway."

Fisk said, "You're missing the most obvious explanation, Joe."

"Religious extremists," Sloan put in.

*Nobody wanted to say* Muslim *anymore, even behind closed doors.*

But Reeder came close: "Islamic fundamentalists. I agree—high on the list of possibles. Venter made no secret of his Born-Again Christianity. That makes him an excellent candidate for al-Qaeda attention."

Fisk asked Reeder, "Is that your instinct here?"

"Not necessarily. Whoever pulled this off . . ." He shrugged again. ". . . a lot of planning went into the thing. Starting with knowing where and when Venter would be in a very public place."

"Terrorists like public places," Sloan said.

"Yeah, but Islamic terrorists want to kill *many,* not just one. The man with the machine gun could have mowed down everybody in the Verdict. Why would a terrorist, wanting attention and credit, go to the trouble of making a killing look like a robbery gone out of hand?"

Fisk was nodding again.

Reeder continued: "Some fairly sophisticated surveillance on Venter is involved here. Did he go to that restaurant bar regularly? Was this his night of the week there or something?"

It was Sloan's turn to shrug. "Unknown as yet. Still digging. But it certainly wasn't his first time at the restaurant."

Fisk said absently, "*I've* been to that restaurant."

Sloan shifted in his chair and frowned at Reeder. "Surely you aren't saying that Islamists aren't capable of that type of domestic intelligence gathering?"

Reeder shook his head. "No, 9/11 proved the opposite all too well. But we're talking about stalking a sitting Supreme Court justice in Washington, DC. You think a bunch of Middle Eastern types wouldn't raise any suspicion in DC? As paranoid as this city is? With all this Supreme Court–sanctioned racial profiling going on? I don't buy it."

Fisk said, "They could have used sympathizers, or non–Middle Eastern Muslims. The Boston Marathon bombing comes to mind."

Reeder said, "It does, but that goes to my point. These al-Qaeda types are grandstanders. That bunch likes *big* targets, lots of people. This is a single target—one important man."

Fisk was nodding.

Reeder asked them both, "Has anyone taken credit for the killing? You know damn well that half a dozen Islamic fundamentalist groups would be bragging this up already, if they were behind it."

Sloan said, "No. None has. Point taken."

With another razor-blade smile, Fisk said, "It sounds to me like Mr. Reeder is just the kind of consultant our task force can use." Her tone said the meeting was over. "Thank you for accepting this position. Do we need to talk compensation?"

"Director, I'm sure you know your history."

That made her frown in confusion. "How so?"

"It's a tradition that goes all the way back to President Wilson. I'll be a dollar-a-year man on this one."

That made her smile, and she extended her hand again. They shook, and something like warmth was in the woman's eyes. That warmth left as she turned toward Sloan, to whom she did not offer a hand to shake.

"And Agent Sloan," she said, "speaking of dollars? I am well aware that buck will stop at this desk. But if it stops here in a way that displeases me, do I have to tell you where that leaves the leader of this task force?"

"You do not," Sloan said with the world's smallest smile.

Soon Reeder and Sloan were on the third floor, Reeder following Sloan down another seemingly endless corridor as unspecific as something out of a dream—it felt like the elevator was back there somewhere, maybe a block away. Then Sloan turned into an alcove and pushed through double doors.

Reeder had expected the typical sea of cubicles, and surely this vast space had been used in that fashion at one time. But right now the expanse had been converted to a command post. Around a central conference table, agents at laptops were hunkered at phones, spiral pads nearby. Wall-mounted bulletin boards kept track of local and cable news, and bulletin boards bore pictures, maps, notes, and more.

Maybe twenty metal desks were scattered around, in no particular setup, some being used, others not. Each one had a computer and a monitor, cords and wires crisscrossing the floor like a nest of snakes.

No one looked up when Reeder and Sloan entered. The only one of a dozen or more worker bees who Reeder recognized was his pal Carl Bishop of DC Homicide. In shirtsleeves and tie, holstered gun on his hip, the brawny, bald detective stood in front of a bulletin board, studying it hopelessly like an anthropologist on Easter Island.

"I've seen better organized Chinese fire drills," Reeder said.

"No argument," Sloan said. "This is what happens when you bring all the great law enforcement agencies into one place—utter chaos. But remember, we've only been a team for about . . ." He looked at his watch. ". . . thirty hours."

"Well, any group is only as good as its leader."

Sloan grinned. "Screw you, Peep."

The SAIC walked to the conference table, and when everyone had noticed their top dog was among them, they quieted down and looked up.

"Ladies, gentlemen," Sloan said, "this is Joe Reeder, president of ABC Security, former Secret Service agent."

Bishop gave him a nod and a grin, but the rest seemed as unimpressed as soldiers at the front taking in their rookie replacements. One cute brunette squinted at him like she'd just spotted a flying saucer out a car window.

Sloan was saying, "You're all old enough to know this man took a bullet for the President of the United States. He's here to help. You may hear me call him *Peep*. It's an old nickname. I'd suggest if you don't have history with him, you make it *Mr. Reeder*."

"Christ, you're killing me," Reeder whispered to his friend. Then to the group: "*Joe* is fine. Just don't call me late for lunch."

Nobody laughed or even smiled at that. But a few people said "Hey"; several nodded.

Sloan didn't let it go at that: "Some of you may know that Peep here is a controversial fellow. There are nasty rumors that he's a Democrat."

That did get a few laughs.

"But before you give him a hard time," Sloan said, "keep in mind that he is here at the specific, special request of Assistant Director Fisk."

That caused a murmur, but then they were all back at it.

"Well," Reeder said, "that was fun. You had to bring up me takin' a bullet, huh?"

Sloan put a hand on Reeder's shoulder, and his blue eyes smiled. "Peep, they did need to hear that. It was a fucking brave thing you did."

"Saving that bastard was the worst move I ever made."

"He was a good president, despite what you may think," Sloan said, "and there are those of us who feel you did the country a great service."

"All I did was my job." Rotating his left shoulder as much as he could, Reeder said, "And anyway, maybe *this* is going to turn out to be the worst move I ever made."

Bishop came up, shook Reeder's hand, clamped him on the good shoulder. "Welcome aboard, Peep."

Returning the firm grip and smile, Reeder said, "Thanks . . . I guess."

"We can sure as shit use the help," Bishop said with a humorless smirk. "We're not coming up with a hell of a lot so far. Any idea how many black SUVs there are in the DC metro area?"

Sloan said, "We'll do a full briefing for everybody in ten minutes. I don't care how many agencies are in on this. We need everybody on the same page."

Bishop, clearly glad to be included, nodded. "I hear you, boss man." He headed to one of the desks.

The flying-saucer brunette approached them. She wore a white blouse under a charcoal suit, had curly hair cut short, brown eyes, a wide nose, full lips, her makeup understated. She was attractive if not pretty in the conventional sense. Cute. Which was probably something of a burden for an FBI agent.

Sloan made the introductions: "Patti Rogers, Peep Reeder."

She extended her hand, her expression still confused.

Shaking her hand, Reeder said, "What?"

She shook her head, clearing the cobwebs. "It's just that Sloan has told me so much about you for so long . . . I sort of figured you'd *fly* in."

"My cape is in the wash," Reeder said with an embarrassed grin.

"Some people reader you are," Sloan said with half a smile. "My partner played you like a kazoo, buddy."

Rogers seemed a little embarrassed herself now. "Nice to meet you, Mr. Reeder," she said.

He nodded. "Why don't you make it *Joe?*"

"All right, Joe . . . There's a desk next to mine. Wanna help me catch a couple killers?"

"Sure," Reeder said, but he glanced at Sloan.

Rogers was already on her way as Sloan said, "Peep, I'm going to partner you up with Patti. You need someone with some actual authority, and Patti is damn good. She's also footloose, since I'll be spending my time running the show."

Reeder nodded.

And then he took his place at a desk on the periphery, away from the big people's table.

"Ethics is knowing the difference between
what you have the right to do
and what is the right thing to do."

*Potter Stewart,*
*Associate Justice of the United States Supreme Court, 1958–1981.*
*Section 5, Grave 40-2,*
*Arlington National Cemetery.*

# FIVE

Patti Rogers knew damn well that Joe Reeder was disliked, even hated, by many of their fellow law enforcement agents, including some here at the command post.

That Sloan had given his friend this chance at redemption reflected well on the man, though she figured neither of these friends looked at it that way.

Anyway, Rogers didn't give a shit what anybody said—not the other agents, not even Sloan, for that matter. She had been assigned Reeder as her temp partner, and she would work with the guy. Any opinions about him would be made starting here and now—on the job. Based on his performance, she would decide whether or not he was the son of a bitch everybody but Gabe Sloan said he was.

Speaking of Sloan, he was making his way to the head of the table gradually, moving from one agent to another, gathering individual progress reports. But shortly it would be time for the briefing.

She glanced at the desk next to her, where her new partner was watching her. He was what they once called "ruggedly handsome," and distinctively so with that white hair and matching eyebrows. Nice tan, too.

"What?" she asked. "Something in my teeth?"

He shook his head.

"What, then?"

"Nothing," he said.

Then it hit her.

"Stop reading me," she said.

"Who says I am?"

"I do."

"Okay, Patti. Or do you prefer Patricia?"

"Everybody calls me Patti."

"That doesn't mean you prefer it. What's your story?"

"I have a story? Why don't you tell me?"

"Midwest. Small town. Farm girl? Figured early on the farm-wife routine that was fine for your mom, God bless her, just wasn't for you. Education was a way out. Iowa State? No, University of Iowa. ROTC?"

"What are you, a male witch?"

"Psych major? Thought so. Three years active duty . . . Marines? Army. Obviously an MP."

"Why obviously?"

"You're in law enforcement. Still in the reserves."

"Okay. I admit it. I'm impressed."

"Don't be." He grinned at her. "Sloan told me all this, the other day, when he said he was thinking of teaming us up."

She couldn't stop herself from grinning back at him. "Why, you son of a bitch . . ."

"That's not much of a read, Patti. Most of the other agents in this room could tell you that . . . Looks like our big chief is ready for his powwow. We better get over there."

Rogers and Reeder, along with other deskbound participants like Homicide Detective Bishop, stood behind those seated at the conference table. This made her feel like an onlooker, but she was confident Sloan would not consign her—or, for that matter, his pal Reeder—to grunt work.

Seated at the conference table over to her right was FBI computer expert Miguel Altuve; short, pudgy, in shirtsleeves (his suit coat over his chair back), bow tie a clip-on, longish dark hair parted in the middle, Miggie could hardly have looked less imposing. But he could do more damage with a laptop than most agents could a firearm.

At Miggie's left were a pair of clean-cut Secret Service agents, their backs rod straight as if even sitting down they were guarding a president. In their dark suits with jackets off, they looked like very well-armed Mormons. Senior Agent Alan Stein had short dark hair and that average look and body type the Secret Service sought. Rogers could offer no evidence that the agent knew how to smile. His partner, Anthony Ho, was tall, muscular—probably a workout junkie. Ho smiled on occasion. Rare occasion.

*Did you get written up when you smiled in the Secret Service?* she wondered. The FBI had a reputation for being humorless, but was *Animal House* compared to this repressed lot.

Over at the table to Rogers's left sat the only other woman in the room, Homeland Security Agent Jessica Cribbs. Taller and trimmer than Patti, Jess had a long brunette ponytail that Rogers secretly coveted. Given that they were members of the same gender minority, at least in federal law enforcement, the two had become friendly, if not quite friends, over the past three years or so.

Jess's partner, beefy, well-dressed Walter Eaton, stood just behind her, arms crossed, his squinty brown-eyed gaze fixed on Reeder, his mustache practically twitching with anger. She didn't need to be a people reader to know how Eaton felt about the new addition to the team. Eaton had just come in from somewhere and hadn't been present when Sloan introduced Reeder to the rest.

*Trouble?*

Detective Bishop's partner, Detective Ed Pellin, stood to Eaton's right like something carved out of a tree trunk by a semiskilled artisan. A former Marine, Pellin was as Semper Fi as it got—hair clipped close, standing at attention out of habit, even if his gray suit was straight out of the hamper this morning. But this was an old-school cop who got results.

The others, including Supreme Court police and a few more FBI, were new to her.

"All right," Sloan said. "Let's get started."

"Not until you answer a question," Eaton said.

*Shit,* Rogers thought. *Insubordination already.*

"Let's hear it, then," Sloan said, with only slightly strained patience.

"What in the hell is *he* doing here?" Eaton demanded, still pointedly staring at Reeder.

Sloan kept his voice reasonable. "I explained that earlier. Let's not waste time going over—"

"That man's presence has not been cleared by Homeland Security."

"No one here has been 'cleared' by Homeland Security, Walt. Joe Reeder is here at the FBI Assistant Director's request. Got that?"

"No. I don't."

Sloan's expression tightened. "Reeder's on board because he's valuable. Because we need him."

"Bullshit," Eaton snapped. "He's a loose cannon that marches to his own damn drum."

*Wow,* Rogers thought. *Wasn't* that *a mixed metaphor, not to mention a collision of clichés.*

Sloan, his voice icy, said, "Reeder's here because I recommended his presence."

Eaton was sneering. "What if Homeland Security doesn't think that cuts it?"

Seated in front of the bitching agent, Jess caught Rogers's gaze and did an eye roll that would have scored a ten at the Olympics.

Rogers gave her a look back that said, *Just the inevitable agency dick-measuring contest. Might as well get it out of the way.*

Sloan, his head to one side, gave Eaton a bland, bored look, as if the Homeland Security agent's glare was unworthy of anything more.

The SAIC said, "The FBI is leading this interagency investigation, which I'm in charge of, and if any of you don't like it, pick up your toys and go back to your own sandbox."

Eaton said nothing.

Nor did anyone else.

Rogers glanced at Reeder, whose expression seemed blank; but somehow she sensed the man was enjoying this.

Sloan smiled in a businesslike fashion. "Now, may we proceed? Or do you think this kind of exchange benefits our investigation, which, by the way, is only into the first-ever murder of a Supreme Court justice?"

DC Homicide Detective Ed Pellin came to everybody's rescue by saying, "I think we may have a lead."

Turning to Pellin, Sloan said, "Let's have it."

"Bish and I got a call from a detective buddy in our robbery division a few minutes ago. He said a pair of stickup artists using this same MO, right down to weapons, has hit bars in Manassas and Falls Church in Virginia, and Bowie, Gaithersburg, and Landover in Maryland. Looks like they've finally made their way to DC."

Sloan glanced at Reeder, then turned back to Pellin. "No one thought of this last night?"

Unembarrassed, Bishop said, "The scores were far enough apart—two states, and robberies, not murders—that nobody put it together right away."

"Any shootings?"

Bishop shook his head. "In Bowie, the guy with the AK broke a bartender's jaw for trying to stop them, but that's the roughest it ever got. They weren't on anybody's radar for murder."

"Well, they are now," Sloan said. He ran a hand over his face like he was trying to wipe away years', not hours', worth of exhaustion. "Okay, Bishop, you and Pellin stay on top of that. Let's ID these bad boys and round their asses up."

"You got it," Bishop said.

"And, Bishop?"

"Yeah?"

"Let's follow this up faster than it came in."

With a humorless smirk, Bishop nodded.

Turning to Eaton and Jess Cribbs, Sloan said, "So . . . is the Homeland Security contingent staying?"

Eaton said nothing, but, seated in front of him, Jess said, "We're on board."

Sloan nodded. "All right. Then it's time to let you know exactly why I recommended that Reeder join us in this operation. You see, he thinks this is not just a robbery—but an assassination."

Coming after news of a holdup team that matched last night's perps, this cast a cloud of confusion over the room. The murmurs combined into the growl of an approaching storm.

Bishop spoke to what everyone was thinking. "Gabe, we have two suspects who—"

"Who we know precious little about. Just because two armed robbers are sticking up bars in nearby states does not mean we have this thing solved. Particularly not considering what Reeder has come up with. Peep! Join me."

Reeder did as he was told. The faces that followed him till he was at Sloan's side were not warm—in fact, many were cold. But even Eaton was no longer openly contemptuous.

"Bring up the security footage on your screens," Sloan told them, then added the time code where they should cue up the video. Those standing leaned in over the nearest shoulder of a seated agent with a monitor.

For half an hour Reeder walked them through the footage, having them pause and go back and generally get to know every square inch of the recording. Rogers was impressed—Reeder's kinesics seemed to be the real deal. She was sold.

And so, apparently, were the rest of them. Not even Eaton argued against the ex–Secret Service agent's interpretation of the footage.

Reeder concluded: "You may say that hanging our entire investigation on my take on Justice Venter's body language is an incredibly foolish tack to take. And I would agree. These holdup men hitting bars in nearby states provide a good lead. I'm sure many of you will come up with others. They should all be run down, with speed and diligence."

Expressions among the agents were exchanged that said to Rogers their new team member had made his case well.

Reeder went on: "But I will stake my reputation . . . which isn't much of a bet in this company . . . on being right."

That actually earned a few chuckles and more than a few smiles.

Sloan stepped up. "If Reeder is right, and I think he may well be, we still don't have a clear motive. Walt, I want you and Cribbs to spearhead looking into the Aryan Nations, Posse Comitatus types, religious extremists, any group that might want Venter dead for racial or religious reasons."

Eaton nodded, still not saying a word.

To Stein and Ho, Sloan said, "Concentrate on Venter's personal life. Is there something there that might have led to this? Keep in mind the sexual controversy that arose in the confirmation hearings. Miggie, run the Justice's financials, give them to Stein and Ho—maybe there's a motive there."

Miggie nodded.

Sloan made a number of other assignments, mostly designating who would back up the individuals he'd already assigned tasks, then finally turned to Reeder and Rogers.

"Peep, much as I might agree with your take on this, these stickup men are our best lead right now."

"Full agreement."

"You and Rogers work with Bishop and Pellin. I want these knockover guys ID'd and brought in ASAP."

If Reeder was disappointed that he'd be pursuing a theory other than his own, Rogers couldn't tell.

Sloan said, "Everybody on top of their assignments?"

Nods all around.

"Good," he said. "Let's get to work."

At the conference table, agents hunkered over their laptops again while those with desks made their way to them. Rogers sat at hers, moving her mouse to get rid of the screensaver.

She glanced at Reeder at his nearby desk, catching him staring at her again.

"Something wrong?" she asked with an edge.

He was clearly appraising her. It wasn't a looking-her-up-and-down kind of thing. But this still made the second time he'd been reading her, and she didn't like it.

Not surprisingly, he read that. "Patti, I'm not doing anything that you and everyone else don't do every day."

"I don't do any such thing."

"Sure you do," Reeder said. "Everybody does. You size up the people around you based on what they give you to work from."

"And what does your sizing up tell you about me?"

"Well, you're practical. That Iowa background of yours."

"You already admitted Sloan told you I was from there."

"True, but the Herky the Hawk bobblehead on your desk would have if he hadn't."

The black-and-gold Herky sat on her desk next to a picture of her folks and brother outside. At the farm.

"And speaking of your desk . . ."

*What now?*

". . . that baggie of carrot sticks says you're health conscious."

"Carrots make me a health nut?"

"If I go to Bishop's desk, wanna bet I don't find a cache of Snickers or maybe Kit Kats? He thinks 'Candy Bar' is a food group."

She laughed a little. Couldn't help herself.

"Your hair," he said.

But now she frowned. "My *hair*? Jesus Christ, Joe. You really think this is appropriate to the workplace?"

"Short is practical, but it also keeps you more in line with this still predominantly male field. Similarly, you take it easy on the makeup."

"I don't wear any more or less than Jess."

"Your friend wears blush and mascara—makes no effort to blend in with the Boys' Club. Actually, she likes to stand out."

Reeder had Jess nailed, all right. The Homeland Security agent had bigger aspirations than fieldwork.

He was saying, "No perfume, either."

"Why all this, do you suppose? So I'll fit in, here in the locker room?"

"I don't know about that. Eaton seems *marinated* in Brut. I didn't know they even still made that shit."

The laugh burst out of her before she could stop it.

But it caught in her throat when he said, "Sloan claims you're brilliant, but I've seen no evidence of that."

"Is that so?"

"Oh, I can tell you're smart. But we need to get at it, so you can demonstrate that side to me. What do you say?"

She sighed, nodded. "I'm up for that. We better check in with those homicide detectives. We seem to be carrying water for them."

He sighed. "If we're going to chase our tails, we might as well get started."

"Chase our tails?"

"I know what I saw," Reeder said. "And it wasn't a robbery. Not really."

"I saw the footage, too," she said.

"What did *you* see?"

"After listening to you? Taking in what you picked up on? An assassination."

He grinned at her. "*Now* you're brilliant."

"Crime and the fear of crime have permeated
the fabric of American life. "

*Warren E. Burger,*
*Fifteenth Chief Justice*
*of the Supreme Court of the United States of America, 1969–1986.*
*Section 5, Lot 7015-2, Grid W-36,*
*Arlington National Cemetery.*

# SIX

For just over an hour, Patti Rogers, munching a carrot stick, had been watching security videos from the out-of-state tavern stickups when something on the Bowie, Maryland, video sat her up straight. The carrot bobbing like a cigarette in her mouth, she rewound the footage and watched again.

The camera was mounted high and angled down onto the bar area. Plenty of patrons, but the joint was not what you'd call packed. The mirror behind the bar, before which rows of bottles stood sentry, gave an illusion of a bigger place, and more people, but finally also a sense of how many others were present.

On her monitor, the two holdup men entered. In black, nondescript but for their ski masks, and of course guns. After an initial stunned response from the clientele, the perps herded the customers away from the counter, and the bartender from behind it, into a group near others seated at tables.

As in the Venter killing/robbery, the holdup man with an AK-47 stood at the bar, near the door, weapon trained on the cowed crowd, while his partner with the pistol relieved the customers of their valuables. With his back to the bar, AK-47 didn't see an employee emerging from the back room into the serving area behind him.

Chewing a last bite of carrot like Bugs Bunny contemplating Elmer Fudd's next move, Rogers paused the video to check her printout of the police report.

This new player was Nick Karlin, twenty-six, another bartender, who—before the robbery began—had gone back into the stockroom. No police record. Husky Nick had been a walk-on with the University of Maryland Terrapins football team; just as the media had made much of Venter's gridiron career fueling his "heroics," Karlin really was an athlete, or anyway a former one. He was also the only person hurt in any of the out-of-state robberies.

She unpaused the video.

AK-47 was standing close enough to the counter that Karlin could reach over and hook the intruder around the neck, jerking him backward.

*Stupid*, she thought. *What if the intruder had started firing, spraying bullets around the bar?*

But that hadn't happened, thankfully. With the counter awkwardly between them, the two men struggled, the gunman using only one hand on his surprise attacker, his other hand maintaining a grip on the AK-47; but at these close, clumsy quarters, the intruder couldn't bring his weapon to bear on the ill-advisedly heroic bartender.

As they grappled, the gunman managed to gradually turn, until finally he was facing Karlin, who tore at the man's mask, pulling it almost off before the gunman broke away, swinging the AK-47 up and jamming its stock in Karlin's face. The bartender dropped behind the counter, a reverse jack-in-the-box.

Rogers knew from the police report that Karlin was unconscious, his nose and jaw broken.

Karlin had almost gotten the intruder's mask off, but at the time his head was buried in the man's shoulder and he had not seen the man's briefly exposed face. And the camera angle didn't help.

Shit.

She watched the two men do battle again, this time in slow motion, and then went through the footage again. Only this time, she observed the struggle in the mirror behind the bar . . .

Frame by frame now, she watched as the pair grappled, the gunman turning as Karlin ripped at his mask. Then . . . *there!*

She froze the video.

In the mirror, the reflection of the gunman's largely revealed face glowered at her.

*"Miggie!"*

Altuve looked up from his monitor, and Rogers waved him over, then turned toward Reeder at his desk. "Joe—you should see this, too."

The two men came over and peered over her shoulders as she pointed to the scowling oval face in the barroom mirror—close-set eyes, lumpy nose, wide mouth with irregular teeth.

"Miggie," she asked, "is that image clear enough for you to use your facial-recognition software on it?"

Altuve frowned in thought. "Maybe. Yeah. Have to reverse it, obviously. Yeah, maybe, possibly."

*Jeez, Mig, could you hedge a little bit more?*

Reeder patted her shoulder. "Gabe said you were smart, kid. Good catch."

She grinned back at her new partner. "Thanks . . . Okay, Miggie—'*do* do that *voo*-doo that *you* do so well.'"

Reeder returned her grin. "Sinatra reference. I like a youngster with a sense of history."

She shrugged. "So we liked the Rat Pack down on the farm."

The computer expert, not much for chitchat, had already slipped back to his station.

Reeder went over to Bishop's desk. Riding the high of finding a real clue, Rogers sneered at the monitor. "Got you," she told the contorted face in the barroom mirror.

She felt, more than heard, Reeder go back to his desk. Before he sat down, he said, "Heads up."

Rogers turned to see something flipping toward her like a *2001* obelisk. Reflexively, she caught it.

A Snickers bar.

"Your reward," Reeder said. "Guess who I begged it off."

She looked over to see Bishop grinning at her. She nodded her thanks to the DC cop, then tore the wrapper with a satisfying rip. Soon the taste of carrot was a memory as chocolate fueled her tedious return to checking security video from the other, probably less significant robberies.

Ninety minutes later, Miggie materialized beside her like a nerdy apparition.

"Something?" she asked, hope rising.

He said, "First, a question."

"Okay."

"How did Bowie PD not see this?"

With a shrug, she said, "Easy to miss. I didn't catch the reflection until I went through it frame by frame—twice."

"Pretty major screwup," he said, "if this is what it could be. I mean, Justice Venter might still be alive."

"Meaning you *do* have something."

He handed her several printout pages. "Facial rec got us a possible in the system."

"'Charles Granger,'" she read from the guy's lengthy rap sheet. "Armed robbery, assault . . . busy boy."

"He seems a dedicated professional, yeah. Check the picture out."

"Looks right. Is this address still good?"

"You know as much as I do. Oh, except for one thing."

"Yeah?"

"That's his mom's house."

Her eyebrows went up. "Charles Granger lives at his mom's house."

"He does."

"An armed robber who's a nerd?"

"*I* live at my mom's house."

She looked at him as if to say, *I rest my case.*

Studying the rap sheet, she said, "Mom's house or not, this address is two years old."

"Best we got, Patti."

"Probably worthless."

"Probably."

Reeder, who hadn't seemed to be listening as he went over security footage, said, "Only one way to find out."

She squinted at him, as if trying to bring him into focus. "I thought you made these guys as a waste of time."

"I could be wrong."

She blinked at him. "That's happened *before*, has it?"

"Sure." His smile was damn near angelic, which somehow went with the white hair and tanned rugged face. "As recently as last year."

She grunted a laugh. "Well, the pair on this bar robbery look like the guys from the Venter hit."

"Looks can be deceiving."

"Let me write that down."

He nodded toward his monitor. "I've been comparing the out-of-state footage to the Verdict stuff, and there are things about how the two holdup men stand, and carry themselves, that don't jibe."

"Oh, really? But then, like you said—you could be wrong."

He got up, took his suit coat from the back of his chair, and climbed into it; he wore no sidearm that she could see.

Then he said pleasantly, "But if I'm right, Patti, why don't we get these clowns out of the way, so we can get cracking on the real assassins?"

She winced. "So . . . shouldn't we go over and tell Bishop and Pellin? It's *their* lead."

Buttoning his suit coat, Reeder thought for a moment. She followed his eyes over to Sloan, seated at the conference table talking with Eaton, the hostile Homeland Security guy. Reeder stared at Sloan and damned if the man didn't seem to sense it. With a glance, Reeder summoned their boss.

Shortly, Sloan was leaning in to study the freeze frame on her computer. "That's not much of an image. You got facial rec on this?"

Rogers said she did.

The SAIC took a long look at the suspect's rap sheet.

"So we have an address," Sloan mumbled.

"We do," she said redundantly.

Sloan called Miggie over, who reiterated that this was a possible match, but not one hundred percent.

A little crossly, Sloan asked him, "What *would* you give it?"

"Fifty-fifty would be a push," the computer analyst said. "Nothing that would hold up in court."

"Not arrest-warrant-worthy?"

"God no."

Sloan nodded his thanks and dismissal, and Miggie went back to his desk.

Reeder said, "Gabe, we don't need a warrant to knock on a door."

The SAIC frowned in thought. "I suppose you two want to check this Granger out."

"Patti here caught it," Reeder said with a shrug.

"But you're backing up Bishop and his partner, what's-his-name."

"Pellin. I haven't shared this with them yet."

The SAIC frowned again. "Why not?"

"Why do you think?"

Sloan and Reeder were talking to each other in a way Rogers couldn't quite follow—the shorthand of agents who'd worked together a long time.

She said, "Maybe we should bring in SWAT . . ."

Sloan grimaced. "Means money if it turns out to be nothing."

Reeder said, "I thought you had carte blanche, Gabe. Supreme Court justices don't get murdered every day, you know."

"Carte blanche," Sloan sighed, "within budgetary constraints."

Rogers said, "Could be a dead end."

Sloan thought about it endlessly, for maybe ten seconds, then said at last, "Okay. All right. Check it out, you two."

Rogers, still not quite following, said to Sloan, "But *don't* take Bishop and Pellin?"

Sotto voce, Reeder said, "Tell 'em and they'll be taking *us* along. You like the sound of that?"

Her head was swimming. "But the out-of-state tavern holdups are *their* assignment."

"Yes, I know," Sloan said. "I gave it to them." He was almost whispering, his manner casual—no one else in the room would guess theirs was a key conversation in the case. "Familiar with the Beltway sniper shootings?"

"Vaguely," she said. "Before my time . . ."

"Peep, you remember what a jurisdictional nightmare that was. I won't put up with that this time around."

She asked Sloan, "What happened?"

But Reeder answered: "October 2002, John Allen Muhammad and Lee Boyd Malvo drove up and down I-95 sniping people from the trunk of their ratty-ass Chevy Caprice. First five victims were in Maryland, number six was in DC proper, then one in Fredericksburg in Virginia, before going back for one more in Maryland, another four in Virginia, then, finally, one more in Maryland."

"My God," Rogers said. "How many victims?"

Sloan said, "Thirteen Beltway victims, and as many as twelve more as far away as Louisiana and Alabama. The whole investigation was a clusterfuck, full of jurisdictional hiccups, piss-poor management, and just plain shitty information."

Reeder said, "The man does not exaggerate."

Still seemingly casual, Sloan said, "In the end, a citizen saw the car, and the two killers were apprehended sleeping in a rest area in Maryland. All the law enforcement in the DC area, and it's a *citizen* who finally tracks them down. Not this time. *We'll* find Justice Venter's killers and be the ones to bring them in."

Half an hour later, Rogers pulled the unmarked Ford in front of a bungalow on Byrd Lane in Groveton, an unincorporated part of Fairfax County. Two modest oaks guarded either side of the sidewalk leading to a front stoop with white pillars, an antebellum anachronism for this glorified shack with its yellow aluminum siding.

They were still in the car when Rogers asked Reeder, "Need a gun? There's an extra in the glove compartment."

"No, thanks."

"We might be facing Justice Venter's killer in a couple of minutes, you know."

"Doubtful, but thanks for the concern."

"Why, do you *already* have a gun?"

She thought maybe he kept one in an ankle holster or some damn thing.

"I own a gun," he said. "I don't have it with me."

"You do know we're on duty here."

"Hey, I'm not law enforcement, remember—I'm just a consultant. We can always call for backup."

She stared at him. He looked as ready for action as a Buddhist monk.

As they got out of the car, she said, "Stay in back of me, then. That's where consultants belong."

They went up the stairs to the stoop, Rogers in the lead as she'd dictated. A screen door protected a varnish-blistered wooden front door whose small window provided no look inside.

She got her pistol out, her other hand on the screen-door handle. With a glance at Reeder, she said, "Ready?"

He was regarding her with a lifted eyebrow. "We left the SWAT team back at the ranch, remember? It's his mother's house. You *could* ring the bell."

She shook her head. *These old-timers.* They always wanted to keep faith with the Fourth Amendment, even though the Supreme Court had rejected it years ago. She'd be damned if she would give up the element of surprise just to coddle a living legend who most people wanted to see drop dead.

With a quick nod to her supposed partner, she yanked the screen open, and it squeaked and creaked like something out of an old horror film. Within, a small dog started yapping.

*Shit*—so much for the element of surprise.

She twisted the handle of the inside door, and it was unlocked but sticking, so she thrust her shoulder against it like a tackle throwing a block. Gun at the ready, she almost tumbled in, Reeder behind her, though he halted as he reached the threshold.

The house smelled of sweat and urine, the latter probably courtesy of the barking terrier that came charging from the kitchen. The dog sprinted past her, as if to attack Reeder, but instead darted between his legs and outside.

As Rogers fanned her pistol around the room, a woman's voice from the back of the house called, "Who is it? Butch, is that you? Damnit, don't let *Yanni* out!"

The little dog, a vapor trail now, did bear a slight resemblance to that long-haired ancient musician.

"*Federal agents!*" Rogers announced, and the back of the house went still.

Then she heard a screen door slap shut somewhere back there. She turned to say something to Reeder, but he was already gone. Circling the house, she supposed, with his no gun and superior attitude.

Nothing to do but follow him, but when she got to the back of the house, Reeder was already three houses away, running through backyards, chasing a youngish long-haired white male in a wife-beater T-shirt and blue basketball shorts and Nikes.

She joined pursuit.

Cutting through yards, keeping them in sight, Rogers pushed herself to close the distance. The guy kept running, lank dark hair flying behind him, the older Reeder staying with the guy—hell, closing in on him.

Rogers was narrowing the distance, as well, but as they neared the end of the block, the guy abruptly stopped, turned to face Reeder, and was pulling something small and dark from the waistband of his shorts—*a revolver.*

Yet Reeder still ran at the guy, suit coat flapping.

*Didn't he see it?*

Feet planted, Rogers brought up her pistol, ready to take this prick down; but she couldn't get a clear shot, not with Reeder between her and the target.

She tried to will Reeder to take one step to either side, so she could drill the guy, but he didn't, and by the time she moved into a better line of fire, it would be too late to do anything for Reeder except maybe avenge him.

Then the ex–Secret Service agent took three more quick steps as the guy was bringing up the gun. Reeder made a whipping motion with his right hand, and something appeared there, like a magician producing a wand.

And it really was a wand, only there was nothing magical about it beyond its stopping power—Reeder had been carrying an ASP telescoping baton the entire time!

Just as the perp was about to squeeze the trigger, the baton struck. Reeder brought the thing down, and, even at this distance, she could hear the guy's forearm snap; and then the perp was scream-ing, a wail that prefigured the police sirens that would surely follow. The revolver plopped to the grass as Reeder kept plowing forward, driving a shoulder into the perp's gut, taking the man off his feet, going down with him, and landing with a *whump*, Reeder on top.

Rogers was running again, sprinting across a backyard to catch up. When she got there, Reeder was already pulling the guy to his feet, the perp's wail replaced by moaning as he cradled his broken forearm.

*Where had that baton come from? How had Reeder managed all that?*

Rogers vowed that she would watch her new partner much closer from here on out.

She was getting cuffs out when Reeder said, "We won't be need-ing those."

"What the hell were you thinking?" she asked, surprised by her own shrillness.

Reeder was hauling the whimpering perp along by an elbow. "He took off, I took off."

"You're a *consultant,* remember?"

"Yes, and right now I'm consulting with Mr. Charles Granger here. That *is* you, isn't it, Charles?"

"Fuck you, man! I ain't done shit. I wanna doctor and a lawyer!"

"How about an Indian chief?" Reeder asked cheerfully, then shook him by that elbow like a rag doll. Granger's eyes rolled, and he howled in pain.

"*Are* you Charles Granger?"

"Yeah, yes! *Gee*-sus!"

Reeder gave her a bland look. "Agent Rogers, meet Mr. Granger. Now I've consulted. Happy?"

"Delighted," she said.

Nudging Granger back the way they had come, Reeder said to her, "Collect his gun, would you?"

Frowning to herself—*why was he suddenly in charge?*—she holstered her pistol and slipped on a latex glove, then bent down, picked up the revolver, and followed her partner and their catch.

With Reeder in the lead now, she wondered if her temp partner was going to cause her any real problems—like maybe get her killed. And she had thought Gabe *Sloan* was a handful of a partner . . .

Yet, for some reason, she was smiling. Pain in the ass or not, Joe Reeder was why they were heading back with, just possibly, one of Justice Henry Venter's assassins.

And he had done this because she had spotted the key clue that brought them here.

Maybe they would make decent partners at that.

"Laws are made to protect the trusting
as well as the suspicious."

*Hugo L. Black,*
*Associate Justice of the Supreme Court*
*of the United States of America, 1937–1971,*
*fifth-longest serving Supreme Court Justice.*
*Section 30, Lot 649-LH, Grid W/X-38.5,*
*Arlington National Cemetery.*

# SEVEN

Through the one-way glass of the darkened observation room of the Fairfax County Adult Detention Center, Reeder took stock of Charles Granger.

Slumped in a straight-back chair, right forearm in a cast, left hand cuffed to a metal ring in the scuffed metal table, the suspect flexed the fingers of both hands. He presented a blank mask of a face, though shifting eyes betrayed anxiety.

Given Granger's hippie hair, this was not likely the "Butch" his mother had called out to, though of course it might be a childhood nickname.

The suspect had been given painkillers at the ER, but nothing narcotic—FBI orders. That meant Granger's forearm would be throbbing like Reeder's shoulder had that day he had taken a bullet for a president he despised.

Maybe he'd used excessive force with Granger—or what used to be considered such, before law enforcement had been granted so damn much latitude. He almost felt pity for the perp— *almost.*

This was, after all, an armed robber, a three-time loser circling the drain on the tavern holdups alone—a small-time stickup artist with the face that went with it: eyes crowding a frequently broken nose (boxing background or just bar fights?), his teeth crooked and yellowed from smoking and lack of care.

*But was Charles Granger a murderer?*

Wasn't as if a hired killer couldn't be a lowlife piece of scum. Few paid assassins were the glamorous figures of espionage fiction or even the real-life cold-blooded, blue-collar hit men who did contract work for organized crime.

No, Charles Granger did not seem to be somebody you might hire to kill a justice of the Supreme Court. Rather, he was the kind of slimeball you met in a bar and offered a few hundred bucks to, to kill your ex-wife who lived in a trailer.

Rogers entered the interview room, her eyes unreadable, her mouth a straight line. She tossed a folder onto the table before sitting opposite the suspect. She opened the folder, glanced at its contents, letting Granger know she was going over his rap sheet. Then she closed the file, placed both her hands flat on the table, and just looked at him, as if waiting for him to start the conversation.

*Good*, Reeder thought.

Granger tried to hold her gaze, but his defiance wilted, and he looked away.

Finally, in a voice as casual as a bored waitress taking an order, Rogers said, "You do know you're screwed here, Charlie, don't you?"

Granger was trembling, just a little, his mouth twitching. Just a little.

"Never mind repeat offender," she said. "We're talking murder . . ."

Granger straightened, his eyes flaring, as he reflexively drew his shackled arm closer, rattling the cuff chain.

". . . and a *Supreme Court justice* at that. We're talking a very special kind of screwed."

"Wait, what?" Granger said, as alert as a deer about to get splattered by a truck.

Reading this guy's surprise and alarm didn't take kinesics training.

"You mean that shit on TV?" Granger asked. "Okay, that was a tavern stickup, but I didn't have diddly to do with that one. Must be one of them copycats."

Reeder smiled. This was a tacit admission that Granger was part of the two-man crew hitting bars in a multistate area.

"Okay, Charlie," Rogers said. "If you had nothing to do with the Verdict robbery, you must have an alibi, right?"

"When . . . when was that?"

"Two nights ago."

". . . Home watching TV with my mom."

"That's what you want to go with? Your mom as your alibi?"

He raised the hand attached to the shackled wrist. "As God is my witness, it's the goddamn honest truth, so help me God."

That was a hell of a lot of *Gods*.

But Rogers clearly didn't buy it. Still, Reeder had been impressed by the relatively quick, confident way the suspect produced his for-shit alibi.

Hearing the observation booth door open, Reeder turned as Sloan and a shaft of light came in.

"Anything?" Sloan asked, letting the door close, returning Reeder to darkness as the SAIC took position next to him.

"Says he's innocent," Reeder said.

Sloan snorted a laugh. "Till we prove him guilty, he is."

Rogers was saying, "No one else saw you that night? Just your mother?"

Glumly, Granger nodded.

Sloan said, "His mother is his alibi."

Reeder wasn't sure if that was a statement or a question.

"Yup," Reeder said. "Bishop and Pellin get anything from her?"

"Old girl had the same story as her baby boy. They were watching *Forrest Gump* on TCM. Mom can barely get out of bed by herself. But Charlie is really a great, great help."

"Our DC Homicide contingent get anything out of the visit, besides a worthless alibi?"

Sloan grinned that very white smile of his. "How about an AK-47 in a closet? Mom said Charlie must be holding it for a friend. Couldn't possibly be his—he's such a good boy. Wouldn't hurt a fly."

"You sure they weren't watching *Psycho* on TCM?" Reeder laughed, once. "I wonder if she thought he was a good boy when he went to juvie, or later, when he went to jail?"

The rhetorical question drew half a smile from Sloan. "Oh, she blames the bad crowd Charlie got in with for her boy's troubles. That's his only fault, you know—too trusting."

"Ah," Reeder said. "Her dog's name is Yanni, but she called out for Butch. Do we know who that is?"

Sloan replenished his smile. "Mrs. Granger claims you heard her wrong. Says she never said 'Butch.'"

"Gee, maybe it was my imagination. And Patti's."

"I've already turned Miguel Altuve loose on Granger's known associates, cell mates, and so on to see if there's a Butch in the mix."

As if she'd been psychically eavesdropping on them, Rogers asked Granger, "Who's Butch?"

Granger's eyes narrowed, his ankles crossed, and he shrank into his chair as much as possible, cuffed to the table. His expression, open before, became guarded.

"I asked for a lawyer," Granger said.

"I didn't catch that."

"Hell you didn't! I told that asshole that fucked me up, by my house? That I wanted a doctor and a lawyer, and he just made a dumb-ass joke out of it."

"No, we got you a doctor." She smiled at his cast. "Remember?"

"I wanna lawyer up," he said. "I'm no fool. I can tell when the shit's gettin' deep."

"That right?"

"Hey, lady, people like me still got a *few* rights left in this country."

Rogers picked up the folder, stood. "If I walk out that door, there's no deal—not now, not ever. You get a lawyer, Charlie, we go to trial."

Granger stared at her in silent sullen defiance.

"Okay," she said pleasantly, "but here's the thing: I'm FBI working with DC Homicide, and do you think we won't figure out who Butch is? That we don't find him, bring him in, and offer *him* a deal to roll over on *you?* First-degree murder of a Supreme Court justice. That's a federal crime, Charlie—slam dunk lethal injection."

She went to the door, taking her time, and was halfway out before Granger cracked.

"Goddamnit, god fucking *damnit!*" Granger yowled. He slammed his cuffed fist on the table. "I'll talk. I'll empty out the damn bog for you bastards. But I want *full* immunity first. I won't say a word more till I got it in writing."

If Granger and Butch were in fact the Verdict bandits, then Rogers was about to make a very good deal, since *Butch* was the suspected shooter. And Granger's eagerness to talk was damn near a confession . . . and yet . . . and yet . . .

Rogers was back at the table in an instant, ready to deal.

Sloan's cell chirped. He withdrew it from his jacket pocket, listened for a moment, then his eyes widened. He rapped on the glass, hard, and Rogers's head snapped toward the sound behind the mirrored surface.

"What?" Reeder asked his friend.

But Sloan, still on the phone, raised a dismissive hand; listening, he made his way out into the hallway. Reeder exited the booth just as Rogers left the interview room, abandoning a pop-eyed Granger to wonder what the hell was up.

Soon, in the corridor, an impromptu conference was under way.

"Gabe," Rogers demanded, "what the hell? I *had* him. He was just about to give us Butch!"

Sloan shook his head. "He was about to enter into a negotiation that means hours of lawyers and paperwork."

"Okay, but then we would have *had* his accomplice."

Sloan was as calm as a priest giving communion. "We'll have him anyway. We don't need Granger. Altuve has identified Butch."

She frowned. "How?"

"Tracked him through Granger's file. He and Charlie go way back, clear to juvie days." Sloan showed them both a mug shot on his cell phone, a baby-faced man with a Curly Howard haircut. "Meet Dwight Brooks—'Butch.'"

Rogers was shaking her head. "But I made a deal with Granger—"

"You haven't made any deal. It wasn't even an offer yet. And now that we know that we don't need him? Good-bye, Charlie."

"Gabe, we just *can't*—"

"Patti," he said, voice sharper, "if we don't have to do an immunity deal with the accomplice to Justice Venter's killer, that's a good thing. That's a *great* thing."

She was still not sold. "I am just not *comfortable* with—"

Sloan's blue eyes, usually so calm, flashed. "Do you think the public will be comfortable, seeing one of this pair walk, even if it does put the Justice's literal killer away? Now *both* Granger and Brooks can feel the full measure of the federal government's displeasure. Understood?"

A vein pulsing in her neck, her entire body rigid, she said, "Understood."

Sloan gave her a businesslike smile. "You stay with Granger. Keep at him. Tell him we can't accept any kind of plea bargain without knowing more."

"He'll probably go back to demanding a lawyer."

"Then get him one. Patti, we don't need his ass. Not anywhere except in a cell. As for Brooks, we have an address, and Peep and I will go calling."

This was rightly Rogers's duty, but she said nothing. *She's good at suppressing rage,* Reeder thought. *Till the day her heart explodes.*

Reeder said, "You should take Patti, Gabe—hell, I'm not even armed. No way I want a repeat of what happened this morning."

Sloan shook his head. "I want you along to give me a preliminary read on Brooks when we haul him in."

"Then don't waste Patti's time here. We all *three* should go."

"No," Sloan said. "I want an FBI presence here with Granger." He withdrew a Glock from his suit coat pocket and handed it to Reeder. "Now you're armed."

"Thanks, no. I've got my baton."

"Take it."

Reeder sighed, accepted the weapon, checked the safety, then slipped it into his waistband.

"We'll take backup," Sloan said reassuringly. "Patti, stay at it."

Rogers nodded, expressionless, and headed back into the interview room.

Sloan drove Reeder back to the Huntington section of Fairfax County, the same mostly low- to middle-class white housing area where Granger's mother resided. Brooks rented half a duplex on Virginia 241, less than ten miles south and west of Granger's home.

On the way, Sloan contacted the two Homeland Security agents to back them up—Jessica Cribbs and Walter Eaton, the former that attractive brunette friend of Rogers's, the latter the jackass who hated Reeder's guts.

Great.

But when they pulled up, there was no sign of Cribbs and Eaton. Reeder and Sloan sat in their unmarked Ford for a while, taking stock of Butch's homestead. The contractor had apparently run low on funds after erecting the brick first floor, an aluminum-sided second story seemingly set on top by mistake. While the apartment on the duplex's right had a nice white-railed front stoop, the left side had an aluminum-sided front porch slapped on as an afterthought.

Sloan nodded. "Brooks is in the shithole on the left."

"He in there?"

Sloan opened his door. "We'll know soon enough."

Reeder, who had thought they were awaiting the arrival of the Homeland Security agents, lagged a little getting out, before falling in at Sloan's side as they headed toward the Brooks half of the duplex. Both men got out their pistols.

Reeder whispered, "Where the hell are Cribbs and Eaton?"

Sloan said, "They'll be here—there's an alley behind the house. Hell, man, this morning really shook you up, didn't it?"

Reeder said nothing.

"Anyway," Sloan was saying, "you ever know one of those Homeland guys to be late for anything?"

"I know one thing."

"Yeah?"

"Eaton is a prick."

"Ah, but a punctual prick," Sloan said, waving his cell as it beeped. "That's his text—he and Cribbs are in position."

"They coming in from the back?"

"Yeah," Sloan said. "They'll take the first floor. You and I will go in and make sure our guy isn't in the living room, then head upstairs and clear the second floor."

They approached the front door carefully, Sloan in front, pistol up. Reeder kept his gun pointed down.

Unlike this morning, no screen protected Brooks's front door, nor was it unlocked. But it was ancient enough that a credit card could open it, and that's what Sloan used.

Nodding to a silent beat, Sloan mouthed, *one, two* . . .

On *three,* the SAIC opened the door wide, barging into the living room, Glock leveled before him. Falling in behind, Reeder was greeted by the smell of day-old pizza. A second-floor stairway was immediately to the right as you came in, while the living room was home to assorted scattered crap, including fast-food bags and piled pizza boxes.

Seconds later, Cribbs and Eaton came in from the back.

Eaton drew very close to Sloan and whispered: "His car's in the alley. Probably home."

Sloan nodded, then whispered back: "Clear the first floor and basement. We're going on upstairs."

The SAIC led the way. Even with the other two agents downstairs, the duplex was draped in a terrible silence that made the hair on Reeder's neck prickle. Like Sloan, he kept his feet toward the outside edge of each step—the well-worn center was more likely to squeak.

At the top, just to the left of the landing, was a corridor that bisected this half of the structure—a door at right, down a ways, a door at left, down a ways farther, and a bathroom, yawning open, at the dead end of the hall.

Sloan pointed at the floor, indicating Reeder should take a position guarding the exit these stairs provided. The SAIC pointed to himself, then pointed down the hallway, indicating he would clear these rooms.

Reeder nodded, and Sloan gave him a raised-eyebrow look that said be ready for anything.

As Sloan entered the first room, Reeder gripped the Glock tight. *Was* he ready for anything? He'd been a field agent, and a damn good one, for a long time; but that was yesterday, and today he, for all his years, was the rookie here.

Then Sloan exited the room, mouthed *Clear,* and was moving past the second door to check the bathroom first. He did so. Nothing, apparently. Again, Sloan mouthed broadly: *Clear.*

Reeder felt himself trembling—not much, just enough to unsettle him and be angry with himself. He watched Sloan enter the final room.

Then came Sloan's voice: *"Federal agents!"*

And Reeder took off down the hall, and he was halfway there when the shot came—*Jesus!*—thunderous in the close quarters. Then the second shot, and a voice he didn't recognize cried out in wordless pain.

"Shit!" Reeder yelled, and he was almost there, the open door just ahead, God knew what waited within—Sloan dead, or dying, a killer with a gun?

Then Sloan came stumbling out into the hall.

At first Reeder thought the SAIC had been hit, but it was something else. Not fear, not even shock—dejection.

"Clear," Sloan said, barely audible.

Behind him, he heard Eaton and Cribbs barreling up the stairs, and Reeder called, "*Clear!*"

Sloan had gone back in.

Reeder peered into a shabby bedroom, where the SAIC, weapon loose and limp at his side, stood at the foot of a double bed. Dwight "Butch" Brooks, in shorts and wifebeater, lay there on his back as if asleep—the kind of sleep indicated by a small round hole in his forehead. The headboard had a lively spattering of blood and brains, dripping like an abstract art piece that hadn't dried yet.

A gun rested in Brooks's limp right hand. Glancing to his left, Reeder saw a bullet hole in the trim by the door, about six inches from where Sloan's head would have been in entering.

Eaton and Cribbs came up behind Reeder, forcing him deeper into the room. Clothes were strewn on the floor, and a dresser was home to beer cans and ancient porn DVDs, though the wall the bed faced had an Ultra HD screen. Big as the one in Reeder's living room.

"Fuck me," Eaton said.

Cribbs let out a long sigh.

"Damnit," Sloan muttered. Then to the corpse, he blurted, "You just *had* to shoot! You just had to shoot . . ."

Sloan slumped, and Reeder put a hand on one of his friend's shoulders. They exchanged glum looks.

Whatever Butch Brooks had known was leaking out the back of his head.

And by now Charlie Granger would have that lawyer he'd requested.

"A man may die, nations may rise and fall,
but an idea lives on."

*John Fitzgerald Kennedy,*
*Thirty-Fifth President of the United States of America,*
*former senator and representative*
*from the Commonwealth of Massachusetts.*
*Section 45, Grid U-35, Arlington National Cemetery.*

# EIGHT

Supreme Court Justice Rodolfo Gutierrez rose precisely at five every morning. He admired precision, considered it a virtue. He would then shave, put on his sweats, and limber up for five minutes, one of his few concessions to turning sixty-eight over this winter past, then—at five-thirty—set out for his daily run.

As usual, Adriana—his wife of forty-five years—accompanied him. Her pink-and-white running suit with New Balance running shoes put to shame his gray sweatpants and white T-shirt, and as a runner she was at least his equal. This morning ritual had gone on for years, and Adriana was every bit as competitive as the Justice. Her hair might be grayer than his, but hers was still the taut, athletic body of the young woman he'd married.

They jogged out of the driveway of their eight-bedroom brick residence to run north along the tree-lined shoulder on Chain Bridge Road at the far end of the Crest Lane cul-de-sac; then they would turn back and retrace their route to the Chain Bridge, before circling north to the house. The forty-one-minute run covered 3.2 miles.

Five eight and 168 pounds, his short black hair graying at the temples, Gutierrez ran with an easy, even graceful gait that—like his wife—gave him the appearance of a much younger runner. There was little traffic this time of morning, so the lack of side-walks seldom hindered their exercise. While their morning work-out helped keep him in shape, what the Justice relished most about it was time for reflection. Today, as every day, husband and wife ran in amiable silence.

Behind them the sun edged over the horizon, the road running more northwest than true north. The Justice's sneakers didn't slap the ground so much as glide, touching down, pushing off. This lovely morning was as quiet and peaceful as an empty cathedral, interrupted only by Adriana's easy in-and-out take of breath and the crunch of her shoes on the gravelly shoulder.

Both good Catholics, the Justice and his wife had raised six children who had given them, so far, half a dozen grandchildren and one great-grandchild. The couple went, well, religiously to confession and Mass, and tithed generously; but Gutierrez knew his greatest gift to the church had been writing the majority opinion returning prayer to public schools.

Creating that document had been the easiest, most pleasurable contribution he'd made since donning the sacred robes of his station. Yes, there had been criticism, but he didn't care—his only desire was that all children, even those unfortunate enough to attend public school, have the spiritual and patriotic underpinnings he'd enjoyed growing up in parochial.

His own success in life had been fueled by his parents' insistence that he achieve academic excellence, and, thanks to them, he had. But praise must also go to the Diocese of Trenton, New Jersey— from St. Joseph Grammar School to Monsignor Donovan High School, he'd received nothing less than a world-class education.

Rodolfo Gutierrez had been a small, frail child, doomed always to be the brightest in his class. Yes, he'd been bullied in Catholic schools from St. Joe's onward—but wasn't that par for the course with a boy of his enviable intellect? And who knew what horrors might have awaited him in *public* school . . .

Discipline was Gutierrez's bedrock principle, instilled by his parents and aided and abetted by the nuns and brothers. This—along with faith and education—was the trinity upon which the Justice had built his life. His children, as they grew older, often joshed him that his traditional "discipline" was, in fact, obsessive-compulsive disorder—but they said so with love and a smile.

Anyway, what was wrong with maintaining a sense of order in one's life? His schedule, and his sense of same, was so precise that he no longer needed to switch on his alarm clock. How many in this life could say as much?

Reaching their Crest Lane turnaround, the couple typically kicked up their speed and ran hard back to Chain Bridge Road, before slowing to their normal stride and turning the corner.

The Justice checked his watch—right on time, of course. He smiled to himself, continuing down the shoulder of Chain Bridge Road, where now a few cars were starting their morning commute, passing by on the southeast-bound side opposite.

"On schedule?" Adriana asked, her first words since starting the run.

"Like you, *Querida*—perfection."

She gave him a little smile—he'd seen that before—and he wondered if she really knew how much he meant it. She was still the lovely dark-haired girl with the olive complexion who'd smiled at him outside Seton Hall and accomplished the impossible: making him late for class.

"Going in today?" she asked between breaths. It was a casual enough question, but there was something calculated about it. Did she wish he would play hooky?

There was no real reason to go to the office—the latest Supreme Court session was winding down, and anyway, with the Venter tragedy, business would be suspended. But Rodolfo Gutierrez went to the office every workday.

"For a while," he said just as casual, punctuating his breathing with clumps of words, "but I'll come home . . . an hour early . . . so we can change . . . before this evening."

He and Adriana would be going to the Venter visitation, the private one for family and friends. By tomorrow Henry's body would lie in state in the Great Hall of the Supreme Court Building. Not all justices lay in state; in fact, few in history had—less than a dozen. This was a rare high honor, but a most worthy one.

Henry Venter had served on the Court with distinction for nearly two decades—not just a respected colleague, but a valuable ally in righteous jurisprudence, a credit to his race, and a damned good friend.

As they neared the Chain Bridge, Gutierrez's sense of loss was heightened by the knowledge that his colleague would almost certainly be replaced by a liberal, thanks to the Devlin Harrison presidency. Conservatives would still control the Court, true, but the balance would now be only five to four.

The concern to maintain conservative control was another reason these morning runs were so important. Gutierrez had to keep up his stamina and protect his health for at least another two years. This clod Harrison gave all the appearances of being a one-term president, but a second term remained a possibility—and a second Harrison term would put the Court's conservative control in serious jeopardy.

Henry's death left Gutierrez the second-most senior conservative member, meaning now more than ever his leadership would be crucial.

After all, the senior member on the conservative side—Ella Caywood Novinger—was pushing eighty. Eighty-one-year-old Edward Curtis Echo Hawk—the Court's first Native American justice—was oldest among the liberals. Gutierrez's opposite in seniority on the liberal side, Associate Justice Stephen Terrell, was a robust seventy-one.

Next down the ladder of age was conservative Chief Justice Whitaker Jackson, two years less seniority than Gutierrez but seven years older. Sylvia McCarren, youngest of the liberals, was in her early fifties, having been appointed by Harrison shortly after his election. She would be a problem for years to come.

The two remaining conservatives—Paul Van Steenhuyse and Grace Sorenson—were both in their fifties and should be around a good long time to battle the likes of McCarren. Like Gutierrez, Steenhuyse and Sorenson were President Bennett appointees, initiating much whining criticism about Bennett "stacking the Court." Gutierrez only wished that great man had stacked it further.

The goal, the strategy, now was clear: Stay in good health, and in top shape, and no matter what awful thing might happen in your personal life, don't even *think* of resigning. The conservative justices needed to maintain the balance of the Court until the right kind of president sat behind the desk in the Oval Office.

This was true whether two years from now or six—the power needed to be maintained. Too many had worked too hard for too long, getting this country back on the right track.

As the couple turned north for the short leg home, Gutierrez knew that sooner or later, he and his wife would have to deal with the elephant in the room—the Golden Age years they had planned. Adriana had long been nudging him toward retirement, and he knew all too well that his lovely wife wanted them both to spend more time with the grandchildren. And then there was travel, and all the things they'd looked forward to over nearly half a century of marriage.

"I love you," he said as they slowed to a jog, as they always did at this point.

She smiled at his unscheduled expression of affection; but there was something sad in it.

"*Querida?* Is something wrong?"

"Rodolfo—I already know."

"Know what?"

"That you can't retire. Not now. Now yet. With Henry gone, you'll have to stay. I've done the math."

Her uncanny ability to all but read his thoughts was proof from God that they belonged together.

"You're not . . . angry with me?"

Shaking her head, beads of perspiration flying, Adriana said, "Not at you—at the men who killed Henry. Petty thieves who not only took a good man's life, but cost us precious time together."

They were almost walking now.

"If our side can get the fool Harrison out after one term," Gutierrez said, "then two years from now? You and I will have everything we've dreamed about. I can walk away satisfied. Job well done."

Making the turn into their driveway, they slowed to a walk, and he checked his watch—forty-one minutes. He glanced smilingly over to tell her, but his wife had stopped at the mouth of the driveway.

She was staring at him.

Unsettled, returning to her, he asked, "What?"

She hugged him fiercely. Not her usual behavior in public, at least not since he'd risen to the Court.

"You are everything I ever dreamed about, Rodolfo."

She kissed him, just a little kiss, with so much in it.

"*Querida* . . ."

"Go feed your birds or you'll get off schedule. I'm going inside to shower."

She moved past him, and he watched her go, lingeringly. He loved her very much, but especially at moments like these.

The driveway was lined with low-lying, geometrically shaped shrubs; so were the front of the house and the southern end of the property. The ample yard looked well tended and green, and gave him a smile—another job well done—admittedly in association with Adriana. He moved around the north side, past the magenta bougainvillea that provided a needed dash of color. Also Adriana's doing—whatever color there was in this life of theirs was thanks to her.

The equally spacious backyard was home to a large patio on the far corner, a tranquility garden near one back corner, and a brick toolshed matching the house. Though hired people did most of the yard work, the Justice liked to mow himself on occasion. This he found as peaceful as his morning runs, and the same was true for his time feeding wild birds, up next in his day.

The shed was a good size, with a second story for Adriana's pots and gardening tools. They had spent years in apartment living, which made the outdoors of their gated paradise precious to them.

The feeder food was in a drum just inside the shed. The drum kept the mice away, should one be brave enough to invade this well-to-do neighborhood. The shed door had no lock—burglars had even less chance than rodents of survival among these estates.

Inside the shed, Gutierrez held the door open with his hip as he lifted the drum's lid and filled the generous scoop. The bird feeder was about eight feet from the shed, giving a better view from the house of feathered guests stopping by for a snack.

The digging of the scoop prompted a rustling—the family of wrens just outside the house built into the shed's second floor. The wrens knew the scoop meant breakfast was soon to be served. By the time Gutierrez eased the shed door closed, they were airborne.

He crossed the grass to the feeder, lifted the lid, dropped the food in. He shut the lid, turned back to the shed, noticing sunlight glinting off something beneath a shrub near the serenity garden, a few feet away.

He had no idea what it was, just that it didn't belong there. He took one step toward it, then pain seared his gut, followed a millisecond later by a shotgun report.

*. . . Had he been out for a second or two, or maybe a minute?*

He didn't remember falling, but suddenly he was on his back on the soft, dewy grass, squinting up into the sun, a coldness in his abdomen. He raised a hand to block out the brightness.

Tried to sit up, couldn't. Somebody had set a big, heavy stone on his chest, only there wasn't any—just the sensation. His fingers walked to his stomach, where they met a throbbing, wet stickiness. Bringing his hand back, blocking the sun with it, he realized his fingers were dripping blood.

His blood?

*Deer slug,* his hunter's mind told him. *But from where? Why?*

He shut his eyes to fight the sun, which felt warm on his face, though every other part of him grew colder, colder.

*He'd been shot*—that much he knew.

Then, in a moment of terrible clarity, his mind stopped its bouncing to tell him he was dying.

There was no fear, no swift parade of memories in his mind, not even a sense of the irony that in moments he would be facing a higher court for final judgment. His thoughts were much more basic. Simple.

The man who had tried to keep everything so neat, so precise, who had always cleaned up after himself when so many men didn't, knew that lovely Adriana, after her shower, would come looking for him in her robe, smiling, because it was their time for their every-third-day sex. But all she would find was the mess that he had, for once, left her.

A bloody one.

"Sometimes history takes things into its own hands."

*Thurgood Marshall,*
*Associate Justice of the Supreme Court*
*of the United States of America, 1967–1991,*
*First African American Justice.*
*Section 5, Grave 40-3*
*Arlington National Cemetery.*

# NINE

Special Agent Gabriel Sloan was having a good morning, considering. In a life that in recent years included losing a daughter and a marriage, such mornings were rare. But this boded to be one of them.

They had the gun taken from Butch Brooks's house, and Sloan felt confident that the shell casing from the bedroom would match the one from the Verdict restaurant bar, where Justice Venter had been slain. Since he'd had to shoot Brooks, for Sloan this would mean vindication of a sort.

Walking toward the task force command post, he saw his reflection glide by in door glass and damned if he wasn't smiling. Things were finally starting to get better.

"Hey, Gabe," a familiar voice behind him said. "Wait up!"

Sloan turned. "Morning, Peep."

Reeder came up fast, digging into his suit coat pocket, his face its usual blank mask, somehow emphasized by his tan complexion and stark white hair. The consultant withdrew the Glock that Sloan had provided him at the Brooks duplex yesterday.

"Here," Reeder said with a tiny sneer of disgust, "take the damned thing."

You'd think Reeder was the one who'd had to kill a man.

Slipping it into his own pocket, Sloan let his smile blossom into a grin. "What an old lady you're getting to be in your emeritus years."

Reeder frowned. "Right—like yesterday didn't bother you any."

"Disturbed the hell out of me. I haven't had many guns pointed at me in my years of service. I know I don't have to tell *you* how *that* feels."

Reeder shook his head. "There's more to it. There's the aftermath. Are you going to see an FBI shrink?"

"Are you kidding? There won't even be a shooting board till this investigation is over."

They were walking, but suddenly in no hurry.

"How did you sleep last night, Gabe?"

"Frankly, like a goddamned baby. Do I love losing the information that Brooks could have given us? Hell no. But do I mind putting a lowlife down so I can go on breathing? Not hardly."

"There's the conservative SOB I know and love."

Sloan flashed a rumpled grin. They continued down the endless corridor.

"Anyway," Sloan said. "That part of it is over. We got the guys. And *one's* still breathing, at least."

"You get the forensics results?"

Sloan shook his head. "Should be soon. Usually the lab takes weeks, even months. But the death of a Supreme Court justice jumps us to the front of the line."

"Don't kid yourself about this, Gabe."

Sloan stopped—the command post was a few doors down. "What do you mean, Peep? If the casings match, Brooks and Granger are our guys."

"Maybe in the sense that one of them pulled the trigger on Venter."

"*Of course* one of them pulled the trigger."

"What I mean is—if they did it, they were hired. This is still no robbery."

Reeder pushed through the command post doors, holding one open for Sloan, who was a single step in when the applause began—the rest of the task force already there. He glanced back at Reeder, who wore a mild smirk, this reception clearly not something Peep found appropriate.

But the clapping grew louder, accompanied by a few hoots and whistles, as Sloan faced a roomful of smiles, everybody on their feet at their desks and at the conference table. Only Patti Rogers, standing but leaning back against her chair, seemed restrained in her smile and lackluster in her clapping—*was she still pissed that she'd been left out of the Brooks raid?*

Sloan gave them a "stop" palm and a grave expression, and the applause quickly died. "Much as I appreciate that, everyone—we're a long way from the end of this."

"Maybe not," Eaton said, jerking his head toward Altuve. "Ask Miggie about the test results he got from the lab."

This sounded like good news, yet Sloan found himself frowning. "I was promised they'd give it to me direct, the second they had something."

"Well," Eaton said with a sly grin, "Miggie *might* have cut a corner or two."

Sloan turned to Miggie, who—despite the group meeting—had already sat down at his desk and was back at it. Or pretending to be.

Sloan said, "Agent Altuve—you hacked our own *lab?*"

Miggie swiveled and smiled sheepishly. "Let's say I . . . identified a security lapse that we now know can be, uh, properly addressed."

"Skip the spin, Mig. Do the shell casings match?"

Miggie nodded. "Yes, they do."

"Which is why," Eaton said, grinning like he'd done the hacking, "you deserve a round of applause, boss man. Well, we all do. *Almost* all of us, anyway."

The beefy Homeland Security agent was looking past Sloan at Reeder. Who said, "You think you have a point to make, Eaton?"

Eaton's head went back and his chin came out, as if daring Reeder to take a swing. "Just that your kinesics bullshit sent us down a lot of needless paths and wasted valuable time. Those casings matching tells us Brooks's gun is the murder weapon—that Justice Venter really *is* collateral damage in a tavern stickup."

Sloan glanced at Reeder, gave him a small head bob that told the ex–Secret Service agent to step forward and explain himself.

Reeder said, "Brooks and Granger are career criminals. Somebody could have hired them to kill the Justice. It's even possible that somebody was sophisticated enough to hire them *because* they were pulling these tavern robberies, and the Venter assassination could be written off as a robbery-related slaying."

A lot of frowns were forming, but the burly Eaton goggled at Reeder.

"What a load of horseshit!" the Homeland agent blurted, eyes rolling. He turned toward the SAIC. "Sloan, you *can't* be *buying* this!"

Calmly, Sloan said, "We've all seen the Verdict security footage, and we all heard Mr. Reeder give us a convincing reading of the body language of both the judge and his killer."

Eaton spat words like seeds: "It . . . is . . . a . . . god . . . damned . . . *robbery.*"

Sloan nodded slowly. "You may be right. Probably are. But we have to make sure. This room is filled not just with representatives of various agencies, but with experts—Joe Reeder is one of them, dispatched here by *my* boss. And as *your* boss, I want to know *why* Justice Venter was murdered and, along the way, build an airtight case against Granger."

The room got quiet. Even Eaton seemed to be settling down.

The group dispersed to their seats at desks or the conference table. They each had jobs to do, and went about doing them. Both the celebration and its argumentative aftermath were over.

Seated at the conference table, Sloan glanced over where Reeder had taken his place at the desk next to Rogers at hers. The SAIC might not have been a kinesics expert, but he could read that Rogers was annoyed with him for leaving her behind yesterday. But he and Patti had been partners long enough for Sloan to know he should give her some space.

He had just booted up his laptop when his cell vibrated, and he checked caller ID: *Margery Fisk.*

*Shit.* Had Miggie's hacking been caught?

He took the call, and the Assistant Director said only three words before clicking off: "My office. Now."

Soon he was standing before her Buick-size desk—she had not indicated he should sit, so he edged in between two visitor chairs opposite her. Fisk was in a gray business suit that matched her complexion. Her dark hair was its usual lacquered self; her aging fashion model's features had a coldness, but her dark eyes blazed.

As if asking him to pass the salt, she said, "Justice Gutierrez has been murdered."

"What? Jesus. *When?* Where?"

"In his own backyard," Fisk said, "within the half hour."

"My God. That changes everything."

"You think?" Her face tightened with barely controlled rage. "Can you tell me, Agent Sloan, why you didn't have Justice Gutierrez under protective watch? Him and every *other* justice?"

He gestured with upraised palms. "Because Venter was the victim in a robbery holdup gone wrong."

"Really? Is that why you had me put Joe Reeder on your team? He was talking assassination, and you were taking it seriously."

"I was. I . . . I still do. Still am."

"Particularly *now,* I should think."

He put a hand on her desk and leaned in. "All due respect, Director—why would the death of one justice be interpreted as indicating other justices were in danger?"

"It would seem a routine precaution. When this investigation is over, another inquiry will follow. You can count on that, Agent Sloan."

*Oh—so that was it: When criticism was raised that the other justices should have been given protection, someone would have to be blamed. And it wouldn't be Margery Fisk.*

She said, businesslike now, "I've already sent guards to the homes of the surviving justices."

"Surviving justices . . . my God, what a bizarre sound."

She arched a perfectly plucked eyebrow. "It's not the *only* bizarre sound we can both expect to hear today and in the coming days. As for now, take your team and find out exactly what went down at the Gutierrez home."

"Yes, ma'am."

He turned to go, but she called out: "And, Sloan?"

He faced her; their eyes met.

"Make sure this is the last justice we lose."

"I'm certain it will be, Director—now that you've seen to it they've been provided with security."

She studied him for a moment, searching for sarcasm; giving up, she said, "Well, I want you to make sure that none of them need it. Find those responsible. ASA-fucking-P."

He nodded and went out.

It didn't take long to fill in the team, considering how scant the available information.

"Rogers . . . Bishop . . . Pellin . . . Eaton . . . Cribbs . . . Reeder— we're going to the scene. The rest of you keep at what you've been doing. Now that two justices have been taken out, look hard at racial hate groups . . . we have an African American and a Hispanic justice as our two victims . . . and also at left-wing fanatical groups."

"Because," Reeder said in the same cadence as Sloan, "it's possible somebody is trying to change the balance of the Court."

All eyes went to the kinesics expert. Things had been moving so fast that no one but Reeder had put it together.

"We just lost the two most conservative members of the Court," Reeder pointed out, "and we have a liberal president sitting in the White House. How do you think those vacant seats will likely be filled?"

Silence draped the room.

Sloan said, "Peep is right. That's a very logical read of the situation."

Reeder said, "Oh, and Agent Eaton? As soon as you apologize, I'll be happy to accept."

Eaton said nothing, but his face was flushed.

Miggie was already machine-gunning at his computer as those Sloan had singled out grabbed jackets and headed for the door.

Sloan called out: "Miggie! We need the Gutierrez address."

"Way ahead of you, boss. It'll be on everyone's cell phones by the time they get to their cars."

"Good." Sloan turned to the conference table. "Oh, and let's not let the jihadists feel neglected. Stay on that thread, too."

Nods over laptop tops saw them out the door.


Drivers in DC are not known for rushing out of the way for emergency vehicles, but this morning, the convoy of unmarked cars, cherry tops flashing, sirens screaming, had even the most hard-nosed motorists heading for the shoulders.

Sloan paved the way by cell with the Fairfax County sheriff, who told him Chain Bridge Road would be blocked at both ends, per protocol. Knowing locals disliked dealing with feds, Sloan put Bishop and Pellin in the lead, and the caravan paused briefly while two DC cops had the deputy check with his boss.

Sloan could see but not hear what was going on, and he was just about to get out and get involved when the deputy stepped back, lifted the chain out of the way, and waved Bishop and the rest of the parade on through.

Already, Gutierrez's street was lined with law enforcement vehicles from every jurisdiction in the surrounding hundred or so miles. Sloan got out, giving his car door a slam as if to announce his presence, and strode toward the Justice's estate, his team behind him like a posse in business suits, Reeder falling in at his side.

With so much local law on the scene, Sloan expected another pissing match, and was ready to let go at whichever local detective was planning to make a career on the back of a murdered Supreme Court justice.

But what emerged from the front door to meet them was a kid, barely thirty, who seemed glad to be approached by someone raising an FBI badge. The kid might have been a younger version of Sloan, military-short blond hair, bright blue eyes, cleft chin.

Hand extended, the young detective said, "Special Agent Sloan?"

Sloan nodded, shaking the kid's hand.

"Detective Tim McCrosky," the young man said, mouth smiling, forehead frowning. "Am I glad to see you. What we have here is well beyond my skill set."

Sloan grunted a laugh. "Who was it said a man has to know his limitations?"

"Dirty Harry," Reeder said, a half step back from Sloan. "First homicide, Detective McCrosky?"

McCrosky shook his head. "Not hardly . . . but the first *big* homicide. The media is already trying to muscle in here and sneak in there—woods edge the backyard, y'know."

Sloan narrowed his gaze. "Detective, we can't have media trampling the killer's route."

The kid raised a gentle hand. "I have uniformed officers back there, in blue booties, shooing 'em off. Plus, we put up a canvas tarp in front of the body."

"Good thinking," Sloan said, nodding. "But you need to cordon off that whole area. Get your guys a shitload of crime scene tape and make sure we keep the media the hell out of there. Got it?"

"Got it, sir."

"And round up any media members that you *know* were back there and confiscate their shoes."

"Their . . . shoes?"

"Shoes. If the path the killer took is through the woods, we have to eliminate all other footprints. That's going to include any members of the media who were back there, and any officers that were there, too . . . at least, pre–blue booties."

The young detective half smiled, nodded, and went over to a uniformed officer, and started delegating.

Sloan said, "Maybe this *is* his first homicide."

"No," Reeder said. "Like he said—just his first big one. He's never had national media tromping around his crime scene before."

When McCrosky returned, he said, "For the time being, if you don't mind, Agent Sloan, I'll be keeping *my* shoes on."

"That's fine," Sloan said with a mild smile. "Let's get started, son. Who found the body?"

"Mrs. Gutierrez. She wondered where her husband was, looked out the window, then ran to him. Called 911 from his cell. She was in her robe. Just been showering."

"That's why she didn't hear the shot?"

"Apparently. Must've had her head under the spray."

Sloan shared a glance with Reeder, then asked, "Who's with her now?"

"Officer Johnson, first uniform on the scene. Been with her the whole time. He's got a nice touch with folks who are in a bad place."

Sloan nodded. "Always a good thing for a cop to have. You interview her yourself yet?"

McCrosky shook his head. "I knew someone with a higher pay grade than mine would show up soon. Pretty much, we just sat tight."

"Well, that wasn't such a bad thing to do, Detective McCrosky. Good job."

The kid puffed up a little.

Sloan gave the detective a dismissive nod. "We'll take it from here."

The young detective went off to supervise his men while Sloan rounded up his team in the front yard to dispatch assignments. As they assembled in a tight semicircle, Sloan noticed Rogers staring daggers at him.

*Shit. Maybe I should deal with this now . . .*

He curled a finger at her, and they stepped off to one side.

She just looked at him. It was an ability Rogers shared with his ex-wife, Beth—waiting him out. Forcing the play on him.

"I can see you're unhappy with me," he said. "About yesterday."

"Why would I be unhappy with you?"

"We don't have time for this, Patti. You tell me."

"All right. I will. You screwed up."

"How exactly did I screw up?"

"You took Reeder along and not me. If I'd been on the scene, with my *recent* field experience? Brooks might still be alive, and we'd have two suspects to talk to."

He let out a world-weary breath. "Look—if I did screw up, it's my weight to carry. You won't be the one in front of the shooting board—*I* will."

But she didn't seem the least bit satisfied by that.

So he admitted it: "Patti, I should have taken you with us."

Her face softened some.

"I have a history with you," he told her, "but I have a longer history with Peep. And in his defense, he did fine on the Brooks raid."

Her chin crinkled. "If I'd been along, you wouldn't have left me to guard an exit. We'd have checked those rooms out together, and—"

"And Brooks would have shot at you instead of me, maybe, and then what? He'd still be dead, right? Or maybe you would be."

"Well, we can't know that."

"That's right, Patti. We can't. If I had it to do over, though, I'd take you instead. Okay? That enough?"

She nodded. It was.

"Now—if we're friends again, could your big, bad boss ask you to please go inside and interview Mrs. Gutierrez? Can you do that?"

She smiled ever so faintly. "On one condition."

"Oh, there's a condition?"

"Never leave me out of the loop again. We cool?"

He laughed, once. "We're cool. While you interview the wife, Peep and I'll check the body while the rest of the team canvasses the neighbors."

"Haven't the local cops done that?"

"The young man in charge seems to have just held down the fort till we got here. Anyway, I want our people on it. We've interviewed more witnesses individually than all these locals put together."

"I hear that," she said.

Within a couple of minutes, the team had dispersed for the neighborhood canvass, while Detective McCrosky accompanied Rogers inside for the Mrs. Gutierrez interview.

Sloan felt a pang for the widow. She'd been taking a shower, such a mundane daily activity, unaware of the tragedy going on in the yard just outside her window. Things in this life could change fast, hard, and forever. Sloan knew that all too well.

In the expansive backyard, with Reeder nearby, Sloan approached the massive canvas curtain the deputies had erected to keep the press from prying. In front of it, lying on the ground, a sheet covering him, was Justice Gutierrez.

While plenty of blue-bootied deputies were in the yard, they kept their distance from the immediate crime scene, and a couple of them waited off to one side with the crew from the coroner's office.

Sloan and Reeder stood over the body for only a second before the SAIC dropped to a crouch and drew back the sheet. Gutierrez lay on his back, a saucer-shaped hole in his abdomen, his T-shirt drenched with blood, already blackening, his eyes staring emptily into the sunny sky.

"Shotgun," Reeder said. "Deer slug."

"Oh yeah."

"That entrance wound didn't stretch the fabric—perfect circle. Looks like a cog bored through. What does that tell you?"

They were both experienced enough deer hunters to know what they were seeing. "Brenneke shotgun slug."

"Bingo."

"Nasty damn way to go," Sloan sighed, dropping the sheet. He stood, his eyes tracing the line of the woods. "Impossible to get any sort of decent sniper setup with a rifle, I suppose. Trees are too thick."

Reeder frowned. "Killer just strolled out of the woods and blasted him?"

"Seems like the obvious way in."

Shaking his head, Reeder walked over past the tarp to get a better look into the forest beyond.

"Doesn't make sense," Reeder said.

"What doesn't?"

"The whole damn thing," Reeder said, frowning into the woods. "It's . . . sloppy."

"Seems to have gotten the job done."

Reeder shook his head again. "No, this is wrong."

"Wrong?"

"Where do these woods come out?"

Sloan considered that momentarily. "There's an access road in Fort Marcy Park. That's what the forest actually is. You could walk in from Bent Twig Road—that borders the park, too."

"Something's just not right."

Sloan had to smirk. "You mean besides a murdered Supreme Court justice?"

"Two murdered Supreme Court justices, remember?"

"Yeah, yeah. Let's stay focused on this one, Peep."

"All right. The two access points into the woods are public—so why carry a shotgun from a vehicle, through the woods, and into the yard, when anyone might see you?"

"There's no traffic in either place at that hour," Sloan said. "Seems safe enough. And maybe it was known that the Justice went out running regularly in the morning. And there are bushes to crouch behind waiting for him to get home."

"Okay. Let's work from that premise. But why carry a shotgun when you could easily hide a pistol?"

Sloan shrugged. "Killer prefers shotguns. Might happen to be the only weapon the shooter owns."

"Not when you're assassinating your second Supreme Court justice in less than a week."

Sloan raised a surrendering hand. "Okay. I see your point."

"Good. Because this group, whoever they are, know what they're doing."

"Group?"

"Has to be," Reeder said. "When this went down, Brooks was dead, Granger in custody. There's more going on here than we know about. It's a conspiracy."

"We have at least three people involved," Sloan granted. "So it's a conspiracy by definition."

"Right." Reeder's voice was as hushed as if he were in church. "They scouted Venter. They scouted Gutierrez. The shooter knew exactly where to be, when to be there. They made the public believe Venter was the victim of a robbery gone bad. The shotgun is a weird, sloppy choice. I mean, they didn't use a shotgun in Dallas, did they?"

Sloan looked down at the bloody corpse. "Maybe they wanted a messy death for Gutierrez, to punish him, make him suffer. Gut shot like that, he didn't die instantly."

Reeder shook his head, then looked from the body to the woods and back again. "Gabe, it's like that damn Verdict shooting all over again. At first, everybody got it wrong. Same thing here. I can *feel* it. We're missing something."

That good morning Gabe Sloan had been enjoying was less than a memory now, as he listened to his friend, not liking the sound of it one little bit.

"The right to revolt has sources deep in our history. "

*William O. Douglas,*
*Associate Justice of the Supreme Court*
*of the United States of America, 1939–1975,*
*longest tenure of any Supreme Court Justice,*
*36 years, 209 days.*
*Section 5, Lot 7004-B-1, Grid W-36,*
*Arlington National Cemetery.*

# TEN

While Sloan entered the big brick mansion to talk to Mrs. Gutierrez, Reeder stayed behind—he wanted to spend a little more time with the late Justice. Elsewhere in the yard, the Fairfax County crime scene team had started its search for clues while the coroner's crew huddled nearby with a stretcher.

Reeder could not shake the nagging feeling that they were missing something. He squatted near the body, pulling back the sheet. Ignoring the late judge's startled expression, he leaned in for a better look at the wound, slowly scanning the bloody shirt—no stippling on the material. Lack of powder burns meant the Justice had not been shot up close. If the assassin had come out of the woods to take Gutierrez by surprise, why had he or she shot from a distance and not crept up to do a point-blank job?

Bending near the wound, mere inches away, Reeder tried to determine the slug's trajectory.

"*Hey!*" somebody shouted. "What the hell are you doing there?"

A man in a Fairfax CSI windbreaker was heading his way—no meek scientist this, more like a Redskins linebacker, six three, muscular, shovel-faced, with a dark flattop and rage in his brown eyes.

"I'm with the task force," Reeder said, rising.

"I don't see an ID," the CSI said, planting himself a few feet away.

Reeder suddenly realized he didn't have an identifying necklace or even a badge to display.

"I'm a consultant," Reeder said, and even to him it sounded lame.

"I'm *not* going to tell you *again*—"

"*He's with us!*" Patti Rogers called from behind them.

They both turned to her. Her FBI badge displayed around her neck, Rogers moved swiftly but carefully across the yard to them.

"He looks like a civilian," the CSI said defensively.

"Take a closer look. That's Joe Reeder, former Secret Service, consultant to the interagency task force on the murders of two Supreme Court justices. You might want to stay on his good side."

Turning to Reeder, the CSI said, "Sorry, Mr. Reeder. I just don't like seeing evidence contaminated."

"I haven't touched the body," Reeder assured him, Rogers falling in at his side. "And I don't want anything contaminated any more than you do. You in charge out here?"

"Yeah. Grogan, Darrell Grogan. Crime scene team supervisor."

"Then you're just the man I need," Reeder said as they shook hands—Grogan's in a latex glove. "I was just trying to determine an approximate trajectory of the killing shot. Can you help?"

Grogan shrugged. "Back in the lab I could."

"I said approximate." Reeder nodded toward the corpse. "Something here just doesn't track."

The CSI let air out, took some in. "Give me a minute—I need a couple things."

"Sure. Thanks."

As the husky CSI strode away, Reeder turned to Rogers and asked, "Anything useful from Mrs. Gutierrez?"

Rogers said, "They went for their morning run, like always, came home, like always. Then she went inside to take a shower and Justice Gutierrez came back around to feed the birds."

"Like . . . always?"

"Yeah," Rogers said. "Justice Gutierrez definitely sounds like a 'like always' kind of guy. His wife calls him 'punctual.' I call him OCD."

Reeder glanced around the yard with its CSI intruders and dead man of the house. "Not tough, then, for the assassin to know where Gutierrez would be, and when."

"Not at all."

"How, exactly, do you figure the assassin knew?"

As if rehearsed, they simultaneously looked toward the woods. Not really hard to hide there.

Rogers said, "Staked him out."

"Yes. And for quite a while, I'm guessing."

"Long enough to get the Gutierrezes' pattern down, anyway."

Reeder gave that a curt nod. "Right till a plan came together— which is why the shotgun as murder weapon doesn't play."

"That what the wound indicates? Shotgun?"

Reeder nodded. "Looks like a twelve gauge. Deer slug."

Her eyes flared. "Somebody wanted to make a point."

"Maybe. But I still want to know why such a big gun, when the woods have public access from the other side. Risk of being seen seems high."

"Maybe the killer wanted to make a *big* point."

Reeder twitched a smirk. "Then why not use a .500 S-and-W handgun, up close and personal? If you're going to the trouble of sneaking up from the woods."

Rogers frowned in thought. "Explain something to me."

"Give it a try."

"You insist the killing at the Verdict was the assassination of a Supreme Court justice hidden inside an armed robbery got out of hand."

"I do."

"Okay. But why bother with that elaborate rigmarole, if you're going to openly assassinate *another* justice, just days later?"

He grinned at her, but the only humor in it was dark. "Because it *is* just days later. These conspirators had everybody looking at Venter's killing through the robbery lens. Had it been read as an assassination, security measures to protect Gutierrez and every other justice would have gone immediately in place."

Rogers nodded. "Yeah, we've already done that for the other justices, now that Gutierrez is down. So it was just that *first* killing that had to fool us."

"Right."

She got a grudging smile going. "Only, you weren't fooled, were you, Joe?"

"No. But it doesn't seem to have done Justice Gutierrez much good."

Grogan returned, drew back the sheet, and went to work with what looked like a dowel, maybe two feet, easing it in, careful the rod did not touch the edges of the wound.

The CSI's head reared back. "Well, hell. Isn't *that* weird . . ."

"What is?" Rogers asked.

Taking in the rod's angle, Reeder said, "Gutierrez was shot from above."

Rogers seemed perplexed. "What, the killer made him *kneel?*"

Grogan, still down there, shook his head. "I don't think so. If the Justice had been kneeling, he probably wouldn't have ended up with his legs straight out in front of him like that."

Reeder said, "No grass stains on his knees, either."

The CSI carefully removed the dowel and got up. He called one of his people over and handed it off.

"So," Rogers said, "if he was shot from a downward angle and *wasn't* on his knees . . ."

They all looked toward the trees behind the property. Had there been a sniper's nest there after all?

"Curiouser and curiouser," Reeder said.

Rogers said dryly, "You don't look like a Lewis Carroll man."

"I'm not. My daughter was a Walt Disney girl. The quote stands—something, a *lot* of somethings, don't add up."

Her eyebrows rose. "Starting with, he was shot at a downward angle."

"Yeah, and I don't care which tree the shooter was in, that'd be a tough damn shot, the Justice standing by the bird feeder, and the shotgun only made it more so . . . if not impossible."

She asked, "Why not use a rifle?"

"Exactly the right question. The shooter likely scouted this job him- or herself, but at any rate knew everything about where to be, when to be there, and the easiest way to do it. Why not take advantage of the available intel?"

Rogers shrugged. "Well, you can't argue with the results. Anyway, that toolshed blocks most angles from the trees, and makes any remaining ones tougher."

Reeder was nodding.

She kept going: "And with a rifle, the assassin could have shot the Justice anytime after he came around behind the house. Why wait until Gutierrez had gone to the shed and backtracked to the bird feeder?"

Reeder said, "Our assassin obviously knew the Justice's OCD schedule. Why not just wait behind the shed with a pistol and a silencer? Pop out when Gutierrez got to the shed, double-tap him, and disappear into the woods?"

The CSI had been taking this all in. "It doesn't make any sense, a sniper in the woods. Why wait until that shed was in the way?"

Reeder glanced at the shed. A wren was balancing on its perch outside the built-in birdhouse that was just below the peak of the structure's V roof. The wren tried to get back inside, but something was blocking the way. It went back to its perch, then repeated its action with the same result.

Reeder squinted as he imagined a line from the birdhouse to where he stood.

"Dear God," he said.

"What?" Rogers asked.

"I may know how this was done."

Grogan asked, "What's your thinking?"

Reeder's only reply was to motion for them to follow as he almost ran to the shed.

He yanked open the door and was met, not surprisingly, by air-less warmth and the scent of soil, albeit with a hint of mint courtesy of a Glade PlugIn in a corner.

Grogan, just behind him, put a hand on Reeder's shoulder and said, "Sorry, sir, but you really shouldn't be touching things without gloves on—fingerprints."

Reeder glanced back with a humorless grin. "Point taken. But if I'm right, this assassin is far too clever to leave any of those . . . and if I'm wrong, it won't matter."

The CSI didn't look happy but gave the FBI consultant no argument.

Rogers, looking around, said, "This is bigger than my first apartment."

The two-story shed was damn near a small garage, with every tool in its designated place, bags of fertilizer and other gardening goodies stacked along walls with a neatness befitting its late owner. Access to the birdhouse was on the partial second floor, beyond the plywood half ceiling.

Reeder was already taking steps to the second floor.

"Mr. Reeder," the CSI called, "what's on your mind?"

The second floor, though only half the width of the shed, was as orderly as the downstairs, made cramped by the A-line roof. A small window let in sunlight revealing stacks of pots of different sizes lining the side walls. At the far end, what had been typically neat stacks of twenty-five- and forty-pound bags of potting soil, fertilizer, and mulch, about thigh-high, had been disrupted so that assorted bags could be restacked into a sort of platform to accommodate a tool that was definitely not intended for gardening.

A shotgun was set up on a bed of the bags, its barrel inserted in, and pointed through, the birdhouse.

Reeder had to bend over some as he moved down the spongy plywood floor. Behind him, Rogers and Grogan had come up and were taking in the view.

"Damn," Grogan said.

Rogers said, "It's a sniper's nest."

Reeder said, "Yes, but do you see a chair or stool? Or a seat made of these bags?"

Rogers said, "What was he, a dwarf?"

Reeder appraised the rig. The weapon was a pump-action twelve-gauge shotgun with wooden stock and pump.

"Remington 870," Reeder said.

Grogan was next to him now. "One of around ten million or so, and this one looks pre-'68—meaning ATF won't have any ownership records."

Rogers was just behind the CSI, the only one of the trio who didn't need to bend. The floor was giving a little—Reeder hoped they wouldn't go crashing down through.

She said, "Not much chance the serial number's still on it."

Neither man argued with her.

Reeder said, "Whoever set this up knew what he or she was doing."

No one argued with that, either: The gun was held in place by smaller bags of potting soil the killer had borrowed from the stacks on either side of the stock and the barrel. Both ends also rested on bags of soil, with one on top of the stock.

The thing that interested Reeder most, however, was the contraption wired to the trigger: a basic electric motorized device with an oval light and a tiny red light, set to pull the trigger when it received a specific radio-wave signal. Reeder stared at the setup for several moments, admiring the ingenuity of the gadget. Its sinister simplicity.

Rogers asked, "So Justice Gutierrez was shot from up here?"

"Yes and no," Reeder said, sliding back past Grogan, who was now inspecting the rig. He was about to similarly slip past Rogers when she stepped in his path.

Rogers said, "Explain."

He pointed toward the steps, and said, "Follow me."

She let him by and did.

When they were back outside, Reeder said, "The shot came from upstairs, through the birdhouse aperture, which is why we couldn't figure out the downward angle at first."

She moved to where she could look up at the birdhouse and the small entrance for its inhabitants. The wren flew back and landed on its perch again.

"The hell," she breathed, her hand acting as a sun visor.

"The assassin," Reeder said, "may have been long gone by the time the Justice was shot. We were considering the riskiness of a killer bringing a long gun through a public access area in daylight—"

Rogers completed the thought: "But he or she could have brought it in at *night*, set it up, and just walked away." She peered at him from under her visored hand. "But did the assassin come back this morning, and wait in the woods, to shoot Gutierrez remotely?"

Reeder didn't answer, his attention on the corner of what he guessed was a serenity garden.

"See something?" Rogers asked, but again he didn't reply, making a wide arc toward the garden.

She followed but was cutting through more direct when he said, "Take my route, Patti, not a straight path."

She smirked at this seeming non sequitur, but she did as he'd said, moving around Gutierrez's body and its shielding tarp.

Reeder's arc around the victim was a precaution: The shotgun hadn't been pumped again, and the round in the chamber had been used to kill Gutierrez . . . but why take chances?

Rogers asked, "Joe, what the hell are we doing?"

Reeder stopped and so did she. He pointed toward a clump of plants near the corner of the garden. "Do you see what's in the shadow of the hostas?"

She strained to see. "I see *something*. But what?"

"Motion detector," Reeder said. "That's my educated guess, anyway. Spot any others?"

She made a slow scan, then shook her head.

Reeder took a step closer to the apparent motion detector. Right into its sight.

There was an explosive sound, but not from a shotgun. Grogan, shouting within the shed: "*Son of a bitch!*"

As Reeder figured, no live round in the chamber.

Moments later the CSI burst from the shed, wide-eyed, sweat flying like tears. The day was heating up in more ways than one, but Grogan's perspiration wasn't due entirely to the small, airless building he'd been in.

"Something happen in there?" Rogers blandly asked the swiftly approaching CSI. Reeder knew she'd put two and two together already.

Grogan pointed back toward the second floor. "God-*damnedest* thing—that frickin' gun just tried to *fire* itself!"

"Really," she said.

"The light came on and the cam rotated, but then nothing. Trigger had already been pulled."

Reeder said, "It didn't try to fire itself. I tried to fire it."

"*You?*"

"Well, anyway . . . this did." He indicated the motion detector on the ground tucked under a bush.

Squatting, Grogan pulled back branches to get a better look. "Motion detector . . ."

"That would be a very safe bet," Reeder said.

The CSI stood. "You're saying the Justice killed himself—when he unwittingly triggered this gimmick."

Reeder nodded. "The assassin watched the Justice from the woods, maybe for weeks or even months. Either knowing or figuring out that Gutierrez was OCD or damn close to it. Came up with this plan and not only pulled it off, left us no fingerprints on the motion detector, the shotgun, or even the damn shell. Or if so, I'd be very damn surprised."

Rogers said, "How often do you suppose Gutierrez filled that bird feeder?"

"Possibly daily, part of his routine. We'll ask Mrs. Gutierrez. But it's likely this motion-control murder wasn't rigged till last night."

She was studying him, as if noticing for the first time that Reeder really existed. "Why do you say that?"

"Well, it's clear Venter was meant to be the first to go, with the kill misread as a holdup gone bad. This kill, however, is obviously assassination. Like we said before, if it had occurred first, all the other judges—including Venter—would've been on high security."

She was thinking so hard a vein stuck out in her forehead. "And you figure these two judges were targeted because they're archconservatives, and somebody wants to restack the Court?"

Reeder shrugged. "That's my read, yes. Doesn't mean we don't keep pursuing other avenues."

The CSI didn't seem to be listening to any of this. He was down having a closer look at the motion detector. He glanced up at them. "Listen, uh . . . I have to get started with the evidence gathering."

"Go ahead," Reeder said. "But I'd keep my expectations low. And be sure to dot the i's and cross the t's."

Frowning, Grogan got to his feet. "Hey, my team and I'll come up with anything else worth finding—believe it."

"I do. But this is a federal matter and an FBI crime scene crew will be here sooner than later. They will second-guess every damn move you make."

Grogan sighed, nodded. Somewhat defensively, he said, "You know, we would have found this motion detector *and* that rig in the shed."

"I'm sure you would."

The two men endured a brief awkward silence, then nodded at each other, trading respectful smiles.

Reeder walked Rogers away from the CSI, found a pocket of the backyard all their own. Too much had already been said in front of someone not on the task force.

He asked her, "How's your rapport with Mrs. Gutierrez?"

"Decent, I think."

"Go back in and get the names and info on her yard-work men. See if any of them, or anybody else, might have been around the shed yesterday. And send Sloan out here so I can bring him up to speed."

Rogers said, "You got it," and went off to do that.

Soon Reeder had not only filled Sloan in but given him a tour including the second floor of the shed with its rigged shotgun and the tucked-away-in-the-bushes motion detector. They stood near the latter and talked.

Reeder said, "This is way past anything Brooks and Granger might cook up, much less pull off."

The SAIC frowned in thought. "But we've got a match on Brooks's gun."

"If they were hired," Reeder said, "it was with the Venter kill *only* in mind . . . and with the intention that they provide a distraction. And get caught."

"Two Supreme Court justices in three days," Sloan said, shaking his head. "At least Fisk has security in place for the other justices."

"May not matter. There's a possibility this is over before it started."

"Huh?"

"If I'm right, Gabe, and this is about reconfiguring the Court, the conspiracy has already done its job. Two very conservative members will be replaced by the President."

Sloan's blue eyes flared. "You're not suggesting the security is *pointless—*"

"Hell no! We can't be sure of their agenda. Maybe I'm wrong. Hate crime is still a possibility, and jihadists are, too. If you were going to thumb your nose at America, killing Supreme Court justices would be a fine goddamn way to do it."

"Not to mention," Sloan said dryly, "outsmarting the FBI, Homeland Security, and Secret Service."

A mild breeze blew in, cutting the morning heat, ruffling leaves in woods where an assassin had likely not long ago approached, tools at the ready.

"Somewhere out there,
beyond the walls of the courthouse,
run currents and tides of public opinion
which lap at the courtroom door."

*William H. Rehnquist,*
*Associate Justice, then Chief Justice of the Supreme Court*
*of the United States of America, 1994–2005,*
*fourth-longest tenure of any Supreme Court Chief Justice.*
*Section 5, Lot 7049, Grid W-36,*
*Arlington National Cemetery.*

# ELEVEN

The gates of Arlington National Cemetery locked at 7:00 p.m. Reeder arrived at sunset, just before eight—while he preferred early-morning visits, Reeder sometimes came at night, seeking a quiet place to reflect. But for the guard at the Tomb of the Unknowns, Reeder would have the place to himself.

He entered through the service complex at the south end of the grounds, then walked north on Eisenhower Drive. Despite the lack of streetlights, there was illumination enough, thanks to half a moon. Traffic sounds barely carried into the cemetery, as if out of respect.

Most of today had been spent at the Gutierrez home. The search for evidence had been profitless with even footprints in the woods eluding them—this had been a dry spring by DC standards, the ground hard. Pairs of agents interviewed neighbors on Chain Bridge Road, then talked to others on Merrie Ridge and Bent Twig Roads, two streets with access to Fort Marcy Park. Sloan even sent agents up to the George Washington Memorial Parkway. By the time all this was done, what they had was what they'd started with: a second slain Supreme Court justice.

Reeder kept a steady pace north, letting silence wash over him and carry his stress away. *The ghosts here couldn't stop giving,* he thought. Whenever Reeder came, they scrubbed him clean.

West on Bradley Drive, back north on Roosevelt, eventually he found himself close to the Tomb of the Unknowns near the amphitheater, and he stayed in the shadows. To the east, a spotlight shone on the tomb of the remains of an unknown soldier from World War I. Three marble slabs laid into the plaza marked the unknowns of World War II, Korea, and Vietnam. Out front, a guard from the Army's Third Infantry Regiment, the designated sentinels of the tomb, "walked the mat."

The ritual never failed to touch Reeder. On a long black mat laid on the plaza, the guard—wearing no sign of insignia, not wanting to outrank the unknowns—strode twenty-one paces south, more or less toward Reeder's spot in the shadows.

At his stopping point, the guard turned, faced east toward the tomb, and stood silent for twenty-one seconds before turning north, switching his weapon to his outside shoulder, counting off another twenty-one seconds before marching twenty-one paces north. After stopping, he turned east, waited another twenty-one, then performed a shoulder-arms to his outside shoulder and paused a final twenty-one seconds before starting his southernly stride.

The switching of the weapon symbolized that a guard always stood between the tomb and any threat, the twenty-one steps and seconds representing a twenty-one gun salute. It all meant something, and that gave Reeder comfort. Ritual, tradition, doing things the right way, was important.

This mirrored a thought that had nagged Reeder at the home of Justice Gutierrez, almost immediately upon his arrival. When he and Sloan were alone just outside the shed, he had shared his thoughts with the SAIC.

"The conspiracy behind these murders," Reeder said, "has us reacting reflexively."

Sloan frowned a little, perhaps taking that as criticism of his leadership. "Well, reacting, yes. But I wouldn't say *reflexively* . . ."

"Gabe, we're one big knee getting slammed with a hammer. Come on. You know how to run a murder investigation—you've done it enough times."

"Of course."

"And it's nothing like this, is it?"

That stopped Sloan like a punch. Then he admitted, "No. It isn't."

"If our victims were ordinary citizens, we'd be interviewing witnesses, talking to coworkers to see if the victims had anything in common other than their jobs, on through the proper procedure. Right?"

"Well . . . yeah. But our victims are Supreme Court justices."

"Whoever is behind these crimes is counting on that. If this conspiracy involves people who know how the government works, maybe they even *planned* on it. And this is DC, Gabe—fucking *everybody* works for the government."

Sloan couldn't argue with that.

Reeder went on: "They have us so busy chasing our tails, getting organized . . . trying to navigate all this interdepartmental bullshit, viewing this as terrorism, maybe international, maybe domestic . . . that it'll take weeks to get properly on our feet."

"We're doing all right."

"Are we? Consider this. Suppose just one of the two justices is the intended victim, and the other was killed only to send us riding off in every direction but the right one."

Sloan's chin lifted, the blue eyes narrowing. "Is that how you read this?"

"It's just one possibility. But whatever is going on, we need to get out in front of this."

Sloan mulled that.

"Gabe, getting a task force up and running and working right is like turning the *Titanic*. You may eventually change directions, but not until you hit the iceberg."

Sloan grunted a laugh. "Okay. Point well taken. We keep in mind these are murder investigations."

"Good."

"I'll make some calls. Won't be a picnic getting Supreme Court justices to sit still for interviews . . ."

"Oh, they'll cooperate," Reeder said. "Two of their brethren are dead. We need Venter's clerk, too—Blount."

Sloan nodded. "We'll make both those things happen before we wrap up here."

But no real progress had been made. Reeder watched the guard walking the mat come back toward him now. Somehow seeing that young man on duty chased away his frustration. He saw in this soldier's face what John Updike, speaking of Ted Williams, had called "the hard blue glow of high purpose."

His cell vibrated and he moved away from the Tomb of the Unknowns, into the darkness.

"Reeder."

"Me," Sloan said. "Patti's on her way to pick you up."

"Yeah?"

"You wanted to interview colleagues. Well, you're going to meet Chief Justice Whitaker Jackson at his home. At eleven."

"Why not go over there right now?"

"You'd find an empty house. All the justices are at a private memorial service for Justice Venter. CJ Jackson won't be home until at least then."

Reeder glared into the cell. "All the surviving justices in one place. Jesus, Gabe, what security is in place?"

"Plenty. But teams to sweep the justices' homes won't be able to go in till tomorrow morning, at the earliest."

"We're still a step behind. I better call Patti and tell her I'm not at home . . ."

"She'll pick you up outside the Arlington service complex. Already told her."

"Maybe you are a detective."

"Peep," Sloan said with a smile in his voice, "we're the FBI—we know everything. You've got twenty minutes or so to get there."

Reeder clicked off, wondering if he should fling the cell into the darkness—damn GPS, anyway. He walked briskly back toward the service complex, enjoying the coolness of the night, a small breeze from the north chasing him down Eisenhower Drive.

Rogers and her unmarked Ford were waiting in the parking space adjacent to Reeder's Toyota Prius. On the passenger side of the unmarked, the door clicked unlocked. He got in.

Fastening his seat belt, he asked her, "How do a couple of second-stringers rate Chief Justice Jackson?"

She smirked. "Everybody from the big-people table is pitching in on security at the memorial service. Look at the bright side—if they blow up the place, we'll *be* the first string."

They were in traffic before Reeder asked, "So where does the CJ live, anyway?"

"McLean—not far from Gutierrez, in fact. Turkey Run Road, off 193."

"Money."

"Lots," she said. "The Chief Justice's shack is appraised at just a shade over five million."

"How do you happen to know that?"

"Real estate records. They're public—all you gotta do is go to the assessor's website."

He just looked at her.

She shrugged, both hands on the wheel. "So I'm interested in real estate. It's a hobby."

"Sounds like you date about as much as I do."

A laugh burbled out of her and he smiled.

Chief Justice Jackson's house dominated a wooded area off Turkey Run Road. Langley High School wasn't far west, and wandering through the woods to the east would eventually put you smack in the middle of the Central Intelligence Agency.

Rogers parked in front of a mostly darkened, looming house, a stone central section with wood-sided wings on either side. On the first floor, nine windows and two doors. Porch light going over the front door. Overwhelming its short hill, the almost mansion spoke success, wealth, and isolation.

She said, "Looks like the CJ isn't back yet."

They sat in silence for a while, Reeder fighting fatigue. Despite himself, he nodded off, and Rogers elbowed him in the ribs.

She was pointing to the far left side of the house.

At first he saw nothing and shook his head, but then he caught it: a shifting beam of light in the woods near the house.

"Call for backup," he said, "then go around the other side in case our friend with the flashlight gets by me."

Reeder was out of the car before she could express an opinion— he wasn't technically in charge, after all—and he trotted at a half crouch across the yard toward the beam, which had disappeared again.

That half-moon was hiding behind a cloud, making it dark enough that maybe the intruder wouldn't see Reeder along the side of the house, moving toward the surrounding woods. When he got there, he made his way in a few steps and froze. No wonder the intruder had risked giving himself away with that flashlight—the uneven ground past the yard was a spooky black world of shadows, exposed roots, uneven holes, and God knew what else, the woods themselves dense.

Reeder backed out of this horror show. He would stay in the yard, move up behind the house, and let this bastard come to him. He could move faster on the grass than the intruder in the woods, flashlight or not.

Straining to hear, scanning the darkness like a searchlight, he did his best to determine if the attacker was alone. But nothing, no sound, no movement.

The intruder might figure the lights were out because CJ Jackson was in bed.

Of course, this assassin most likely knew damn well where Jackson was, and would wait inside for his return from the memorial service. With the nearest neighbor a quarter mile away, the assassin should have it made. A security system would be about it. He or she would already have checked the property for FBI watchdogs, seeing nothing—Reeder and Rogers propitiously arriving *after* that precaution . . .

Reeder kept low, moving as silently as possible, getting the lay of the land on the fly. The backyard sloped gently to the woods, which formed a black wall in the night. Reeder picked the spot where the intruder would emerge, were he the one trekking through that ominous space.

In a fleeting thought, Reeder remembered Sloan's comment that a security sweep of the justices' residences would wait till tomorrow. *Might he run into another motion-detector trap?*

The ASP came off his belt and into his hand as if the weapon had willed the action. Still, he did not extend the baton—the sound might alert the intruder. He didn't hear Rogers but assumed she would be coming along soon.

He came down the lawn low till he reached the dead-center spot where the intruder might likely emerge, staying back a few yards so he could maneuver if he was wrong. He slowed his breathing, tried hard to melt into the shadows.

*Rustling in the woods.*

The flashlight was off now, but the assassin was moving his way, closer, closer—Reeder could hear the man's labored breathing. He held his. He'd guessed right about where to position . . .

Far off, sirens wailed—help on the way, but like the old movies, this cavalry would arrive much later than needed, and right now served only a negative purpose, a distant siren song that reached the intruder just as the figure in black made it to the edges of the woods, nosing the air like a nervous deer.

Reeder crouched lower, made himself small, screaming in his mind at Rogers, willing her not to step out into the backyard. Risking a glance at the house, Reeder at first saw nothing, then caught

Rogers peeking around a corner, then ducking back. Smart woman, not giving anything away.

With the moon tucked behind a dark cloud, the stars a universe away, even the barest whisper of a breeze now seemed on Reeder's side, downwind of his quarry as he was. Everything slowed, including Reeder's breathing, a hunter in his element now.

The sirens stopped. Not the cavalry after all—probably just an ambulance. Or maybe a smart cop who decided not to help a bad guy.

At any rate, this false sense of security inspired the intruder to take one slow step out of the woods, and then another. Tall, skinny, dark long-sleeved shirt, black jeans, white eye circles in a black ski mask, something metallic in his right hand—*a gun?*

Reeder snapped the ASP to its full length, and the snick alerted the intruder, who spent a startled millisecond considering a return to that snarl of woods but instead emitted an animal howl, of dismay more than anything, and charged, throwing himself at Reeder, swinging the metallic object—the flashlight, unlit, not a gun—catching the edge of the ASP shaft as Reeder swung it.

Then the man was on him, clutching Reeder around the shoulders and taking him down on the grass, and he landed hard on the flashlight in the intruder's hand beneath him. The gangly shape on top of him reared back, eyes in the ski-mask holes dark and wild, pulling his arm free from under Reeder and whapping him alongside the head with the flash, not a hard blow but damn distracting, and then the guy scrambled onto his feet, reconsidering those woods, turning that direction. Only the intruder hadn't taken a step before Reeder, on his back, lashed out with the ASP.

"*Shit!*" the intruder cried.

The sickening crack of the baton against the man's shin got swallowed in a scream, and the intruder was on the grass, his hands gripping his broken tibia as shrieks shredded the night.

Over this noise, Reeder—getting to his feet, back and shoulder hurting a little, side of his head not much at all—could make out a chopper coming. Rogers materialized over the fallen man, her gun sweeping the woods for accomplices.

Reeder said, "By himself, I think."

"You okay?"

"He bruised my pride."

She trained her pistol on the fallen intruder, on his back like a bug, rolling but not righting, as Reeder frisked him—no weapon. No ID, either.

She was saying, "You have the right to remain silent . . ."

But the intruder wasn't at all silent—he was moaning in a loud, jagged manner, like a lawn mower motor that couldn't quite catch: moan, *cough*, moan, *cough*.

Reeder yanked the ski mask off and saw a hawk-nosed, pock-marked thirtysomething loser with the same kind of lank, stringy dark hair as Charles Granger.

The *whup-whup* of the helicopter grew ever louder, as did the sirens, a cacophony conspiring to drown out Rogers's voice as she completed the Miranda warning.

She had to shout for Reeder to hear as she indicated the baton: "How many suspects are you going to bust up with that thing?"

"He jumped me on his way to kill the Chief Justice."

The intruder interrupted his moaning to say, "Fuck . . . I wasn't gonna kill *nobody*."

Reeder and Rogers both glanced down at him.

"I got no weapon," he said, eyes big in the narrow face. "What was I gonna kill him with, the sterling silver? What are you fucking *talking* about?"

Rogers knelt, cuffed him, patted him down again—she came up only with a small pry bar.

"What were you going to do with that?" Reeder said, indicating the pry bar.

"For the French doors," the intruder said, sitting like a sidelined football player hugging an injury. "Homeowner's out of town. In friggin' Bermuda."

Rogers asked, "Who told you that?"

The chopper came into view, the spotlight underneath shining down on the house, taking only a hovering second to spot the group on the lawn, blades churning air noisily.

Below, the cuffed trespasser turned his head away to avoid the glare.

Getting a radio from her pocket, Rogers shouted into it, "*Clear, clear! Suspect in custody!*"

For several excruciatingly loud moments, the helicopter paused in midair, then backed away. Flashing lights on the street visible on either side of the big house announced police cars. A lot of them.

Reeder said, "What's your name?"

"Marvin."

"First or last?"

"Tom Marvin. Thomas J. You'll find me in the computers, but no violence. I never hurt nobody on a job."

*Tell that to my back,* Reeder thought. Then he repeated Rogers's earlier question: "Who told you the owner was in Bermuda?"

"*He* did," the guy said, and pointed toward the near mansion.

"What, the owner?"

"Yes, yes, yes!"

"The owner told you he was going to Bermuda and invited you to invade his home?"

"*Yeah*. Hello? Insurance scam! E-mailed me a picture of a painting, said the thing was covered for hundreds of thou, plus he had a buyer, some underground collector guy. Said he'd make out like a bandit."

Reeder said, "You're a bandit, Tom. How do you think you're making out?"

"Screw you and that fuckin' whip of yours."

Rogers said, "How much did he promise you? The owner of the house."

"One hundred k. For the simplest boost in the world. He even told me what wire to snip to kill the alarm system."

"What's his name, the owner?"

"Jackson. Whitaker Jackson."

Reeder and Rogers exchanged glances.

Reeder said, "Ever hear of him before?"

No longer moaning, probably settling into shock, Marvin said, "No. Do I look like I hang around with guys who live in houses like that?"

"What did he look like?"

"He didn't look like anything. He was just a voice on the phone."

"He called your cell?" Finally, a break maybe, though it would probably lead to a burner phone.

Shaking his head, Marvin said, "No, I don't have one. Well, I mean . . . I do now. This one just showed up in my hoodie pocket, couple weeks ago. Guy's been calling me on it ever since."

Rogers asked, "Phone just . . . showed up?"

Marvin shrugged. "Riding the Metro, I get off, it's ringing in my pocket. First time I knew it was there."

Reeder said, "And you just take this call, from this cell phone that shows up in your pocket?"

"Yeah. I freelance, you know? Gotta take a flier now and then."

Rogers asked, "What did he sound like, the guy on the phone?"

"Well-spoken type. Businessman, sort of." Marvin raised a shaky finger toward Reeder. "Like that guy."

Reeder grunted a laugh. "You heard *my* voice on the phone?"

"Didn't say that. But it could've been. Whoever it was sent me that picture by e-mail and five grand cash."

Rogers asked, "How was the cash delivered?"

"Came in the mail. Kinda risky doing that, but it was his money, and it came."

Reeder ran a palm over his face. "All this sounded kosher to you?"

"The five grand was kosher, and the ninety-five more sounded kosher enough."

That was about all Reeder could take. He needed to find some Tylenol for his goddamn back, and the old collarbone injury was screaming. No medicine existed to cure this pain in the ass they'd just busted. But he had one more question to ask.

"Tom," Reeder said, "would you happen to know a guy named Charlie Granger?"

Marvin frowned.

"Easy question, Tom. Granger. Charlie."

". . . Okay, yeah. I do. So what?"

"How about Butch Brooks?"

Nothing.

"Know him, Tom? Won't be hard to track."

A reluctant nod. "I know him."

The uniformed cops were coming down the back lawn, and Reeder let Rogers bring them up to speed.

Reeder looked into the woods. Was the assassin, or perhaps the mastermind behind the assassinations, watching from there, right now? If so, he or she was too well camouflaged.

Then Sloan was at his side, and Reeder explained what had happened.

"Obviously," the SAIC said, "this wasn't a burglary you interrupted."

"No. I don't figure the Chief Justice hired Tom Marvin to help on an insurance scam."

Sloan chuckled dryly at the thought.

Reeder said, "This was about putting us through our paces. Testing us."

Sloan frowned. "They had to know we'd put on more security after Gutierrez."

"Right, but they wanted to know how much, what our response time would be, and so on. They knew this was how it would play out, and they wanted to see what we would do. Now they know."

Sloan said, "Sounds like we're still one step behind."

"Well, Gabe, we better catch up . . . because next time? I don't think it'll be a test."

"I'd like to be known just as a good worker in the vineyard who held his own and contributed generally to the advancement of the law."

*Harry Blackmun,*
*Associate Justice of the Supreme Court*
*of the United States of America, 1970–1994,*
*author of the* Roe v. Wade *decision.*
*Section 5, Lot 40-4, Map Grid V/W-36,*
*Arlington National Cemetery.*

# TWELVE

Attendants loaded the suspect, now wearing an Aircast on his broken tibia, onto a gurney. They strapped Marvin down, then slowly rolled the stretcher across the lawn past Patti Rogers, the man's face knotted in pain. The night had cooled, but a sheen of sweat pearled the perp's face in the rolling lights of the police cars.

*Had Reeder overstepped?* she wondered. *Two perps with broken limbs in as many incidents.*

Of course, these were easy questions to ask now that they knew Marvin was no assassin. Reeder's assumption—that the man in black, emerging from the woods behind the Chief Justice's house, was a probable assassin—had been sound.

*And yet . . . and yet . . .*

The last time Reeder had been in harm's way, he'd taken a bullet for a president. No doubt shrink time had followed. After that, a desk and ill-advised words about the man he'd saved, finally resignation . . . then of late thrust into fieldwork of an extreme nature.

*Was he guilty of misjudgment?* she wondered. *Of excessive force?*

Sloan and Reeder were talking just out of earshot. Normally she might take her concerns to Sloan, her longtime partner; but Sloan was Reeder's longer-time *friend.*

They were coming toward her now, Reeder a little ashen, though his face was its usual indifferent mask; still, he looked a little sick. Stress? Conscience?

Sloan said, "Patti, let's hear your take on tonight."

She raised an eyebrow. "Somebody was checking to see how much and what kind of security we set up."

Sloan nodded. "Peep's view, too."

She caught a hint of a smile from Reeder, pleased perhaps that they'd read the burglary attempt the same way.

"That'll do for an overview," Sloan said. "But what's your version of the events?"

She started from spotting the flashlight in the forest. Wrapping up, she said, "When I got close enough to see—very damn dark out here, before these lights, Gabe—Joe was on the ground and the suspect was just taking off into the woods. Joe lashed out with that baton and brought him down."

"Appropriate amount of force, would you say?"

". . . Yes."

Sloan sighed. "Good. I just want all our ducks in a row. This is the third assault on a justice in four days."

Reeder said, "At least we didn't lose one this time."

She nodded toward the house. "Where is the CJ now?"

The SAIC said, "Until we can sweep the property and make sure it's safe for his return, Chief Justice and Mrs. Jackson are in a hotel under Secret Service protection."

She nodded. "What about the other justices?"

"Covered. Very well covered."

Reeder asked, "Did our team interview any of them?"

Sloan rolled his eyes. "Yes, for what good it did. Worse than interviewing straight citizens! None of the other justices have any idea why Venter and Gutierrez might have been singled out—other than your theory, Peep, that this may be to rid the Court of two archconservatives."

Reeder frowned. "Nothing personal in the lives of either man that any of their colleagues can come up with?"

Sloan shook his head. "Not a thing. Or any controversial judgments that spring to mind out of the many. Without their clerks, high and mighty can't tell you where they were this morning, let alone what their schedule is tomorrow."

"I'd be lying," Rogers said, "if I said that surprised me."

Sloan eyed her. "Peep thinks this may be an inside job."

With a smirk, she said, "What, one of their clerks?"

"Not *that* inside," the SAIC said, "though Christ knows the justices have probably provided their lackeys with enough motives. No, somebody in the federal government."

"Not exactly how I put it," Reeder said.

Sloan gave him a cut-the-bullshit look that Rogers knew too well. "You all *but* said it, Peep. And I know you well enough to read between the lines."

Reeder's notion rang true to her—and, anyway, the consultant had been on top of this all along.

But she asked Sloan, "What do you think, boss?"

"The person or persons behind this," he said, "seems to understand our usual responses and tactics, all right. But I'm not convinced the killer is someone inside the federal government."

Reeder shook his head. "I never said in the *federal* government—although it could be."

Rogers squinted at him. "Meaning?"

The consultant shrugged. "Start with the three suspects we picked up."

"Okay," she said.

His eyes traveled from her face to Sloan's. "Do we think any one of these three shit-for-brains is the mastermind of a plot to change history?"

Rogers and Sloan shook their heads.

"Well," Reeder continued, "the late Mr. Brooks aside, the others both seem to have been set up. Do we believe either of 'em can convincingly lie to us?"

Head shakes all around.

"So let's assume," Rogers said, "they're telling the truth. Granger was watching TV with Mommy. Marvin was doing the bidding of a voice on a cell phone."

"Which would mean," Reeder said, "the ringleader is one smart bastard who knew one or likely three of these small-timers going in."

Rogers nodded. "Someone they knew in prison, maybe."

Sloan cut in, saying, "What con, smart or stupid, would want to suffer the kind of heat we're going to bring? Anyway, if Peep is right, this is political. Maybe even . . . ideological. I mean, it's not some mob guy mad at the Supreme Court for sustaining his damn conviction."

"Not a mob guy," Rogers agreed. "A bitter politician in the slam, maybe, who feels betrayed?"

"We rule out nothing," Reeder said. "But we stick with the notion that someone knew one or all of these lowlifes . . . most likely from the other side of the glass."

Rogers frowned. "A cop, you mean?"

Sloan said, "That theory only takes in about half the population of the metro area, if you factor in all the fed agencies, police departments, correctional department employees . . ."

Reeder said, "Don't forget the lawyers."

"Oh, I won't," Sloan said. "After all, every third person in DC is a goddamn lawyer, and we wouldn't want to leave them out . . . Nice going, Peep. You've pared our list of suspects down to four million."

Blandly, Reeder said, "It's a start."

They laughed a little. They could all use it.

By cell, Sloan got Miggie Altuve out of bed to get the computer expert started on making connections between Granger, Brooks, and Marvin.

Leaving the crime scene to the techs, Rogers drove Reeder back to Arlington National Cemetery, and his car.

"The answer is maybe," Reeder said, as they drove through darkness.

"Huh?"

"Did I use excessive force back there? Is this a troubling pattern, me breaking one suspect's arm and another's leg? The answer is maybe."

She flashed her eyes from the road to Reeder, saying, "How the hell do you *do* that?"

"Know what people are thinking? I don't always."

"You do often enough to be a pain in the ass."

"It's a gift." He shrugged, looking out into the night gliding by. "Or maybe a burden."

She glanced over again. "So how *do* you manage it?"

The silence dragged on, and she wondered if he had gone to sleep over there.

Finally, he said, "At first, starting maybe junior high . . . I just sort of *felt* things. It was just the way my mind bent. Then later, seemed like I could see things that a lot of people simply didn't. Or didn't bother to."

"When was this?"

"Well before the Secret Service. College, I guess. Of course, once I was in the Service, they trained me to use this . . . *leaning* even more. I wouldn't call it a talent or even an ability. Maybe a tool."

"I would."

He ignored that. "Eventually I studied kinesics, body language, and sharpened the tool even more."

"Can you turn it off?"

When he didn't answer right away, she glanced over again. Their eyes met and she saw pain.

"Sometimes," he said, and it was almost a whisper, "I wish I could."

". . . But it's useful."

"Not in a marriage."

The intimacy of that shook her.

Trying to sound light, she said, "Well, uh . . . speaking as a different kind of partner, I think it's an entirely positive thing. Even if it is sometimes . . ."

"A pain in the ass? My wife hated arguing with me. Said I was always two, three steps ahead of her. I was obnoxious, she said. No, I *can't* turn it off."

She said nothing for a while, just driving toward Arlington, little traffic at this hour. They rode in silence for several minutes.

He said, and it was not a question, "You think I might be out of control, at least a little."

". . . Are you?"

"I don't think so. Only to the extent that being afraid qualifies as being out of control."

"Every officer confronting a dangerous suspect is afraid."

He huffed a humorless laugh. "I don't have to tell you I've been out of the game for quite some time, before Gabe threw me back in the thick of it. Patti, both times I was scared shitless."

This seemed absurd coming from a big, rugged guy like Reeder. But he clearly wasn't kidding.

He said, "The first time, with Granger? I just lashed out. He had a gun, and I had a baton, and the adrenaline must have . . . I hit him with all the force in me."

"And the second time?"

"Our friend Tom? I had to stop him. If I didn't take him down, all the way down, he might have shot me."

"He didn't have a gun."

"We didn't know that."

"No," she admitted. "We didn't."

Reeder said, "In my position, you might have shot him."

"A wounding shot."

"Are you sure, in the excitement, in the near dark, that you wouldn't have aimed at maximum body mass? And risk killing him?"

". . . I have a feeling you already know the answer to that one, Joe."

"I believe I do."

They drove a while.

Then she said, "This is a lot to share with a partner of a couple of days."

"The key word there is *partner*. Look, I know I can be remote. That I lapse into this . . . 'people reader' mode. Since I'll be your partner for a while, I'd appreciate you cutting me a little slack on that score. Okay, Patti?"

She smiled at him. "Okay, Joe. You okay from that scuffle? Need a doc to look at you?"

"No."

When they got to his car, they agreed to meet at the office.

"In how long?" she asked.

"Five hours," he said. "Between the two of us, we should at least be able to catch eight."

The smiles they exchanged weren't exactly warm, but they both knew one thing: Joe Reeder and Patti Rogers were partners now, for as long as this frustrating and important case might last.

Five hours later, give or take a minute, Patti Rogers parked her unmarked Ford in the Hoover Building ramp. She had slept, showered, and even managed to change into a fresh suit, a nice gray Donna Karan number; but she felt like she'd come straight from under a bridge abutment after a night in a refrigerator carton.

She saw Reeder in the rearview mirror, headed her way. He might be just back from a week's vacation in the Bahamas. No ashen color now—rested and ready. Crisp suit, darker gray than hers, white shirt, black tie.

As he closed the distance, she powered down the window and called back to him: "I wish I felt like you look."

"Same back at you, Patti. Good morning. Don't get out—you're driving. We're meeting the Chief Justice in twenty minutes."

She got them to the Supreme Court Building without resorting to the siren, and they were soon being led by a clerk dressed better than either of them into an expansive, dark-paneled office where law books filled built-in bookcases and history hung in the air like smoke.

Chief Justice Whitaker Jackson sat behind a mahogany desk somewhat smaller than his home state of Rhode Island. Two visitor's chairs waited before the desk.

Though in his seventies, Jackson enjoyed timeless masculine good looks, like Randolph Scott in the old westerns, gray hair worn a little long, prominent cheekbones, a long but well-carved nose. His light blue eyes bore a red filigree, and his black suit and white shirt had a rumpled aspect—had he been up all night, in the aftermath of the break-in at his house? His silk tie with its black and gold diagonal stripes made a loose noose. He looked exhausted, and it wasn't even 10:00 a.m.

But there was no weariness in it when he rose as they entered. He was tall, well over six feet, taller even than Reeder.

They did not immediately sit—formalities needed attending.

"Thank you, Mr. Chief Justice," she said, "for seeing us on short notice. I'm Special Agent Patricia Rogers, and this is task force consultant Joseph Reeder of ABC Security."

"Been too long, Peep," the Chief Justice said, his voice weary, though he managed to give Reeder an energetic smile.

"Good morning, Your Honor," Reeder said.

The men shook hands.

Reeder knowing Chief Justice Jackson was no surprise to her. His Secret Service duties would have put him next to the most powerful people in DC—for that matter, the world. She and the Chief Justice shook hands, as well.

"Special Agent Rogers," Jackson said. "A pleasure despite the circumstances. You must be very good at your job to be on this particular investigation . . . and in such skilled if, uh, controversial company . . . right, Peep? Won't you two have a seat?"

Now, finally, they sat, though the two men waited for her. Rituals. Traditions. Customs. DC.

"So, Special Agent Rogers," Jackson said in the warm, rich baritone that had flowed from the bench so often, "I understand you're not here to discuss the peculiar doings at my home last night so much as to explore these tragic murders—the loss of my friends Justices Venter and Gutierrez."

"That's correct, Your Honor."

"May I ask, first, if you've made any progress in your investigation?"

"We have a dead suspect and two arrested ones. But promising as that sounds, we don't feel we are anywhere close to assembling the real picture from the puzzle pieces available. That's why we're here."

"Feel free to ask any questions you like."

She smiled, nodded. "Let's start with the obvious: Do you have any notion of any individual who might wish Justices Venter and Gutierrez any harm?"

His grin managed to make his face both rumpled and more handsome. "Special Agent Rogers, at one time or another, pretty much everyone in the country wants to see one or all of us dead."

She sat forward. "So, for example . . . there hasn't been a particular case, one ruling, that you think might have incited someone to this level of violence to those two justices?"

"Certainly."

"Good. Which case do you have in mind, sir?"

"I have a hundred cases in mind, Agent Rogers, a hundred rulings. Take Roe v. Wade. Before it was overturned, nearly a dozen murders were tied to that decision, as well as two dozen–some attempted murders and hundreds of death threats. The thing is, not one of these very real attacks was perpetrated against any of the justices voting in favor of what was once called a pro-choice stance."

"In fact," Reeder put in, "no Supreme Court justice had ever been assassinated before this week."

"Quite true," Jackson said.

Rogers said, "One theory our task force is exploring, Chief Justice . . . and please do not be alarmed . . . is that some group may be declaring war on the entire Supreme Court."

But rather than alarm, amusement colored the Justice's expression. "Oh, I hardly think that's the case, Agent Rogers."

"Oh?"

"Henry Venter and Rodolfo Gutierrez were both conservatives . . . as am I—and I'm the third justice touched by this, by way of the attempted break-in at my home."

"Hell," Reeder said.

She and the Chief Justice both swung their eyes to her partner. "What?"

"Something, Peep?" the Justice asked.

"*Maybe* something." He was frowning in thought. "Would you consider joining us in a little . . . brainstorming about the case, Your Honor?"

"Glad to. My background is criminal law, after all."

Jackson had been a very successful prosecutor in his day.

Reeder said, "Justice Venter's murder was stage-managed to make his assassination look like the byproduct of an armed robbery got out of hand."

Jackson nodded.

So did Rogers.

"Next," Reeder went on, "Justice Gutierrez was killed by an automated device, and we realized the circumstances of the first assassination were contrived to mislead us just long enough for the second one to be successful. Now bear with me—I'm going to speculate."

Rogers shifted in her chair. "I'm not sure you should . . ."

He grinned at her. "Okay, then—*you're* going to speculate. Agent Rogers, what would have happened if we'd arrived at Chief Justice Jackson's house shortly *after* Thomas Marvin broke into the house?"

The Chief Justice, a little lost now, interrupted the exchange, asking, "What would have been different? I still wouldn't have been home yet."

But Rogers knew just what Reeder meant. "We'd have found the suspect inside the Justice's house."

"Right," Reeder said. "Where we would have assumed he was an assassin."

She frowned. "And if he'd made any wrong move—"

"You would have shot him, Patti. Just like Sloan shot Butch Brooks. And we'd have two out of three dead suspects."

"Maybe."

"*Maybe* is enough. *Maybe* is a good bet. If I'm right, somebody would have just as soon seen Marvin dead, too. Hell, Justice Gutierrez had been killed by a booby trap in the morning, right? We'd just dealt with Granger and Brooks . . . Last night, we were on edge."

She was nodding. "Okay. Yes. Tensions were running high. Tom Marvin could very easily have wound up shot to death."

Reeder glanced at the Chief Justice, who was listening raptly, and said, "Your Honor, I ran a theory past our SAIC. I'd like to run it by you."

"Certainly."

"Do you mind if I use the Socratic method?"

"Please do."

"What happens if, at this point, the killings end?"

"Well, I can't answer as to your investigation . . ."

Rogers asked, "May I take that question, Your Honor? In that case, we would think that our three suspects, Granger, Brooks, and Marvin, were the assassins, and that we'd stopped them."

Now the Chief Justice did seem a little alarmed. "Would you cease investigating?"

"Once it became clear," she said, nodding, "that the assassinations had run their course . . . probably, yes. There would be those, like Mr. Reeder, who would posit conspiracy, who would suggest that a mastermind or a group of powerful players might have put these . . . these *pawns* into motion. But such thinking rarely gets traction in our circles. And the practical reality is . . . it would soon be 'case closed.'"

Reeder said, "I am convinced our three suspects are patsies in the grand Lee Harvey Oswald tradition. Even if one or more of this trio really committed the crimes, they sure as hell did *not* come up with the plan—someone else did."

"Your mastermind," Chief Justice Jackson said.

"Two Supreme Court justices murdered," Rogers said, feeling sick to her stomach, "and those really responsible getting away with it."

"Not just *any* two justices," Reeder said. "Two *conservative* justices."

"Who," Jackson said, "will be replaced by a liberal president. Giving us two liberal justices . . . with lifetime appointments."

Rogers was aware of Reeder's theory, but hearing it in this office, and taken seriously by the Chief Justice himself, shook her.

Reeder said, "Right now, the balance is six to three, conservatives. Take two off the majority, add them to the minority—"

"And," Rogers said, "you've changed the entire balance of the Supreme Court, possibly for decades."

"*Likely* for decades," Chief Justice Jackson said with a terrible solemnity.

Reeder leaned back in his chair, tenting his fingers. "Three presidents—Andrew Jackson, Abraham Lincoln, and Franklin Roosevelt—appointed justices whose cumulative time served spanned over a century. If that happens here, we're talking about substantially changing one of the three pillars of the republic for over one hundred years . . . with just two murders."

Rogers, rather numbly, said, "Two murders that will impact everybody in the United States for the rest of their lives."

"And if I'm right," Reeder said, "those truly responsible may well walk away from this untouched."

His face drained of blood, Jackson said, "It would be an unprecedented coup of the judiciary. And only your mastermind and his cronies would know . . ."

Reeder's cell vibrated and the conversation paused while he read a text.

Rogers asked, "What is it?"

But Reeder directed his response to the Chief Justice. "I'm sorry, Your Honor, we're going to have to cut this short. There's been a development, and my partner and I are wanted at the White House."

*The White House!* she thought.

But she said, "What development?"

Reeder said, "Security sweeps of the other justices' properties turned up two more devices."

"Damn," she said.

Jackson said, "May I ask where?"

Reeder said, "Justices Van Steenhuyse and Sorenson."

"My lord, man . . ."

"But they're both safe, Your Honor."

The Chief Justice's eyes tightened. "Peep, Van Steenhuyse and Sorenson are *also* conservatives."

Rogers swallowed. "Maybe . . . maybe it *is* a war."

"Well," Reeder said, rising, "at least we know for sure who's under attack."

"I'll be damned if I am not getting tired of this.
It seems to be the profession of a president
simply to hear other people talk."

*William Howard Taft,*
*Twenty-Seventh President of the United States of America,*
*Tenth Chief Justice of the Supreme Court.*
*Section 30, Grave S-14, Grid Y/Z-39/40,*
*Arlington National Cemetery.*

# THIRTEEN

At the White House, Reeder and Rogers joined Sloan outside the West Wing entrance, where a pair of armed Marines standing guard were ignoring him. The SAIC had a sleep-deprived look, his posture suggesting he was about to attend his own beheading.

Reeder asked, "Why are we here? We should be with the crime scene units at the Steenhuyse and Sorenson homes."

Sloan's smile was ghastly. "Here I thought you'd be pleased to be back on your old turf, Peep. I have to tell *you*? When the President wants an update, the President *gets* an update."

"Isn't that Assistant Director Fisk's job?"

"Sure it is. Which is why *we're* here, shit rolling downhill as it does. Shall we answer the clarion call?"

Sloan led them through the maze of offices, bullpens, and bustling staff members. Reeder had practically lived here, and Sloan was an old veteran of West Wing briefings; but Rogers couldn't quite hide that she was as impressed as a high school history buff taking a White House tour.

Before long, the task force trio were at the Oval Office's reception area, where head secretary Ms. Curtis served as gatekeeper at the most important door in America. She rose behind a desk rivaling Chief Justice Jackson's, a slender woman of medium height, sixtyish, her gray suit a shade darker than her short-cut hair, her demeanor as dignified as the Lincoln Monument.

Sloan was in the lead, and she acknowledged him with "Special Agent Sloan," bestowing a smile and nod before leading the SAIC and his little party to the threshold, adding, "If you'll just wait inside. The President will be joining you in a moment."

Sloan's thanks seemed a shade obsequious as Ms. Curtis held the door open.

To Reeder, the last of the party, she whispered, "Nice having you back in the building, Mr. Reeder."

He smiled over his shoulder at her. "Let you know a little later if it's nice to *be* back, Emily."

She followed them in, indicated two facing sofas and a few chairs at the center of the room, letting them sit where they wanted among those options.

Then she positioned herself at the door. Protocol did not allow anyone but key staff (and cleaning crew) to remain in the Oval Office without the President present.

These famous surroundings were essentially the same as when Reeder worked presidential protection, with a few minor differences—plusher, less formal sofas, their upholstery patterns less busy than the previous First Lady's choices; and a different selection of historic paintings, heavy on the Revolutionary and Civil Wars, no doubt picks of the President.

Sloan and Rogers shared opposite ends of a sofa while Reeder took one of several hardwood but well-padded chairs. Quietly, Reeder said to Sloan, "You look like you could use a weekend at your cabin."

"You look like you could use a getaway, too," Sloan said. "Maybe when this is over, we can go up there, a few days. No TV. No cell service. Heaven."

"A little hunting, little fishing," Reeder said wistfully. "Knock back a few beers . . ."

With her mouth in a wry twist, Rogers said, "Alcohol and ammo. You boys *do* know how to party."

The door nearest the desk swung open, and Ms. Curtis slipped out as President Devlin Harrison entered at a brisk walk.

They all rose.

The tall, slender African American President, second in US history, did not look happy. Normally cool and affable, Harrison—his brown suit perfect yet not ostentatious—presented an unblinking, slightly hooded gaze and a down-turned line of a mouth on which it was hard even to picture that famous smile.

Entering a beat after Harrison was his chief of staff, Timothy Vinson, a stocky, balding, mustached man in his fifties, impeccably dressed in charcoal pinstripe. The much-feared Vinson had waged many a political war from the safety of a general's vantage point. He, too, seemed less than pleased about the meeting they were about to have.

The President strode directly to Reeder, acknowledging him by name and saying, "I'm glad to finally meet you—your reputation precedes you."

Of course, Harrison looked anything but "glad," and this presidential greeting was decidedly ambiguous.

The Commander-in-Chief offered Reeder a hand to shake and he took it and shook it, saying, "An honor, Mr. President. I only wish it could have been under better circumstances."

"That's one of the realities of the job, Mr. Reeder. Meeting people you admire in less than ideal ways."

That was ambiguous, too, wasn't it?

The President turned toward Rogers, and—Sloan seemingly struck mute—Reeder said, "This is Special Agent Patti Rogers, Mr. President. She and I are partnered on Agent Sloan's task force."

"Agent Rogers," the President said with a curt nod, and gestured for everyone to sit.

They did.

The President sat back on the sofa across from Sloan and Rogers with his arms folded, legs, too.

*How fucking guarded could one man be?* Reeder wondered.

The chief of staff, who had not been a part of the introductions and had spoken to none of them, sat on the same sofa as the President but gave him plenty of room. His expression was openly sullen.

Harrison's expression, on the other hand, was as unreadable as his body posture was telling. "Agent Sloan . . . Gabe . . . suppose we begin with you telling me just what the hell is going on."

Sloan swallowed and said, "Mr. President, our investigation is ongoing."

Everyone in the room, including the man who had spoken them, paused to consider the lameness of those words.

The President, his eyebrows flicking up and then down, said, "Well, that's a relief to hear, since we have two murdered Supreme Court justices, not to mention another whose home was about to be invaded, until Mr. Reeder here stopped it."

"We have two suspects in custody," Sloan said, scrambling, "and another deceased, and all three are subjects of intense scrutiny. Our task force is looking into every conceivable group that might—"

Vinson almost snarled as he said, "Skip the soft soap, Gabe. Is our national security at stake? Do we need to be breaking out the drones for al-Qaeda, or are we looking at a specific foreign govern-ment? Why don't we have CIA representation on this task force?"

That list of questions might have gone on, but the President raised a hand like a slightly bored traffic cop, and Vinson resumed his glower.

Sloan said to Harrison, "Sir, we're confident this is strictly a domestic situation."

The President's frown said he wasn't convinced.

The chief of staff sat forward in an accusatory manner. "Agent Sloan, have you taken out any time to look at the media? To them, this is very much a matter of national security. There are calls for a national state of emergency, for sequestering the rest of the justices in a bunker until the assassins are captured, with the *New York Times* suggesting we shut down the Stock Exchange for a post-9/11-style cool-down period."

Vinson sat back.

*Good cop, bad cop,* Reeder thought. He'd seen several presidents use their chiefs of staff similarly. And plenty of ranking detectives used their partners the same way.

No one responded directly to Vinson, but Sloan turned his ear-nest gaze on the President.

"Sir, such wild speculation and irresponsible media behavior has been with us as long as the twenty-four-hour news cycle. The public still thinks Justice Venter died a hero. The FBI and the other agen-cies involved have pointedly *not* confirmed that the two murders are tied together."

While his chief of staff rolled his eyes, Harrison merely shook his head gently. "Agent Sloan . . . really. Now that there's been some kind of attempt on the Chief Justice, the linkage will be obvious, no matter what statements we might issue."

Reeder sat forward. "I agree, sir. But Agent Sloan is right—evidence strongly indicates that not only are the perpetrators domestic, they have a high level of knowledge of both our tactics and techniques—a knowledge base bigger than outsiders might reasonably possess."

Harrison frowned. "Mr. Reeder, are you suggesting this scenario emanates from inside the federal government?"

"Not necessarily, Mr. President. But we are dealing with a conspiracy whose leader or leaders display a comprehensive understanding of interagency procedures uncommon among the general citizenry."

The President actually smiled a little. "Mr. Reeder, just because you're seated in the Oval Office doesn't mean you have to sound like a politician."

Reeder flashed a grin. "Sorry. But we live in a one-industry town, Mr. President, and that industry is the government. Not just federal, but local and the surrounding states, and how many DC-area citizens are *former* government employees?"

Sloan said, "I've explained to Mr. Reeder that he has not exactly thinned our suspect pool."

Reeder said, "And Agent Sloan is right again, Mr. President. But at the same time, the indications are strong that while this is a domestic threat, it is not likely a KKK or Posse Comitatus–type group."

Vinson, frowning, said, "You keep saying *group* and *conspiracy* . . ."

"Mr. Vinson, Mr. President . . . I'm not much for conspiracy theories, although we can discuss Lee Harvey Oswald and Jack Ruby at your leisure, assuming either of you have any. I'm available for golf dates."

Sloan winced, but the President was smiling again.

Reeder went on: "Our three suspects, one deceased, are small-time criminals who are hardly capable of the kind of plotting and logistics displayed here. Nor do any of them appear to have any hate group or other ideological leanings."

"*Somebody,*" the President said, "has set them in motion."

"Yes. Three bad guys who *somebody* sent to do their bidding." He looked pointedly at Vinson. "And, yes, it's a conspiracy. A group."

The President exchanged somber glances with his chief of staff, then said to Reeder, "All right. Go on."

"I believe this is a small, sophisticated cabal that has an ideological purpose. Some in the media are already speculating that it's no coincidence that the justices targeted are all conservatives."

The President said nothing, his brow furrowed, his eyes moving. "You are actually suggesting, Mr. Reeder, that a domestic left-wing terrorist group is trying to reconfigure the Supreme Court by removing its most conservative members."

Reeder said, "They aren't trying to reconfigure it, sir. They expect *you* to. Surely that's obvious."

Sloan sat forward. "Mr. President, this is only one possible theory we're pursuing. But there's no denying that these tragedies will wind up changing the balance of the Court."

The President's smile had a sneer in it now. "Wonderful. By lunch the conservative talkers will be saying I've launched a death squad to tip the Court my way."

Reeder said, "Not all of them will say that, sir."

Harrison's eyebrows rose.

"Some," Reeder went on, "will say you plan to kill all *six* conservatives."

Sloan winced at that and began, "Mr. President—"

But the President cut him off, saying, "When Henry Venter seemed to have died a hero's death, the public felt good about its government for once. But Justice Gutierrez's killing caused a . . . correction in the stock market. And when the public finds out an intruder was caught outside Chief Justice Jackson's home, who can say what will follow? And God forbid *another* justice should die . . ."

Everyone in the Oval Office was old enough to remember 9/11 and its immediate aftermath—the stock market shutting down; no planes flying; a country sitting vigil before their televisions, waiting for any new information, watching the same images of death and destruction again and again. Then the Patriot Act, opening so many dangerous, terrible doors . . .

"As it is," the President said, "I have to appoint two justices. And when I appoint two liberals, I'll be understandably accused of taking advantage of tragedy. People on the right and independents will be outraged, and even my own party will have a sour taste."

Sloan said, "Every president for as long as anyone can remember has done what you're about to do, Mr. President."

Tentatively, Reeder said, "It's not really my business, but . . ."

Harrison nodded for him to go on.

". . . there *is* another precedent."

All eyes were on Reeder.

"What Agent Sloan said is not exactly true—not for those who recall John F. Kennedy."

Reeder was well aware that JFK was a hero of Harrison's.

He continued: "Kennedy was the last liberal president not to nominate a clearly liberal justice. Byron White, admittedly a long-time Kennedy supporter, was not strictly speaking a liberal. For most on the left, White was much too conservative. Of course, the conservatives thought him too liberal, which, to my mind, made him—"

"The ideal choice," Harrison said very softly.

Reeder shrugged. "Some might say so, Mr. President." The President's expression, for the first time on this visit, took on a calm, even relieved aspect. *Did he already have someone in mind?*

Elsewhere on the President's sofa, however, party loyalist Vinson was staring daggers. *Too bad, Vinnie,* Reeder thought. *I might be ex-Secret Service, but I still serve the President, not his goddamn chief of staff.*

Then Harrison's face clouded again. "Gabe, Mr. Reeder, Agent Rogers . . . I am depending on you not only to catch those responsible, but to ensure the safety of our surviving justices . . . How chilling to hear those words: *surviving justices.*"

No one said anything.

The President rose and so did they all.

"If you need anything," he said, "anything at all, contact Tim here."

Grudgingly, the chief of staff said, "Feel free."

"Thank you, Mr. President," Sloan said with a nod, and then another nod for the chief of staff. "Mr. Vinson."

Then, oddly, the President locked eyes with Reeder and said, "I'm depending on you to wrap this up . . . ASAP."

Reeder said, "An honor to serve this president, sir."

Vinson went over to open the door for them, less a gracious gesture than a sign that they had just been dismissed.

Outside in the sunshine, Sloan said, "You sounded pretty damn confident in there."

*Was Sloan irritated that the President, at the end there, had treated Reeder not like a lowly consultant, but the man in charge?*

"What else could I say, Gabe? I stopped short of telling him the conspiracy had accomplished its goal and this was already over."

Sloan squinted at him. "Is that what you really think is going on?"

"If changing the balance of the Court is the motive for the murders, why not? Those three dumb-ass flunkies are strictly there to take the blame, right?"

"Then what do you suggest, Peep? We just call it a day and give up?"

"Hell no. I might be wrong, and anyway, the conspiracy may stop killing, but that doesn't mean they can't be caught."

"Well, I'm relieved to hear that," Sloan said archly. "But do you mind if I interrupt your postgame wrap-up with a question? If the move on the Jackson house was just a smokescreen, how do you explain the *other* two devices?"

"I'll have a better idea after I've seen them," Reeder said. "Now that we've paid our presidential respects, can we get back to the real work?"

Rogers said, "I second that."

On the half-hour drive up Connecticut Avenue to Chevy Chase, Maryland, Rogers was at the wheel with Sloan in front and Reeder in back, Miggie having texted them Justice Van Steenhuyse's and Justice Sorenson's addresses.

Reeder asked, "How is Miggie doing with that list of police or agency personnel who've intersected with any or all of our three suspects?"

The SAIC shook his head glumly. "Slow going. Hell, half of DC law enforcement is on the list, and our team is not exempt. Actually, Peep—*you're* on that list."

"The hell. Never laid eyes on any of 'em till we went to bust them."

Sloan glanced into the backseat. "Oh no, you're on the list, all right. You identified Marvin and Granger in separate incidents."

Reeder sat forward. "Gabe, I never saw *either* of them before."

"Well, according to Miggie, you ID'd 'em both."

"That's *impossible* . . ." But thought for a moment, then: "Actually, it's not. ABC operatives probably ID'd Granger and Marvin for crimes committed against clients of ours. I routinely sign every report. Company policy."

Looking at Reeder in the rearview mirror, mildly amused, Rogers said, "Well, *that's* embarrassing."

Sloan said, "Yeah, well, don't get too cocky, Patti—we're on that list, too."

"We *are?*"

"Remember the Henson kidnapping, back when we first partnered?"

"Sure. Five-year-old boy. Got him back, glad to say."

"Well, a person of interest in that case was a suspected child molester we early on crossed off the suspect list."

She took her eyes off the road to glance at Sloan. "Gabe, we had dozens of leads like that."

"Well, one of them was Dwight Brooks."

Leaning up again, Reeder frowned. "Our boy Butch?"

Sloan gave him a tired nod. "The one and only."

"Jesus," Rogers said, shaking her head, eyes a little wild. "We never even *talked* to him!"

"Nope," Sloan said, "just a name in some paperwork."

Reeder asked, "Anybody else on the task force connected to the suspects?"

"Almost the entire first team—Bishop and Pellin, for one . . . or two. Eaton, from his job as a deputy sheriff before Homeland Security. Even your Secret Service brethren, Stein and Ho—Granger was questioned about passing a counterfeit twenty a while back. Probably got it in one of those bar heists. Nothing came of it, and Granger sold the boys a story about getting the bill back as change in a bar. Just another citizen interview of many."

Rogers, shaking her head again, said, "So Jess Cribbs is the only one of the task force field agents who *didn't* somehow trip over these creeps?"

Sloan nodded. "Her and Altuve—though Miggie's not a field agent."

"I don't envy Miggie his job on this one," Reeder said. "Either this is a huge dead end or we're all suspects in our own investigation."

"Small damn world," Sloan said.

Lenox Street, where expensive homes looked smugly across at each other, was just one of many such tree-lined lanes in the bedroom community of Chevy Chase. Right now Rogers had to nose down the middle of the normally quiet street, its either side lined with emergency, crime scene, and other government vehicles, sidewalks bustling with reporters, TV crews, and nosy neighbors.

Reeder said, "I'd say the word is getting out."

Rogers squeezed into a space a block down. On the sidewalk, as they knifed through onlookers and media, Reeder—who had belatedly been given a task force ID necklace—slung his on, the others having already done so.

The houses on Justice Van Steenhuyse's side of the street had expansive backyards that were, like those of Justices Gutierrez and Jackson, bordered by trees.

Rogers, noting that, asked Reeder, "Woods again?"

He shook his head. "Chevy Chase Club—tennis courts, golf, horseback riding. Upscale fun. Little out of all our leagues . . . Could make a nice point of entry for an assassin, though."

Sloan, Rogers, and Reeder went up the walk of the Justice's two-story brick home—not as mansion-like as the other two justices' residences, but nonetheless impressive. Two uniformed cops were out front, screen door closed, inside door open—probably detectives inside.

Reeder asked Sloan, "Who's handling the interviews?"

"Eaton and Cribbs," Sloan said. "They're inside talking to the Justice and his wife. I should probably head in there. I'm here to supervise, after all. You two are on site strictly to eyeball the device—isn't that what you wanted?"

"Exactly what I wanted," Reeder said. "But, Gabe—take a look out back before you go in, okay?"

"Okay," Sloan said with a shrug.

The trio circled to the backyard, where uniformed officers from the Village of Chevy Chase and crime scene technicians from the Maryland State Crime Lab milled about, waiting for the hotshot task force investigators to give a go-ahead to bag the evidence.

Unlike the motion detector at Justice Gutierrez's, this one (disconnected now) was damn near in plain sight, on the ground and nestled in a flower garden under a window onto a breakfast nook.

Across the wide, flat expanse of lawn that ended at a tree line thirty yards from the house, two cops stood within the trees near where the weapon was set up.

As the three crossed to it, Sloan said, "Remington 30-06."

Rogers said, "Perfect—another gun common as dirt."

Already, Reeder wasn't liking this. The rifle was hidden well enough, just beyond the edge of the wooded area, but the angle looked a little off.

Rogers saw it, too. "Trickier shot than Gutierrez."

Reeder asked the crime scene techs, "Done with this, fellas?"

The nearest tech, a young guy with a shaved head, said, "Yes, sir. Next step is bag and tag."

*Fresh back from the Army,* Reeder thought. "Anybody touch the weapon?"

"No, sir."

"Thanks," Reeder said, and crouched near the rifle. He frowned at it.

Sloan asked, "What?"

"Something," Reeder said.

He dropped into a prone position to look through the scope, and found it aimed high. Very damn high. "How tall is Justice Van Steenhuyse, anyway?"

"Six one," Sloan said, "six two."

"Does he make a habit of standing on a chair in his backyard?"

"Probably not," Sloan said.

Looking through the scope, Reeder said, "Well, this rifle is set up to execute a perfect head shot . . . if the target was six five and standing."

Sloan said, "Maybe somebody nudged the rifle," and went over and spoke to the techs about it.

In the meantime, Reeder slid aside for Rogers to drop into his spot.

"Shit, Joe," she said, goggling at him. "You're right."

"Don't sound so surprised."

Sloan came back, looked down at his prone colleagues, and said, "Techies say nobody touched the weapon. But that doesn't mean somebody didn't jostle it and just doesn't want to advertise the fact."

"Gabe," Rogers said, "get down here and have a look yourself."

He did, then rose, dusting himself off. "One of the crime scene guys *has* to have knocked it off line."

"Or," Reeder said, getting up, Rogers too, "it's a dummy."

"A dummy?" Sloan asked. "Don't be ridiculous."

"You're right that it's possible somebody knocked it off line. But *this* out of whack? Listen, can you get Eaton or Cribbs out here?"

"Sure," Sloan said. "Why?"

"Please. Need to ask a couple questions."

The SAIC used his cell to summon the burly, mustached Eaton, who strode out into the backyard and up to them.

"What do you want, Reeder? We're in the middle of a goddamn interview."

"Could you ask the Justice who does the gardening back here?"

"Well, that already came up. I mean, with this rifle aimed in that direction. They both do, Justice and Mrs. Van Steenhuyse."

"Good. Thanks. Sorry to interrupt."

"Uh, okay."

Mildly confused, Eaton glanced at Sloan, who nodded, and the burly Homeland Security agent headed back inside.

Looking from Sloan to Rogers and back again, Reeder said, "Think about the degree of intel gathered before the Venter and Gutierrez kills. How the patterns of both men were studied and utilized. Now, explain a motion-detector kill that might just as easily have taken out the Justice's wife as the Justice."

Forehead tight, Rogers said, "Precise before, sloppy now. Makes no sense."

"That's right. No sense at all. Now, factor in that the motion control could've been triggered when either of them knelt to tend the flower garden, firing a gun *already* aimed too high, had the Justice been standing."

Sloan waved the young, shaved-head crime scene tech over. "Son, you *sure* no one touched this?"

"No one, sir."

"So, then," Reeder said, "you don't even know if it's loaded."

"Affirmative, sir."

Reeder knelt again, worked the bolt, and a brass shell gleamed up at him. He grunted to himself, stood. To the tech he said, "You want to collect this evidence?"

"Yes, sir."

"Then we'll get out of your way."

The trio walked until they were out of earshot.

"A live round," Sloan said, eyebrows up. "Still think that's a dummy?"

"Why not?" Reeder said. "They've been screwing with us since the very beginning. That crap might have been set up to keep us chasing our tails."

Sloan's eyes flared. "For what the hell purpose?"

"To keep us focused on an ongoing threat, and keep the bad guys out in front of us. Remember, if the only motive is to tip the balance of the Court, then we might be chasing conspirators who've already slipped back into their normal lives."

Sloan gestured to the rifle. "You don't think *that* represents a real threat?"

"Well, obviously we treat it like one," Reeder said. "But as long as we're worried about what they *might* do, attention is taken away from what they've *already* done."

A long, weary sigh seeped from the SAIC. "Jesus, Peep. How do we figure out what's real and what's being used just to bluff us?"

Rogers shrugged. "Checking out that device at Justice Sorenson's," she said, "would be a start."

Sloan gave that a second of thought, then said, "Okay. You two go out there now. I'll check in with our team members here, then catch a ride and see you soon. Go."

They went.

"Things do not happen. Things are made to happen."

*John Fitzgerald Kennedy,*
*Thirty-Fifth President of the United States of America,*
*former senator and representative*
*from the Commonwealth of Massachusetts.*
*Section 45, Grid U-35,*
*Arlington National Cemetery.*

# FOURTEEN

On the way to Justice Grace Sorenson's residence in Alexandria, Virginia, Patti Rogers didn't mind that her passenger had lapsed into an almost brooding silence. DC-area traffic always demanded attention, and, anyway, she was never one to feel conversation was necessary just because you were riding with somebody.

Finally, though, she asked Reeder, "Something?"

He didn't answer right away, just kept staring out the window at the passing city. *Had he even heard her?* She was about to repeat her question when his head swiveled her way.

"What," he asked, without any inflection at all, "do you know about Jessica Cribbs?"

"Well . . . she's a friend. Why do you ask?"

Even as she returned her attention to the road, Rogers could sense Reeder's eyes on her. Reading her.

"*What*, Joe?"

"What can you tell me about her?"

"I told you about her before."

"Not in detail."

She flashed a frown at him. "And now, what? You wanna see her X-rays?"

His shrug was barely perceptible. "Everybody on the task force is DC law enforcement, Patti. Cribbs is the only one who's never brushed shoulders with our three suspects."

"Which puts her in the clear."

Under the white eyebrows, the dark brown eyes were as hard as his tone was light. "Normally. In this particularly odd circumstance, it's a kind of . . . red flag. What's her background?"

She huffed a laugh. "Jess isn't part of any goddamn conspiracy."

"Then let's get this out of the way. Where's she from?"

". . . Minnesota. Jess was a state trooper before she got recruited for Homeland Security."

"That alone explains why she never had any dealings with our three perps. She's not longtime DC law enforcement. How about you?"

"What about me?"

"How long have you worked in DC?"

"Six years or so."

"Straight from your MP stint?"

She nodded.

He asked, "How long has Cribbs been in the area?"

"Two, no, more like three years. Judging when we started having interagency dealings, anyway."

"Then she could have been here longer?"

Rogers shook her head. "Don't think so. She was still grousing about housing prices and snarled traffic when we first met—not used to the city yet."

He was giving her that blank gaze of his.

She frowned. "What?"

"Was that so hard?"

"Jesus, Reeder—do you suspect *everybody?* You think I don't know you were checking on me, too?"

His eyes went to the window again. "I don't suspect anybody—yet.

You know the drill—ask questions about things that break an already established pattern."

"Is that right?"

"You know it is. Cribbs is the only one on the team without prior contact with the suspects—no matter how flimsy some of that is—which breaks the pattern. So it's incumbent upon us to look into why."

"No argument," Rogers said wearily. She was starting to hate how right he was all the time.

"Anyway," he said, "Miggie will keep looking into all of us, Cribbs included, I suppose, but it's just . . ."

"Just what?"

His eyes were on her again. "Occam's razor—know it?"

"Sure. Simplest explanation is usually the correct one."

"Exactly. This case?"

"Yeah?"

"Just the opposite."

Mount Vernon Circle was yet another exclusive tree-lined street in a quietly wealthy area, but at least Justice Sorenson didn't have woods behind her home. The Dogue Creek inlet that fed into the Potomac River was back there, which Rogers knew from the satellite photos Miggie had sent.

They rolled up in the Ford and parked at the curb, the long, wide driveway already crammed with police cars and crime scene vans. The massive two-story brick home might have been some exclusive bed-and-breakfast, not a house occupied by a married childless couple. A portico with four white columns protected a porch and its wide concrete stairs.

"That creek," she said, "will make it hard to trace any entry."

"More like impossible," he said. "But we'll check it out anyway."

"Why not? Maybe we'll spot a deer back there, and you can tell it what forest it was raised in."

That may have been too openly sarcastic, but got a smile out of Reeder just the same.

The pair made their way along the edge of the driveway to where a two-car garage stood open. Matching Jaguars nestled there, vanity plates reading "HIS" and "HERS."

She made a face. "Maybe you better put me back on the suspect list."

"Something against Jags?"

"Something against vanity plates. Anyway, I'm more the muscle-car type. GTO, Charger, Stingray."

"Ah. An all-American girl with vintage tastes."

"Damn straight." She frowned as she glanced around. "Joe, my apartment isn't this clean."

"Nobody's is."

The garage appeared pristine, not so much as an oil smudge on the concrete floor—no rakes, lawn mowers, or power tools against the walls, the Jags more like props than vehicles. Any CSIs who came up with something in here would earn their pay for a week.

Reeder led the way through a door at the rear onto a patio of polished white stone tiles surrounding an Olympic-size swimming pool with a blue electric cover. Beyond, a vast lawn fell to a long pier, where a motorboat and a Jet Ski were moored.

Rogers asked, "How many years would I have to work to get a setup like this?"

"Two or three lifetimes," he said absently, his attention on the diving board, where two techs in Virginia State Crime Lab polos were on its far side. A line of cones was set out on the patio to require a wide berth, and—under the board, in the shade—was a motion detector, barely visible.

Rogers and Reeder joined the two techs, one of whom was the muscular supervisor from the Gutierrez crime scene, Darrell Grogan, who she thought was kind of hot.

Grogan introduced them to his coworker, a skinny female, but nobody shook hands—the techs were in latex gloves.

Reeder asked, "Where's the weapon?"

"No gun this time," Grogan said. "And that motion detector is legit—the Sorensons had problems with neighbor kids sneaking into their pool."

Rogers said, "Disadvantaged types whose parents don't have a pool, huh?"

Everybody smiled a little, which was all that deserved, and Grogan went on: "The motion detector is pointed—"

"At the power switch for the electric pool cover," Reeder said, getting it.

Rogers asked, "Then why did you put up cones around the motion detector?"

"Just a precaution," Grogan said. He pointed toward the other end. "You see, somebody rewired the pool-cover switch. It triggers something *else* now."

Rogers frowned. "You mean, something . . . explosive?"

"Something that goes boom, yeah—we're waiting on the bomb squad."

Reeder walked down and knelt at the small power box, which was maybe six by nine inches, with a button-style switch for the pool cover.

Grogan and Rogers caught up with him.

Reeder said, "Can't be a very big bomb to fit in that little thing."

Grogan said, "How big does it need to be to kill somebody?"

"Not very," Reeder admitted. "How do you *know* there's a bomb?"

The tech held up a sealed plastic evidence baggie with a small piece of wire in it. "One of my guys spotted this on the tiles nearby, opened the box . . . and found the bomb. Oh, and shit himself."

"Metaphorically, I hope," Reeder said. "This being a crime scene."

Rogers asked, "Why *didn't* the bomb go off?"

Grogan said, "Bomb is hooked up to the switch that retracts the pool cover. Pushing the 'open' button appears to be the only way to set it off."

Reeder asked, "How long have you been waiting for the bomb squad?"

"Couple hours," Grogan said. "There was a suspicious package at the Smithsonian."

Rogers smirked. "When isn't there?"

No one argued with that.

Reeder pointed back toward the diving board. "Why didn't the motion detector get tripped when the bomb was planted?"

"Wires were cut," Grogan said. "Obviously, the intruder knew about the motion detector and the pool-cover switch arrangement going in."

"No surprise," Rogers said. "These people have known every damned thing about the justices, so far."

"Somebody's been working on this," Reeder said almost to himself, "for a very long time."

Sloan, Eaton, and Cribbs came out onto the patio and joined them. Reeder brought everybody up to speed. That was really Rogers's job, but she didn't mind. The man really did know what the hell he was doing.

"I suggest calling AD Fisk," Reeder concluded, "and get an FBI bomb squad out here, *now.*"

"I can handle it," Eaton said.

Everybody looked at him.

The burly, mustached cop said, "Hey, I went to bomb disposal school in the service."

Sloan frowned, asked, "How long ago?"

Then, before Eaton could answer, Sloan got out his cell and walked a few feet away to make his call.

When Sloan returned, Reeder asked, "ETA?"

Sloan said, "They'll get here when they get here."

"Really? Why not let Eaton look at it? Grogan's guys already opened the box—that's how we even know there's a bomb in there. You have to push the button to trigger it, Gabe."

Sloan sighed, mulled that, then turned to Eaton. "Just take a look, okay? Open it up, like the other guy did . . . but otherwise don't touch *anything.*"

"Roger that," Eaton said.

Sloan instructed Grogan to get his people inside and away from the windows, which the tech did.

Then the SAIC turned to Reeder. "We're going down to the other end of the pool, Peep. Back of the diving board. Rogers, Cribbs . . . you, too."

Reeder said, "I'm going to stick with Eaton. If he needs an extra pair of hands at some point, I'm the guy who got him into this."

Sloan said, "Absolutely not."

"Then fire me," Reeder said.

Sloan looked at his old friend with open dismay. Eaton, on the other hand, was looking at the consultant with something that might have been newfound respect.

Sloan said, "Have it your own goddamn way," and headed down to the deep end.

Rogers paused to give Reeder a little squeeze of the arm, and they exchanged nods. Then she got the hell away from there.

But from what was likely a safe vantage point, she had a decent view of the gray power box on its short pole, conduit running up the back. In the front was the "open" button and a clasp to keep the door/lid closed. Push the button once, and the cover opened; push it again, it closed. Pretty simple stuff.

*Then why was her heart in her throat?*

Eaton squatted in front of the box on the pole, loosened his tie, and undid his collar button. A guy had a right to get comfy when he was risking getting blown to hell.

She clenched a fist as Eaton undid the clasp and eased the door open and swung it past the switch . . .

Nothing happened.

Reeder called out: "Come have a look!"

Not moving fast at all, Sloan, Rogers, and Cribbs joined Reeder and Eaton, the latter still squatting. They stood close enough to see that the "bomb" was a small vial filled with gray powder, like metal shavings. The lid of the vial was a blasting cap, with two wires running to the back of the "on" switch.

"Simple device," Eaton said, gesturing. "When the button's pushed, one wire serves as a ground—other carries current to the blasting cap. When the cap blows . . . boom."

Rogers asked, "What's in the vial?"

"Likely Tannerite," Eaton said.

Sloan asked, "You sure?"

"That or something similar."

Rogers asked, "Lethal?"

"Lethal enough," Eaton said, and stood. "What's in that little metal box could make it rain shrapnel."

Cribbs asked, "Is it stable?"

Eaton said, "If I take off the wires and the blasting cap, Jess, we could play catch with the damn thing. Hooked up like this, no, stable is not what I'd call it. Let's back away, shall we?"

They did.

Reeder was shaking his head.

"What?" Sloan asked.

"This perp doesn't make a mistake—I mean, not one damn mistake, then boom . . . if you'll pardon the word . . . suddenly two goofs in one day?"

Eaton asked, "*What* two goofs?"

"At Jackson's, the rifle was out of alignment with the target," Reeder said. "And now, a piece of wire is left on the ground in plain sight."

Sloan said to everyone, "We don't *know* that rifle at the last house didn't get knocked off target by a tech, and a half-inch piece of wire left behind by a guy working in pitch black doesn't seem like much of an error to me."

"Besides," Eaton said, "don't we *want* these guys to fuck up?"

"*If* they're fucking up," Reeder said.

Eaton's frown was a near scowl. "Meaning?"

"Meaning they've been throwing us off track from day one. Based on the first two kills, these people don't make mistakes. Now—*two*. Somebody likes us out chasing our tails. Somebody likes us good and damn distracted."

Eaton was shaking his head. "Reeder, you ever *seen* Tannerite go off?"

"I know it's dangerous," Reeder said. "And I know there's enough there to kill Justice Sorenson, all right. Or her husband."

"Her husband?"

"This is like the Van Steenhuyse place—even if that rifle *was* jostled, the setup could've taken out the spouse as easily as the supposed intended target. Look at Venter and Gutierrez, how specifically those kills were contrived. This . . . *this* is careless . . . sloppy. Another dummy. We're being played."

"Bullshit," Eaton said.

But Sloan said nothing.

Reeder said, "This bomb was likely put in position when the Sorensons were at the Venter memorial service. When they were away all evening."

Eaton almost snarled, "So fucking what?"

Rogers decided to stay out of this—the brief alliance between these two alpha males had been replaced by the old pissing contest.

"The assassin knew they'd be gone," Reeder said, quiet but firm. "Had plenty of time. Cut the wires on the motion detector in the dark, got into the switch box, wired a bomb to the switch, also in the dark, and wanna bet didn't leave so much as a fingerprint? Yet managed to drop a half-inch piece of wire onto the patio without realizing it. Really?"

Sloan said, "That's how we catch criminals, Peep. They make mistakes."

"Look, I'm not saying there isn't a continuing threat . . . but we have the justices under protection. The bad guys getting to them now will be next to impossible. The two rigs found today were set up *before* our security measures were put into place."

Sloan frowned. "What do you suggest?"

"Solid, old-fashioned investigative technique. We need to get back to our surviving suspects. One of them knows *something*, even if he doesn't know it . . . and then there's our eyewitness."

Eaton smirked. "*What* eyewitness? We don't have an eyewitness."

"Sure we do. The clerk, Nicholas Blount, was with Venter when the Justice was shot. We haven't really interviewed him in the kind of depth he deserves. Or the other notables present at the Verdict that night."

Rogers said, in support, "Because we've been chasing our tails."

Reeder nodded, exchanged smiles with her. "Because we've been chasing our tails is right."

The discussion ended with the FBI bomb squad showing up. They disabled the device in less than five minutes, the agent who'd done that, Lawson, bringing the device over in a bag. He was slender, thirtysomething, with ancient eyes.

"Simple device," he said. "Like—dirt simple."

Sloan asked, "Would it have worked?"

"Powerful enough to destroy the box it was in, at least. Would've made a hell of a bang, and spit some nasty shards."

Sloan said to Reeder, "Still think it's an empty threat?"

"I never said it was an empty threat, Gabe. I just think we need to start playing offense, not defense."

Sloan sighed, nodded. Then he said to the Homeland Security agents: "Eaton, you and Cribbs take a run at Granger and Marvin. They've seen enough of Reeder, Rogers, and me."

Eaton nodded, and he and Cribbs headed out.

Very quietly, Sloan said to Reeder, "I brought you in to consult, Peep, because I value your opinion. But I can't have you taking over."

"Not my intention."

"Then don't undermine my authority."

"Understood."

Sloan was a little flushed, while Reeder seemed as placid as the pool under its electric cover.

She half expected the SAIC to belabor the point, but he didn't. The pair had been friends a long time, and whatever passed silently between them, she wasn't privy to.

Reeder said, "How about Rogers and I interview Nicky Blount?"

"Sounds like a plan," Sloan said quietly.

In the car, putting on her seat belt, Rogers turned to Reeder. "You *weren't* trying to undermine his authority."

"Doesn't matter."

"I've never seen him like that, and we were partners a long time."

Reeder caught her eyes and held them. "Gabe's under incredible stress, Patti. This isn't just about solving murders. You were in that meeting with the President. This is a political nightmare, and he's AD Fisk's fall guy. Things in DC are *never* black and white."

"Oh, I know," she said. "Everything's gray . . . except murder."

"No," Reeder said, shaking his head. "*Especially* murder."

"To get what you want,
*stop* doing what isn't working."

*Earl Warren,*
*Thirtieth Governor of the State of California,*
*Fourteenth Chief Justice of the Supreme Court.*
*Section 21, Lot S-32, Grid M-20.5,*
*Arlington National Cemetery.*

# FIFTEEN

On the way to the Supreme Court Building, Reeder used his cell phone to scroll through police reports on Granger, Marvin, and the late Butch Brooks.

He said to Patti Rogers, "None of these guys has the smarts for what went into all this."

"And yet they're in it up to their eyeballs," Rogers said, glancing over from behind the wheel. "Which means they're flunkies."

"And," Reeder said, "flunkies report to somebody. Somebody a lot smarter."

He kept going over the reports. Something was itching at the back of his brain—tied in with his people-reading skills was an ability to sense something small that was wrong in a big picture. Unfortunately, that was just a sense. An itch. But he kept scratching at it . . .

Then, in Brooks's file, as he skimmed through the name, address, and other info, something tiny popped.

He said softly, almost to himself, "The AK-47 was at Granger's house."

"Right," Rogers said. "So?"

"So it's apparently a weapon from the out-of-state robberies. And we found the Verdict murder gun at Brooks's, too . . ."

"What about it?"

"Well, the police report says Brooks was left-handed."

She flashed him a frown. "Which is significant why?"

Reeder didn't immediately respond. He was replaying in his mind the Verdict Chophouse security video.

He said, "The gunman at the Verdict was right-handed."

She frowned at him again. "You're sure?"

"No question about it."

"Not that I doubt you," she said. "But why don't we ask Nicky Blount for confirmation?"

"Let's do that."

Entering through the front door of the Supreme Court Building on its west side proved trickier than anticipated. Justice Henry Venter's body now lay in state in the Great Hall, the funeral ceremony having taken place earlier, the line of mourners still extending through the front doors and down the stone stairs.

As they flashed their credentials to a guard near the door, Reeder said to Rogers in a near whisper, "He'll be buried a hero."

"Is that so terrible?" Rogers asked as they stepped inside, catching some glares from those in line who figured they were cutting in.

"Not terrible," he told her, "but still wrong. This is a criminal matter, and any commonly accepted inaccuracy can lead to a miscarriage of justice."

On either side of the marble-hewn Great Hall were sixteen columns between which were busts of past chief justices. Rogers's shoes clicked on the marble while Reeder's were barely audible.

She said, "Sloan says you didn't like Venter."

"Venter was a pompous ass," Reeder said. "But there's a lot of that in this town."

"So that's not why you didn't like him."

His voice low, maintaining a surface respect for a man he respected very little, Reeder replied, "He made this country a worse place to live in, and we both know he died a coward."

They were near the Stars-and-Stripes-draped coffin now. Some people were crying, others were dry-eyed, but all were somber—Reeder and Rogers included.

As they climbed the stairs to the second floor, Reeder said, "Maybe it won't have to come out. A lot of people in our history who did worse than Henry Venter are remembered as heroes."

The door to the outer office of Venter's chambers stood open, revealing walls paneled in heavy polished wood, one given over to law-book-bulging bookshelves. Four clerks, including Nicholas Blount, were at work at their respective desks. It might have been any other busy day here, except this was one of tidying up, of concluding affairs.

Nicholas Blount stood out from his peers (two males, one female), but not because he was a senator's son and carried a special bearing—rather, it was the blackened left eye and the bandaged left cheek, the expected result if the gunman who'd pistol-whipped him had been right-handed.

Due to his injuries, Nicky Blount was currently basking in the late Venter's reflected heroism, a jurist who'd "given his life to save his valued clerk, his trusted friend" (as Sean Hannity had put it). The media seemed to be cuing Nicky up as a rising political star.

*Would the younger Blount prove as reprehensible as his old man?* Reeder wondered. After all, Senator Wilson Blount and his good-ol'-boy cronies were the worst kind of pork-barrel, backward-thinking politicos.

Reeder approached the clerk, saying, "Mr. Blount? This is Special Agent Patti Rogers with the FBI. I'm Joe Reeder, task force consultant."

They were expected.

"We certainly appreciate your efforts around this office," Blount said with a businesslike smile, shaking hands with both.

Injuries aside, Blount had the blond, plasticine good looks of a career politician, or maybe a functionary in the Hitler Youth. His charcoal suit and white shirt with subdued dark tie were properly somber.

The clerk ushered them to visitor's chairs at a desk in one corner. Everyone sat.

"We are sorry for your loss," Rogers said, "but I'm afraid we've already put this interview off longer than we should."

"Thank you. I understand," he said with a nod. "I'm sure Justice Venter would applaud your efforts."

She gave him her own businesslike smile. "We shouldn't have to take up too much of your time, Mr. Blount."

"Fine. Whatever is necessary, Agent Rogers."

"Could you give us your account of what happened that night at the Verdict?"

He ran a hand across his forehead and sighed deeply. "Reliving that tragedy, I fear, won't be a problem. I've done it a thousand times or more, and I only wish I had acted more quickly. But Justice Venter beat me to the punch."

*Okay,* Reeder thought. *He's written his script and has it memorized.*

Nicky Blount would be telling this story until the day he died, needing to make himself look as good as possible, despite having pissed his pants in fear (a detail unlikely to be provided in this account). And the Justice would come across as a combo of Bruce Willis in a *Die Hard* movie and Davy Crockett at the Alamo.

Nonetheless, Reeder listened closely as the young man gave his version of events. Actually, it didn't stray far from what had been on the security footage . . . aside from the crucial moment, where in the Blount account Venter died a hero.

Rogers asked a few predictable follow-ups, and her interview was coming to a close when Reeder asked, "Why didn't the holdup man shoot you?"

"Well, isn't that obvious?"

"Is it?"

The clerk shrugged, then nodded vigorously, two oddly contradictory responses. "Didn't Justice Venter give his life for me?"

"Interesting question."

"Not a question, Mr. Reeder. A statement. He gave his *life* for me."

This was stated with the certainty of a Christian affirming that Jesus had died for his sins.

There was no arguing with a zealot, so Reeder asked, "In which hand did the shooter hold the gun?"

*Let us see,* he thought, *how accurate Nicky is in remembering a detail like that . . . as opposed to reciting the epic poem of the heroic death of Justice Henry Venter.*

Momentarily surprised, Blount said, "Well, uh . . . his right."

"You're quite certain of that?"

"Quite certain," Blount said defensively. Like any liar, he became indignant when one of the true parts was questioned. "*Absolutely,* his right hand. I mean, for Christ's sake—he pointed the thing in my face!"

"Thank you, Mr. Blount," Reeder said. "Now, picture that hand, that gun, pointed right at you . . . however uncomfortable that might be. What *else* do you see about the shooter?"

Blount caught on quick, closed his eyes, thought for a moment. "Gloves, black shirt, black ski mask."

"Any hair visible around the edges of the mask?"

". . . No. None."

"Eye color?"

Blount's eyebrows furrowed. ". . . Blue eyes."

"Quite sure?"

"Quite sure."

Frowning a little, Rogers said, "Mr. Blount, you didn't mention that to the police."

"I didn't think of it at the time, and I wasn't asked about it, not directly. I hope I haven't screwed anything up. I was in the ER getting stitched up, and . . . um . . . I was badly shaken."

"You urinated in your pants," Reeder said.

Blount glared at him, embarrassed. "Have *you* ever had a gun pointed at you?"

"Yes," Reeder said.

The clerk blinked a few times. "Oh. You . . . you're *that* guy, aren't you? Sorry. You took a bullet. You're a hero. Like the Justice. I *wasn't* a hero. But I never claimed to be."

Rogers flashed Reeder a dirty look and said to the interviewee, "We don't have any intention of embarrassing you, Mr. Blount. We just need every fact, every detail, to get as complete a picture as possible."

"I get it. I understand. It's just . . . it was goddamn *frightening*."

Reeder asked, "How tall was the gunman?"

"That much I *did* give the police—average height, average build."

*Average* was a word that no investigator relished hearing from a witness, a worthless word that meant something different to everybody on the planet.

Reeder asked, "Can you estimate a height, Mr. Blount?"

"I think so. Five eight or nine?"

"Weight?"

"One fifty maybe, one sixty?"

"Muscular build or slim?"

"Muscular."

"Any paunch?"

"No. No beer gut."

"Good. What about the other robber?"

Shrug. "He's more just an impression than the one who was right there *on* me."

"What was your impression, then?"

"Tall guy, big gun."

"Do the same thing with him you did with the other one. Visualize him. Start at the gun and work back."

Blount tried, but then shook his head. "He was way across the room, the one with the AK-47. I just didn't get a good enough look. I'm sorry."

"But you saw that it was an AK-47."

"That made the *real* impression."

Reeder wished they'd gotten to Blount sooner—they should have. The DC detectives that night had interviewed Blount while he was still in shock, with no follow-up till now. Like he'd told Sloan, these task forces were always a clusterfuck in early days.

Trying to find anything new to latch onto, Reeder asked, "What did they *sound* like?"

"Sound like?"

"Think back. Hear it. Characterize it."

Blount closed his eyes, listening to his memory. ". . . Loud, angry, aggressive—like they meant business and were ready to kill somebody if necessary. Which is what they did, isn't it?"

"Do you know music, Mr. Blount?"

"Well . . . yes. Some, I guess."

"Ever sing in a choir?"

"Yes. Sure. As a kid."

"Were their voices *different,* the holdup men? Was one a baritone and the other a bass? Was one a tenor?"

"I get you. I'd say baritones. Both baritones. One a little gruffer than the other."

"Which was gruffer?"

"The AK-47."

"Good. Very good, Mr. Blount. How about an accent? Foreign?"

"No."

"Regional?"

". . . No."

"On the security footage we saw, the gunman said something to you. Right after he shot Justice Venter. What was it?"

This threw Blount.

They were discussing the most traumatic event of his roughly thirty years; he'd been threatened, witnessed a killing, been pistol-whipped.

And Reeder had touched the rawest of the raw nerves, the angriest of the wounds; had found the one crucial thing that Blount had shared with no one, and perhaps hadn't allowed himself to dwell on, either.

Justice Venter's clerk looked down at the blotter on his desk, fingers of one hand fumbling idly with a flash drive. For a while, they just sat there. When Blount finally looked up, tears were welling.

"He . . . he said it was my fault—the gunman, he said Justice Venter's death was on me."

Rogers sat forward. "What do you think he meant?"

"That . . . that if I had handed over my wallet faster, Justice Venter wouldn't have tried to intervene. That if it wasn't for me, the Justice would still be alive."

Rogers remained professionally composed, but her eyes asked Reeder a terrible question: *Could Venter's slaying be the result of a robbery gone wrong after all?*

He shook his head almost imperceptibly, and, after a beat, she nodded back the same way: The subsequent murder of Justice Gutierrez and the possible attacks on the other judges almost certainly ruled that out.

Reeder returned his attention to Blount.

Having come into this interview with at least a vague dislike of this smooth son of a redneck politician, now all he needed was a guilt-ridden victim.

"Mr. Blount," he said, "I can't share with you any specifics—this is an ongoing investigation, after all, and of the highest sensitivity. National security concerns and all that."

"I do understand . . ."

"*But*—I can assure you that you weren't responsible in any way for Justice Venter's death."

"That's . . . generous of you. Kind."

"No. It's the truth. Follow the news over the coming days and months, and you'll have proof of that. Thank you, Mr. Blount."

Everyone rose, and another round of shaking hands followed. Washington was nothing if not ritualistic, after all, from this farewell to the Justice lying in state downstairs.

Out into the afternoon sunshine, Rogers asked Reeder, "Why in the hell would that holdup guy say that to Blount?"

Reeder grunted a wry laugh. "Might just have been screwing with his head."

"Is that what you think?"

"No. I think the bad guys wanted Nicky Blount feeling guilty and buying into Justice Venter trying to save his ass."

She smirked. "To keep us chasing our tails."

"Yes, and to muddy the waters from the git-go."

As they walked to the car, Rogers posed the obvious question. "Was Brooks ambidextrous?"

"Not if the police reports are to be believed."

"Then why was the gun in his *right* hand when he shot the Justice?"

Reeder stopped, and she stopped and faced him. A cool breeze was at his back and warm sun was on his face.

He said, "Who says *Brooks* shot the Justice?"

"Well, we've assumed from the start . . . oh shit. We *assumed.*"

"We've assumed that Brooks is the shooter because the gun showed up there, but what if Brooks and Granger weren't under those ski masks? And who was driving the getaway car outside the Verdict? Marvin? Or somebody else entirely?"

"That's a lot of questions," she said, looking as stunned as a freshly clubbed baby seal.

He grinned at her. "Isn't it though?"

"Maybe we need to talk to Granger and Marvin, like, right away."

"No maybe about it."

In separate interview rooms at the Fairfax County Detention Center, Rogers sat down with Tom Marvin while Reeder arranged an audience with Charlie Granger.

But when Granger saw Reeder already seated at the table, the prisoner froze—right arm in a cast, no cuffs, his orange jumpsuit looking lived-in.

The guard nudged Granger into the room, but the prisoner protested. "Hey, I got *nothin'* to say to this clown. Not without my lawyer, I don't."

The guard closed the door in Granger's face.

"I want my lawyer!" Granger yelled, pounding on the door with his good hand.

"You don't need him," Reeder said.

Granger kept his back to the seated Reeder, facing the door. "I got nothing to say to you."

"Will you answer one question?"

Silence.

"Was Butch Brooks ambidextrous?"

That turned Granger around. "What the fuck?"

"Ambidextrous—was your buddy Butch ambidextrous? You know what that *means,* right?"

Granger sneered. "Yes, I know what it means, and maybe when it come to jerkin' off he was, but otherwise no. He was *left*-handed. He drove one-handed like that."

"Oh, was he a driver? Decent wheelman?"

"He was a hell of a wheelman. Why?" His curiosity aroused, Granger shuffled over and took the chair across from Reeder. "Go ahead. Ask another."

"You really *weren't* at the Verdict Monday night, were you, Charlie?"

"What the hell have I been *tellin'* you, you and everybody, includin' my goddamn lawyer. No, no, *no,* I wasn't fucking at the Verdict Monday night. I was with my mom, helping her out."

"Like a good son."

"Like a very goddamn good son."

"You know something, Charlie?"

"What?"

"I think maybe you were."

Reeder got up and walked out, leaving Granger sitting there like everybody else in his card game disappeared.

In the hallway, Rogers came up to Reeder.

"Anything?" he asked.

She nodded, smiling like she had a secret but couldn't keep it. "Our friend Marvin? He's scared of somebody."

"He tell you that?"

"No. I *read* him. I've been hanging around with you, remember? Marvin isn't talking to anybody about anything. Very scared, our boy Marvin. How about Granger?"

"Well, he didn't want to talk at first. He did confirm that Brooks wasn't ambidextrous."

"Are you sure Granger doesn't think that means a land-and-water animal?"

226

"No. He knows the definition, all right. Butch Brooks was left-handed."

She thought about that. "So . . . does that mean Brooks didn't kill Venter?"

"It means Brooks didn't pull the trigger. Granger says Brooks was a wheelman—maybe Butchie was at the curb in the getaway vehicle."

She was frowning. "Then how did the gun get in Butch's house?"

"Maybe they passed weapons around in that robbery ring. Or possibly it was provided by whoever Marvin's afraid of. It's a conspiracy and we're dealing with the flunky side of things, remember."

She thought about that, then said, "Remind me what color Granger's eyes are."

"Blue."

"So *Granger* could have been the shooter."

"Could be."

She gave him the tiniest of smiles. "But you don't think so."

Reeder sighed. "He wasn't the guy wielding the Glock in any of the out-of-state robberies. And Butch's fingerprints are on the pistol. Is there any reason that Butch Brooks might have used his right hand, when he was a leftie?"

She shook her head. "Not that I can think of."

"Makes even less sense when you read Butch's rap sheet."

"Oh?"

"The late Butch Brooks had brown eyes."

She held up her hands in surrender. "Hold on. Why would this sophisticated conspiracy you keep talking about enlist these known repeater criminals to do their dirty work, and then not use them to *do* their damn dirty work!"

"Curiouser and curiouser," he said.

"Don't start that again," she said, rolling her eyes. "But goddam-nit—you're right."

They walked to the Ford. Time to call it a day, and Reeder could only wonder if they'd taken as many steps forward as they had back.

"Beware how you take hope from another human being."

*Oliver Wendell Holmes Jr.,*
*Associate Justice of the Supreme Court*
*Section 5, Grave 7004,*
*Arlington National Cemetery.*

# SIXTEEN

Amy Reeder lay in a fetal ball on her sofa, a couch cushion hugged tight to her chest as if a life preserver. Which seemed appropriate, since she was drowning in a sea of her own tears. That the cushion smelled of Bobby's shampoo was at once solace and torture. She inhaled deeply from it, and then the tears started again.

*Damnit,* she thought, *why am I not cried out yet?*

Her eyes were red, dry, and itchy, which was what bawling for the better part of two hours got you. But at least the tears weren't coming as hard now—this was just residual overflow, trailing down her cheeks, an accompaniment to the gnawing ache in her belly.

Tonight should have been special. She'd had no confidence she wouldn't screw it up, but never *dreamed* she'd make so spectacular a botch of it. This was to have been the first night of several in her extended birthday celebration, which would include going away for the weekend to (finally) consummate the Amy/Bobby relationship. But after much toss and turning and soul-searching, she'd come to the reluctant conclusion that it just . . . wasn't . . . *time* . . . yet.

Over the past several days, both on the phone and in person, she had tried to tell him. She just could never find the way in. Finally, she'd been left with tonight as the only real option—after all, you didn't go off with a guy for the weekend and suddenly announce you want separate rooms as you pull up at the hotel.

Despite his casual style, Bobby was unfailingly prompt, and tonight was no exception. He arrived for dinner, right at seven, a small bouquet of yellow and white flowers in hand. They kissed at the door and went to the kitchen for her to put the flowers in water.

She had dressed up a little tonight—a short black skirt and matching jacket over a retro tee with Taylor Swift on it. Bobby was strictly a jeans and T-shirt type, which was fine by her. She was more interested in the warmth of his personality and the sharpness of his intellect than in the brand of his sweater or slacks.

Likewise, he had never seemed mainly interested in just her body—and he'd always been understanding about the old-fashioned sexual morality she clung to.

As he watched her at the sink, he said, "Smells great."

"Flowers or the food?"

"Food. Flowers, too, I guess. And you. You, uh . . . look fantastic by the way. Maybe you should wear skirts more often. Let those nice legs show."

"You're sweet," she said, a little embarrassed.

Okay, so he wasn't *not* interested in her body.

That was nothing new—she'd been hit on as early as junior high and knew she could attract males, and Bobby was nothing if not one of those. But knowing that so many guys couldn't see past her good looks had made her cautious, even gun-shy, about their intentions.

Bobby's intentions seemed clear. They had been a couple since October and still hadn't slept together half a year later—if having sex with her was his only goal, he'd have split before Christmas, right?

She handed him the flowers in a little vase. "Put these on the table, would you? And I'll serve you up."

"You got it," he said, taking the flowers into the little dining room.

Bobby was a vegetarian, so she'd made spaghetti with marinara (she had made and frozen some meatballs for herself, to go with the big batch of sauce she made up). She was no great shakes as a cook, but her mom had taught her a few things, and her dad kept her bank account flush, so she could always afford good ingredients. Still, she rarely cooked for Bobby and was anxious. They started with a tossed salad, the dressing purchased from a restaurant they both adored.

Through the meal, conversation typically covered how their respective days had gone—they didn't share any classes, and he was a poli sci major and she was undeclared, so that took a while. She looked for an opening to discuss her decision with him, but it just wasn't there. He did say, "And she can *cook!*" Which was a relief, if an overstatement.

He helped with the dishes and talked about some problems his folks were having—like her parents, his were divorced. Along the way, he said something that made her tummy clench.

"Do you suppose," he said, wiping a plate, "that our parents were once normal humans who got along like we do, only to have work and kids and all of that derail them?"

"I don't know," she admitted. "I do remember my parents loving each other. Being cozy and walking arm-in-arm and that."

"When was this?"

"Well, I don't remember noticing that kind of lovey-dovey thing after grade school. My father worked weird hours and he was kind of . . ."

"Remote?"

She sighed, nodded. "Yeah, and he could be spooky."

"How so?"

"He could just . . . *look* at you and know what you were thinking. But you could never tell what *he* was thinking. Drives my mother crazy."

He nodded. "Passive-aggressive. My old man's like that."

"No, it's not that, exactly. It's *similar* . . . but it's not that."

When the dishes were put away, they moved to the sofa. She put some music on, a romantic ballad channel on iTunes Radio. This might be asking for trouble, but evenings they often sat there, sometimes semireclined there, making out. As usual, the apartment was mostly dark, and they were in each other's arms almost at once.

They had done a lot of things on that sofa, including her satisfying him with her hand and even her mouth, but they always stopped short of intercourse. At one point, months ago, he pressed her on it. Not physically—that wasn't his way. He wanted to talk it out. That was one of Bobby's few failings: He was under the impression you could deal with emotions intellectually.

He said, "We've established you're not a virgin."

"That's right. I'm not."

"And you're . . . obviously not shy."

The "obviously" referred to the fact that Bobby's pants were around his ankles.

"Not shy."

"Then what is it?"

"Pull your pants up and I'll tell you."

"You drive a hard bargain."

But he did.

And she did, telling him how her best friend, Kathy, in high school got pregnant and had an abortion from some sketchy pseudo doc and died horribly. Since then, Amy hadn't had sex, and she'd only been with two guys before that, anyway. She was on the pill, but she knew that wasn't infallible. Mostly she just liked having her periods regulated.

"We'll be together," she'd assured him.

"On our wedding night, you mean?"

"That sounds a little sarcastic for a marriage proposal."

"It wasn't a marriage proposal. It *is* sarcasm."

She had pulled away and started to cry, which she hated, but thoughts of Kathy did that to her, and then she apologized, and he apologized, and she said for now they could "fool around" but that was all, and he said fine, fine, he would follow her lead.

Since then, whatever sexual fun and games they'd had never quite reached intercourse, unless dry humping counted. Lately, though, marriage talk for real had kicked in, and she was starting to think, to *really* think, that Bobby was who she'd wind up with in life.

And this had led to the planned weekend getaway with Bobby, to celebrate her nineteenth birthday. Just the kind of milestone to get rid of this millstone.

Funny how her father, usually so good at figuring people out, completely missed the boat on Bobby, disliking him for no specific reason beyond not wanting to share his little girl with another male. She had long ago given up on trying to convince Daddy that Bobby really was wonderful. Sooner or later, her dad would come to see that for himself.

On the sofa, she was naked to the waist and he was kissing her breasts. She had unzipped him and was working him, slowly. Under the skirt, Bobby's hand was traveling up her thigh and then her warmth was in his hand, his fingers probing. His lips left her breasts and found her mouth, and his tongue explored even as his fingers did the same.

Between heavy breaths, he said, "Hell . . . with . . . the weekend . . . we've *decided,* haven't we? . . . Why wait . . . a few . . . frickin' . . . *days?* . . . Let's *do* it . . . Sweetheart, we *have* to *do* it . . ."

She let go of him and pushed him away. "No. No. No!"

She pulled her T-shirt back on, and he looked at her in pain, his passion sticking out. "What?"

"You *know* I'll do anything but that."

"Sweetie, I've been so patient . . ."

"You have. You *have.* I need a little more time. Just a little more time."

"But your birthday trip . . ."

"Not then, either. No. We can have fun, but . . . no."

His eyes went all deer-in-the-headlights. "What *happened?*"

She shrugged, arms folded over her breasts. "I thought about it, and it's not right yet . . . I . . . I have to be *sure.*"

"You have to be sure? You're not sure about *us?*"

"I am, but . . ."

"But you're not."

Clumsily, comically, he put his wilting self away, zipped up, stood, and gathered what little dignity was available.

"Well," he said, clearly wounded, "I guess this is better than hearing about it in the hotel lobby. Thanks for that consideration, anyway."

She gazed earnestly up at him. "Bobby . . . I was going to tell you tonight. I was just . . . waiting for the right time."

*"Fuck!"* He almost screamed the word. He gestured to the sofa, where they'd already done things illegal in several states. "In the

middle of *that*? *That's* the right time? I've been patient, Amy, but really . . . this is *crazy*. This is ridiculous. We're grown-ass adults."

"Please, Bobby . . ."

*"Please?"*

"I'm just . . . not . . . *ready.*"

He pressed his hands to his head as if his skull were about to explode and maybe he could somehow hold the pieces together. He took in a long breath, then let it out, his expression pained.

He said, "Amy, I love you, but I can't do this anymore. I'm committed to you, but it's pretty obvious you're not committed to me. And it just . . . just hurts too much to be around you."

"Bobby . . ." She smiled up at him lamely and patted the sofa. "Please. I'll take care of you."

Anger flared in his eyes. "I don't want to be bought off, Amy. I want to take care of you, and I want you to take care of me, and I'm not talking about sex, not at all . . . Please. No calls. No texts. *I* have to work this out now. Myself."

He headed to the door and she flew off the sofa, but he was already well down the stairs to the street. She followed anyway.

From the doorway, she called, "Bobby . . . *Bobby!*"

He didn't look back.

When he was gone, she did two things: She moved the vase of yellow and white flowers to a place in her little living room where she could see them, and she returned to the sofa, where she'd been crying ever since.

*It wasn't that she didn't* want *to make love to him. She wanted that very much. The time just wasn't quite right, was it? And look how* mad *he'd gotten tonight. What if she got pregnant and instead of taking her in his arms, he just got pissed and stormed off, and then she would be a mother whose child had no father, or maybe she'd wind up dead and bleeding like Kathy . . .*

She sat up, hugged her legs to her, rocking.

*Were they broken up?*

He had left so abruptly, but he did say he was going to try to work it out. She thought of the crazy old movie: *So you're tellin' me there's a chance . . .*

If they were broken up, they'd ended with a whimper, not a bang, and when the joke of that came to her, she began to laugh, a harsh laugh more like a cough, summoning still more tears.

Then the realization came: *She didn't want to lose him.*

Something in the dark part of her mind said, *Oh, so you're ready, are you? To buy him back with sex?*

But that wasn't it, was it? What she knew was that she loved him. He was worth taking the risk, and anyway, the "risk" was really just some stupid psychological barrier she'd built up—the odds of pregnancy with birth control were minuscule, and, besides, Bobby would stand by her. She knew that.

She would text him, no matter what he said. She would call him, too. She would keep it up till he gave in. She could fix this— she knew she could, because she *was* ready. Robert Landon was who she wanted to be with. Maybe spend her life with.

*If only she could get him to listen.*

She sent a text: SORRY. SECOND CHANCE?

She left a voice mail: "I'm wrong, you're right—can we please still do the weekend? Can you forgive me and can we please, please, *please* celebrate my birthday together?"

She went back to the sofa, cell in hand, waiting. Shaking—one moment confident he'd call, the next certain he wouldn't, and back and forth and back and forth . . .

Then came a knock at the door.

She grinned, sucked in breath, tossed the pillow aside, and went to answer it.

But when she did, it wasn't Bobby.

"I never moved into combat without having
the feeling of a cold hand reaching
into my guts and twisting them into a knot."

*Audie Murphy,*
*most decorated soldier of World War II,*
*Congressional Medal of Honor winner.*
*Section 46, Lot 366-11, Grid O/P-22.5,*
*Arlington National Cemetery.*

# SEVENTEEN

Just outside the door of his town house, where Patti Rogers had dropped him, Reeder wanted nothing more than a Heineken, a shower, and his bed. Exhausted, he was not up to sorting through thoughts that might add up to something, tomorrow morning. He had taken them as far as he dared on the ride home with Rogers, but these were half-formed ideas not yet worth sharing, puzzle pieces without a shape to fit them in.

He was barely inside when his cell phone chirped. He didn't recognize the number on the caller ID and ignored it at first, then reconsidered. With all that was happening, he better take the call.

"Reeder," he said.

The voice that came out of his phone was mechanical, obviously filtered through an antirecognition program.

*"We have your daughter. You have one hour to verify, after which you will receive further instructions. Involve no one else, or suffer the consequences."*

The call clicked off.

Such things could chill the blood, it was said; but with Reeder, the opposite occurred: His temperature spiked and sweat popped out like a thousand blisters.

He pulled up *Contacts* on the phone and punched Amy's number, but the call went straight to voice mail.

"It's Dad, honey. Call me. It's important. Never mind the hour."

He fought back panic. He was not prone to it, though not immune, either, not with his daughter at stake. Should he call his ex-wife? Ask Melanie if she'd heard from Amy? No. Not yet, anyway—he didn't want to risk panicking her. That would do no good, and if she got wind of what was up, she might call the authorities and . . . well, he wouldn't call her now.

The Prius made the already short drive to Amy's in a record four minutes and a few seconds. Speeding and ignoring traffic laws had an oddly calming effect on Reeder, a response he'd not felt since Secret Service days. In a tense situation—after a first burst of adrenaline—everything inside him would ease, and he'd settle into a zone. That feeling fell over him now, the hysterical parent caged up somewhere deep within him.

He parked in front of Amy's, glancing up and down the block with seeming unconcern. If someone was watching her building for him, they were goddamned good—he didn't spot anybody on the street, or in parked cars.

She lived on the third floor, and street entry was by numbered keypad only, no getting buzzed in. But his company had installed the alarm system, which had an embedded master pass code that only Reeder and a few top ABC employees knew. He could get into scores of residences all over the DC area, but this was the one that counted.

Inside, he took the carpeted stairs two at a time to the third floor. Breathing a little hard, he stopped and knocked once, in the desperate hope that Amy was on the other side of the door, in the small living room. He didn't give a shit if she and her hippie boyfriend were humping away like rabbits on the floor, if she would just take a break and open that damn door.

He knocked again, louder, longer.

Nothing.

He brought out the key that Amy didn't know he had. He had it, all right—he paid the rent, didn't he?—but he'd promised himself to use it only in an emergency, which this sure as hell was.

The lights were off, the room quiet. As he stepped inside, the apartment had an empty feel.

"Amy!" he called, keeping alarm out of his voice.

Silence.

He closed the door behind him, flipped the switch, triggering an overhead fixture that she rarely used, preferring table lamps and a generally muted lighting scheme. The overhead made the living room seem overly bright, like an autopsy room. Everything seemed in place, though two sofa pillows were on the floor. Some yellow and white flowers on an end table looked fresh.

Damp towels in the kitchen spoke of a home-cooked meal, as did the familiar smell of the marinara sauce that Melanie had taught their daughter to make. *Amy had been in this kitchen this evening.* The dining room table was set for two. *Had Bobby been here with her? Maybe an early birthday celebration?*

*Was he here when she was abducted?*

The realization of that likelihood uncaged the crazed parent for a few moments. He always thought Melanie leaving him had ripped him apart worse than any physical wound ever could. And that was true enough. But this was worse.

Recaging the crazy man, Reeder returned to the living room. The two couch cushions on the floor of the otherwise undisturbed area were not enough to indicate a struggle. She had left under the barrel of a gun, most likely, or perhaps had been lured out by some trusted figure, a cop maybe, with news of a nonexistent accident.

On the coffee table, Amy's cell phone spoke silent volumes—she would *not* have left that behind. Someone had quickly, suddenly, gotten her out of here. His fists clenched—the cell's presence meant there would be no tracking her by GPS.

He was doubting now that Bobby had been here when she was taken. He looked around to see if the boyfriend's phone was anywhere, on the floor maybe, but didn't find it. On her cell, he found the Landon kid listed first in her contacts—that hurt a little—and tried his number. Straight to voice mail.

"This is Amy's father. I'm looking for her. Call me when you get this, no matter the hour."

Her cell didn't tell him much. The numbers in her call log were all ones he recognized—him, her mother, and a bunch of calls and texts to Bobby. Her e-mail account looked normal, and so did everything he could access on her social media accounts. No contact with or from anyone out of the ordinary.

He returned the cell to the coffee table.

In his daughter's bedroom, he found nothing apparently out of place—not that he would know. The only time he'd been in this room was when he helped her move in. Her closet seemed fairly full, a suitcase out but empty, as if she was planning to pack for an upcoming trip.

Bathroom looked normal. Her toothbrush there, hairbrush, all her toiletries.

Then he walked through every room again, absorbing the awful emptiness. Nothing about it confirmed that she'd been taken, but circumstantial evidence combined with cop instincts screamed it: *They had her.*

Nothing left to do but call Melanie. He would try to elicit from his ex-wife any information she might have without alerting her that their daughter might have been abducted.

"Hello, Joe," she said in that awful, neutral tone reserved for phone solicitors and ex-husbands.

"Hi, Mel." *Keep it light.* "I'm trying to get ahold of Amy, and her cell goes right to voice mail. Heard from her tonight at all?"

"No. Not for a few days, actually. But then she's been very caught up in midterms, and of course that boyfriend."

"Right."

"She doesn't always answer the phone, you know. Text her—I know you hate doing it, but she always responds right away to my texts, even when she's blowing off my calls."

"I'll try that."

"What's the matter?" That tone for ex-husbands disappeared. It was the old voice. The voice of someone who loved him. "Honey, you sound a little off."

*She* was the real people reader in the family, at least where he was concerned.

"I was just a little worried when Amy didn't pick up," he said. "We had kind of an awkward meal out the other night, with her and her boyfriend."

*Would she buy it?*

"Joe, don't worry about it. She and Bobby probably just went to a movie. Isn't this five-dollar night at the art theater they go to?"

*She bought it.*

"Hell, I don't know," he said, and forced a laugh. "I don't keep track of the artsy-fartsy stuff those kids like."

"Joe, what's *wrong?*"

*Whoops—he'd tried too hard.*

"They pulled me in on the Venter investigation," he said. "The security footage came from one of our cameras. I'm pretty stressed, back in the federal frying pan."

When in doubt, punt with the truth.

"You don't need that kind of crap anymore, Joe. How many times have I told you? You have to learn to delegate."

*An image popped into his mind: He was with Melanie and Amy, age ten, on vacation, at Mount Rushmore. Looking at giant presidents, Amy thinking carving up that mountain was awful, Mel talking about* North by Northwest, *him loving them both. And probably not show-ing it enough.*

He said, "Good advice. Mel, listen, if you get ahold of Amy, or hear from her or whatever—tell her to give me a call, will you?"

"Sounds kind of urgent."

"Well, I need to change some birthday plans with her."

"I will. Joe?"

"Yes?"

"Don't overdo. You're not a kid anymore."

She clicked off and he clicked off. Then he sat on the sofa and cried into his hands for maybe thirty seconds.

It was all he could spare.

Eventually, Melanie would have his ass for not telling her what was going on, but he knew he'd just done her a kindness, and him-self a favor. She could make phone calls that would only hamper him on his mission to get Amy back. And when he got her back—not *if*, fucking *when*—Melanie would forget all about anything except that she was holding her daughter in her arms.

His watch said only a few minutes remained before that second call with "further instructions."

He needed help on this, and he needed it right now. But calling Gabe would not only violate the no-cops demand, it would automatically put Joe Reeder on the sidelines. Sloan would have no choice but to bring in the full force of the FBI even while keeping Reeder out of the search for Amy—AD Fisk would insist, as would anybody in her place.

Hell, even if Amy was quickly found, Reeder would be yanked off the task force—she had almost certainly been targeted because her father was looking into the murders of the two justices. And if the kidnapping had no connection to the murders, he would *still* get sent to the showers, an investigator whose daughter had been recently kidnapped . . . even if she'd been recovered.

*Even if she'd been recovered.*

He couldn't allow himself to think that way.

His DC Homicide pal Bishop was in some ways a better short-term option, but that also went against the kidnapper's demand, and anyway Bishop didn't have the tools at his disposal that Reeder needed.

That left only one real choice.

"Patti Rogers," said the voice in his ear.

"Can I trust you?"

"Well, I'm fine, Joe. How are you?"

"Can I trust you?"

"What the hell . . . ?"

"Before I tell you what's going on, I have to know. We haven't been partners long. It's a fair question."

For a while her only answer was silence, but he didn't prod her with any more words. He just waited.

Finally she said, "Short of risking my career for you? Yeah. I'm there. What do you need?"

"My daughter has been abducted. I think there's a reasonable possibility that the conspiracy took her."

"Jesus fuck," Rogers blurted. "Reeder, we have *got* to call Sloan."

"Not now, not yet," Reeder said. "I need to track the kidnapper myself. I don't want to be sidelined, and that's what Gabe would have to do."

"What would you say to any other father in your position?"

"Let the FBI handle it. Patti—am I 'any other father'? This is my daughter, yes. But I'm damn near certain it's part of this judicial coup we've stumbled onto."

Silence again.

Then: "Okay. Goddamnit. I'm sorry about your daughter . . . Amy, right?"

"Right."

"Joe, what can I do? Name it."

"I thought you said you wouldn't risk your career for me."

A shrug was in her voice: "Risk it, make it. One of those should happen."

He almost smiled. "Look, I'm expecting the kidnapper's second call in, like, six minutes. Can you get a trace set up on my cell in that time?"

"On it," she said, then clicked off.

Nothing to do now but wait.

Reeder fell back onto the sofa and pressed his fingers into his temples. *Why Amy?* This *had* to be about the justices—no way this was a coincidence. But why attack *him* instead of someone else on

the team? Everybody had vulnerabilities, *something* they loved—
fathers, mothers, daughters, sons, wives, a goddamn dog!

What threat did Joe Reeder present to the conspirators that
nobody else on the task force did? Or was this big enough that they
could go after *all* their families?

*No, no—that was crazy . . .*

But wasn't killing Supreme Court justices to reconfigure the
court crazy?

Then his phone trilled and, for all his training, he damn near
jumped out of his skin. He took a deep breath, exhaled slowly, whispering a silent prayer that Rogers had the trace set up, and said, "Reeder."

He waited for the mechanized voice. Here in his daughter's
deserted apartment, he pledged to her and himself that no matter
how this turned out, the person on the other end of this call would
never stand trial.

*"By now, you know we have your daughter."*

Reeder's voice was as cold and mechanical as his adversary's:
"She isn't here, but that doesn't mean you have her."

*"Don't speak unless you're asked a question."*

"If you have her, let me talk to her."

*"No."*

Reeder hung up on the bastard.

He stared at the phone in his sweaty palm, forcing the crazed
parent back in his cell. They hadn't made a demand yet. They would
call back. Otherwise, kidnapping Amy had been for nothing, and
this was not that kind of situation, not that kind of crime.

The cell rang.

"Reeder."

Rogers said, "Not long enough for the trace."

*Fuck!*

"Hang up," he snapped. "I'm waiting for him to call back. I'll call you."

He clicked off and stared at his cell again.

They let him sweat longer than he would have ever imagined. But that was smart, wasn't it? Time allowed doubt to take root and grow.

*Had he overplayed his hand? Was he gambling with Amy's life?*

He wanted to hear her voice, he *had* to hear her voice, to let her know everything was going to be all right.

To let him know she was still breathing.

Thirty minutes after he hung up on the kidnapper, he began to wonder if he was ever going to hear her voice again.

Finally, the cell rang.

"Reeder."

*"This will be your only opportunity to save your daughter. By the way, we also have her friend."*

So they had Bobby, too. Or did the voice on the phone mean someone else?

*"Your choice is simple. Just listen. If you hang up again, or make any demands on us, or even ask one question . . . your daughter's death will be on you."*

Almost the exact phrase that Justice Venter's killer had spoken to Nicky Blount: *It's on you!* He was dealing with one of the conspirators, all right.

Reeder said nothing. The mechanical coldness of the voice-disguising software was matched by a real coldness in the original. He would take this man's threat seriously.

*"Your silence is the correct response. Tomorrow morning, you will resign your position with the task force looking into the Supreme Court killings. Do you understand?"*

"Yes."

*"After the coming weekend, we will disappear, our work done . . . and your daughter will be released unharmed. Do you understand?"*

"Yes."

*"Failure to comply means death for your daughter and her friend. Do you understand?"*

"Yes."

The phone clicked.

For a moment he just sat there. He felt numb. He hit the number for Patti Rogers.

He asked her, "Anything?"

"The call was from the cell of a Georgetown student."

"Bobby Landon," Reeder said. "Amy's boyfriend. They seem to have him, too."

"Could *he* be in on this?"

"Very little chance. He's been dating Amy since October."

"Okay, but how long has the conspiracy been working on this thing?"

"Doesn't matter, Patti. They couldn't know I'd be asked to consult with the task force. No, the Landon kid must have been with Amy when they grabbed her. They claim he's alive, too."

"Well, his *phone* isn't—went dead right after the call. So what's our next step?"

"Your next step is to have Miggie send me everything he has on the Supreme Court investigation."

"And nobody can know, I suppose."

"You can know. Miggie can know. I can know."

She sighed. "Okay. That's *my* next step. What's yours?"

"I have to quit the team."

"Trouble creates a capacity to handle it."

*Oliver Wendell Holmes Jr.,*
*served thirty years*
*as Associate Justice of the Supreme Court.*
*Section 5, Grave 7004,*
*Arlington National Cemetery.*

# EIGHTEEN

Seated at her desk in the task force command post at the Hoover Building, Patti Rogers felt a hyper uneasiness that had little or nothing to do with this, her second grande latte of the morning. She sipped at it. Granted, she'd come into the office early, but that was two hours ago and still no sign of Reeder. Over at the conference table, Gabe Sloan would occasionally glance from his watch to Reeder's empty desk and back again, and frown a little, before getting back to work.

The weight of what Reeder had shared with her last night—two kidnappings, both apparently still unreported—had her wondering if her new partner had left her to twist in the wind today. If it became known that she had withheld that knowledge of such crimes, she really *could* lose her job. Hell, she could face obstruction charges . . .

Around her, most of the rest of the team was working away, oblivious to what had gone down last night.

Hunkered over his laptop, Miggie Altuve—who'd also done Reeder a clandestine favor—had thus far cast not a glance her way. Was he hiding in his work, or just obsessive about it? In any case, he was blissfully unaware of the kidnappings that were burning a hole in her conscience.

Rogers could not allow the abductions to stay off the books much longer. If Reeder didn't show up in the next thirty minutes, she would have to go to Sloan, career be damned . . .

On cue, Reeder pushed open one of the command post's double doors; but he did not come in. He just motioned to her, then pointed toward Sloan. Heads started popping up around the room, but when she and Sloan rose to go out, everybody got back to work.

A confab in the corridor made sense. Reeder would hardly want to face the SAIC in front of the entire team. Despite the tragic circumstances, the consultant seemed placid as a mountain stream. Or was that a slight tension around his eyes? In Reeder's case, that was tantamount to a nervous breakdown.

When the three were alone in the corridor, Sloan spoke up first: "Why so late for work, Peep? I have several fresh leads for you and Patti."

Without preamble, Reeder said flatly, "Amy's been kidnapped."

Sloan gaped at him. "Jesus, no. This *morning?*"

"Last night," Reeder said with a head shake. "I sat on it till now."

"Oh, Christ, Peep, no. You *know* that's no way to—"

"I went to Amy's apartment first. I needed to make sure this wasn't a false alarm."

"And it was no false alarm."

"Apparently not."

Sloan huffed a sigh. "When did the call come in?"

"Just as I was getting home. I was given an hour to determine for myself whether Amy had been taken. Her boyfriend, Robert Landon, also a Georgetown student, was likely also abducted."

Sloan's eyes flared with irritation. "And you waited till *now* to bring us in?"

"The caller told me not to involve anyone else. I took that to mean no law enforcement."

"Shit. You know *better* than that! The more time you allow to pass, the more likely—"

"On reflection, obviously, I've come to the same conclusion. I'm here, Gabe. I'm here now."

The SAIC shook his head, teeth bared like a growling animal. "And it took you this long to come to your senses?"

"Well, I went to Melanie's last night. Amy's mother had a right to know what was going on. I wasn't about to tell her something like this over the phone."

Sloan's angry visage eased to one of concern. "How's Mel doing?"

"What do you think? She's a wreck. We went through all the stages of grief, including a new one, where I got pounded on."

"Shit. Shit shit shit."

"We talked for hours, working through it, figuring things out, deciding exactly how I should play this."

The irritation returned. "Peep, you don't have that luxury. *We* decide that now. The FBI. You *have* heard of it? How much does the kidnapper want?"

"This isn't a ransom deal. He wants me to resign from the task force—walk away from the investigation."

Sloan frowned in confusion. "What the hell?"

"I have no idea why. It's not like we seem to be getting any-where. But that's what they're asking. And, frankly, I wouldn't be coming to you now if I hadn't been told to."

Sloan's hands went to his hips, his eyebrows raised. "Don't kid yourself, Peep. Your background doesn't qualify you to take this on alone any more than *any* distraught parent. Leave this to us. We'll go after the bastards."

The SAIC turned to go back into the command post, but Reeder stopped him with a hand on an elbow.

"I'm not finished," Reeder said.

"What?"

"When the creation of this task force was announced to the media," the consultant said, "I wasn't a part of it. That came later. An afterthought. An add-on."

Sloan blinked at him. "Yes. Right. So?"

"The media's been kept away from us. If I was spotted at a crime scene by a news crew, nothing's come of it. Far as I know, I've stayed strictly under the radar."

"What's your point?"

"My point is . . . how many people even *know* I'm part of this task force? Have you considered that?"

Shrugging, Sloan said, "Well, no, I haven't. I've given it no thought at all. Why should I?"

At Reeder's side, Rogers said to Sloan, "Start with the people we've interviewed—Nicky Blount, the Chief Justice, Charlie Granger, Tom Marvin. We spoke to a few people at the White House, including the President and his chief of staff. It's a limited number."

Sloan didn't seem to be following.

Reeder took over for her: "Granger and Marvin are behind bars. They didn't kidnap Amy. Blount's a victim himself, and the Chief Justice seems an unlikely snatch artist. I think we can rule out the President, although I wouldn't put much past Vinson, his chief of staff."

Sloan, frowning, said, "Well, who the hell *does* that leave, Peep?"

But Rogers answered, pointing toward the nearby double doors. "Everybody in that room."

Sloan goggled at them. "You think one of our *own* is part of . . ." He couldn't even finish it.

Reeder said, "I don't think anything yet. But someone who knows I'm working with the task force took my daughter. Keep that in mind."

"I will," Sloan said. "I don't share your paranoia, but I will. And I'm going to do you a big favor, Peep. I'm not going to press the issue that you waited to report this. But I'm taking this to AD Fisk, right now."

Reeder nodded. "Yes, by all means. Get an FBI kidnap team over to Melanie's—I told her to expect that. Alert Bobby Landon's parents, too—they live in Arlington. They have a right to know what's going on."

Sloan eyed him suspiciously. "All right. But where do you come in?"

"I don't come in. I go out."

"What . . . ?"

Reeder pointed a finger at his friend's chest. "*You* need to go in— go in there and tell the team I'm leaving, that I'm off the task force as of now. Tell Fisk, too. Inform the President, while you're are it. I need to make a show of walking out of this building and going home. I'm off the Supreme Court investigation."

"That'll raise a lot of questions from everybody you just mentioned."

"Tell them I have a family emergency. Nothing more. Anyway, it won't take long for word about Amy to get around the building, once you've told Fisk and kidnap teams are dispatched."

"You're right, of course." Sloan gripped Reeder's arm. "Peep, I promise you that we will do everything in our power to get Ames back to you."

"I know you will."

"Go home and wait by the phone. I'll keep you posted, all the way. Do I have to tell you what that daughter of yours means to me?"

"I know. I know."

Sloan swallowed thickly, opened the door, holding it open for Rogers, who said, "You go. I'll walk him out."

The SAIC nodded, gave his old friend a sorrowful smile, and headed in.

She and Reeder headed down the endless corridor toward the elevator.

About halfway there, Rogers said, "Before we teamed up, I heard a lot about you."

"That I'm an arrogant son of a bitch, you mean?"

"Pretty much. I don't necessarily think that assessment is too far off base."

He smiled a little. "Oh, don't you?"

"No. You're at least half crazy and could obviously use a decent round of therapy."

"I'll take that under advisement."

"But you're a hell of an investigator, Joe. You see things nobody else does, and I appreciate that."

"Well, I appreciate you saying it. You're okay yourself, Patti. Sloan was right that you're smart, and you've got good instincts. Learn to listen to them."

They were at the elevators.

She stuck out a hand and they shook.

"Joe, I would work with you again in a heartbeat."

"Thanks, Patti." The elevator came and he stepped on. "But who says we aren't still working together?"

"Wait, *what* did you say?"

She hadn't been planning to ride down with him, but the car was empty and she hopped on.

As usual, his face gave nothing away. "You don't *really* think I'm going to stop working on this, do you? My daughter's kidnapping? The conspiracy behind all this shit?"

She shook her head. "Now you *are* talking crazy. You need to stay out of it, Joe, and let the experts do their job. The FBI'll get your daughter back, and nab all of those responsible. Bank on it."

He gave her a bland smile. "Actually, the rate of return of kidnap victims when the FBI is called in is slightly lower than when not. Oh, and thanks for having Miggie e-mail me those case files."

"You're welcome, but—"

"I'm not going to put you and your career in undue peril. I'll work alone . . . but I'll feed you anything I find."

The doors opened onto the lobby. He stepped out; she stayed on.

"Patti," he said, holding the door open, "they've already killed two Supreme Court justices. Do you *really* think they plan to release Amy?"

Her inability to give him an answer was answer enough.

Then she heard herself say, "What can I do for you?"

"Eyes and ears open. Trust no one. There's a very good chance somebody on the task force is a conduit to the conspiracy."

He let the doors close on her.

The morning rushed by in a blur as Rogers sifted through a mountain of information culled from the crime scenes. A diligent digger, she couldn't come up with one useful new avenue to pursue. Around her, team members were mining for clues, too—Eaton was in the field, as were the cops, Bishop and Pellin; but Cribbs, Secret Service agents Ho and Stein, and computer expert Miggie worked away at their laptops and phones.

Just before noon Sloan, back from a meeting with AD Fisk, approached her desk. Maybe he had those leads for her that he'd mentioned earlier. But his expression seemed awfully grave.

"Patti, were you with Reeder when he talked to Granger at Fairfax Detention yesterday?"

"Yes, with him at the lockup, but no, not in the room. I was off questioning Marvin."

The SAIC dragged the desk chair away from Reeder's empty station and sat close, leaning in closer.

He said, "Eaton went over to see Granger first thing this morning for a follow-up interview. It never happened—prisoner was dead in his cell."

"*What?* How?"

"We won't know till the autopsy—no physical signs of violence. Could be somebody slipped him a get-out-of-jail-free pill."

"Jesus," Rogers said. "Suicide?"

"Or so we're supposed to think. A prisoner figuring he was facing a long, slow ride to lethal injection *might* take an earlier exit . . . Any idea what Reeder said to Granger in that interview?"

"Not really."

Sloan's eyebrows flicked up and down. "Well, Reeder was the last person alone with the prisoner."

"Are you . . . implying something?"

The SAIC spoke softly, almost whispering, glancing around to make sure their small conversation in this big room stayed private. "What I'm saying is that the last person who had a chance to slip something to Granger seems to be Reeder."

She smirked dismissively. "That's crazy. What about guards or other inmates? Morning meal . . . ?"

"Eaton's sticking around to check into that," Sloan said. "But right now it's looking like . . . do I have to say it?"

She was shaking her head, wide-eyed. "Not Reeder. No. There *must* be another explanation."

"With any luck," Sloan said, "Eaton will find it."

*Eaton fucking* hated *Reeder!*

Sloan was saying, "Before we go down a road I really don't want to, Patti . . . I need to know something. You've been working with Reeder for the last few days. I can't be objective—he and I've been friends too long. What's *your* take on Reeder's current state of mind?"

She shrugged. "He doesn't show it, but he *must* be going crazy over his daughter's kidnapping."

"If that's what it is."

"What else could it be?"

He ignored that, then repeated, "Patti, what's your take on him?"

"He's not an easy guy to, well . . . read. Plays it close to the vest. I guess when you know how to read other people, you learn how to guard them from reading you."

"Agreed."

"And he's a hell of an investigator. I mean, every decent break we've had in this case is due to him."

"Also agreed."

"But . . . nothing."

"Go on."

"Well . . . he's badly injured two suspects with that baton of his. I worry that this violence may be an inappropriate response. Could have something to do with his being shot as a Secret Service agent. PTSD, maybe. But, hey, I'm no damn *shrink* . . ."

Sloan frowned in thought. "Could he be . . . out of control?"

"He seems almost too *much* in control . . . except for those violent outbursts, where the situation called for at least *some* aggressive response."

"I see."

She leaned closer. "You don't think he passed that pill to Granger, do you?"

Sloan frowned, slowly shook his head. "What, and told him it was an aspirin? Or talked him into killing himself? Ludicrous. Of course . . ."

"What?"

The SAIC's eyes tensed. "If Reeder's part of the conspiracy, he could have passed the pill along with some *threat* attached. Take this and we won't kill your mother, maybe. Or maybe there's a girlfriend."

She was shaking her head vigorously. "You can't believe that, Gabe. Joe is the one who convinced the rest of us that this *is* a conspiracy!"

He sighed. "All I know is Reeder was the last one to see Granger before Eaton came around this morning. It's not exactly a smoking gun, and there are guards and other prisoners, but we need to investigate it. Investigate *everything*."

"Investigate *Reeder,* you mean?"

A shrug. "Like you said, he's gone to every crime scene and read it like a book. A book he wrote, maybe? Did he fake his own daughter's kidnapping to buy time? And there's *other* circumstantial evidence implicating him."

"Such as?"

"Such as Reeder owns a shotgun like the one that killed Gutierrez."

"That doesn't even rate as circumstantial evidence, Gabe. We're talking the bestselling shotgun in the USA."

"Patti, what two things is he best known for?"

"Well, he saved the President's life."

"What's the other thing?"

". . . That he hated the President he saved."

"Right. How did he feel about Justice Henry Venter?"

"Not a fan."

"'Not a fan' understates it. Reeder is a liberal, and our victims are conservative justices of the Supreme Court. Did you know Peep was my daughter Kathy's godfather?"

"I didn't."

"When she died at an abortionist's hands, he took it damn near as hard as Kathy's mother and me. The President Reeder saved was the driving force behind the repeal of Roe v. Wade."

She spoke so softly even she could barely hear: "And Justice Venter wrote the majority opinion."

He nodded. "Patti, do you know why I'm telling you all this?"

"No."

"You were my partner. And you were *his* partner—however briefly. I know how loyal you are. But if you know where Joe Reeder is, you need to tell me."

"He's not at home? Or his office?"

His frown was almost a scowl. "What do you think? My guess is, he's asked for your help. Well, the best way to help him is to let us know where he is." Huge sigh. "Shit, just a few hours ago we were out in the hall with him. But now I need to bring him in. Just for questioning. But *now*."

"I don't know where he is."

"You're sure?"

"Gabe, I'd tell you if I did."

The SAIC gave her a long, appraising look. "I've left a message on his phone. If he gets back to me, I'll have him come in. If you hear from Reeder, tell him he needs *not* to ignore my request. Otherwise, I'll have to put a BOLO out on him."

Was it possible that Sloan's handpicked investigator was part of the conspiracy? If she called Reeder herself and told him to get his ass in here and straighten Sloan out, he'd be Daniel in the lions' den, but with much worse odds.

If Reeder was right, there was a leak on the task force who would be watching. The kidnappers had told him to quit the team, to walk away. Returning, even only to submit to questioning, might well endanger Amy.

On the other hand, if Sloan's suspicions were correct, Reeder could be preparing for the next justice murder, or making his way to a nonextraditable country while the task force chased its tail.

*Which side was Reeder really on?*

The only thing she knew for sure was that his parting advice had been sound: *Trust no one.*

"Law not served by power is an illusion;
but power not ruled by law is a menace."

*Arthur J. Goldberg,*
*Associate Justice of the Supreme Court, 1962–1965,*
*United States Secretary of Labor,*
*United States Ambassador to the United Nations.*
*Section 21, Lot S-35, Grid M-20.5,*
*Arlington National Cemetery.*

# NINETEEN

On the second floor of his town house, in his home office, Reeder sat sifting through crime scene photos on his computer monitor. His cell buzzed, a new text coming in.

Message from Sloan: YOU OKAY? CALL ME.

Reeder ignored it. Right now, he didn't want to talk to anybody, not even Sloan—nobody who didn't have information to help get his daughter back.

The conspiracy of killers thought he was a hell of a lot closer to bringing them down than he really was. That might have been to his advantage, had it not led to Amy's abduction. But it at the very least told one thing: He should be closer than he was. And he *could* be closer, if he knew how to read the evidence.

The answers were buried in what they already knew, what they already had. So he went back to the beginning. What *did* he know? Not just surmise, what did he *know?*

He looked hard at the out-of-state jobs pulled before the Verdict Chophouse hit. In those, the pistol-wielding holdup man was clearly left-handed. Butch Brooks was left-handed, all right, but he seemed to be the driver—Granger had said as much ("hell of a wheelman").

Reeder opened a window on Marvin's rap sheet—*he* was left-handed, too! Two left-handed players in the Granger crew. A little odd, maybe. But not as odd as one of them turning into a *right-handed* gunman in the Verdict footage . . .

The gun that shot Justice Venter had been found with Brooks, so they'd all assumed Butchie Boy was the shooter. But he wasn't—hell, he wasn't even the guy on the crew who waved a pistol around in the earlier robberies. Butch was the driver. The killing weapon had been left with him strictly to connect the Granger crew to the Verdict shooting.

Reeder watched the murder footage again, zoomed in. Like Nicky Blount had said, the shooter was right-handed and blue-eyed. Was there any way it could be Tom Marvin? A left-handed man could, after all, hold a gun in his right hand; it didn't violate a law of physics or anything. He went back to Marvin's rap sheet and checked eye color—*BROWN*. Scratch him, unless he was wearing colored contacts.

Then, going back to the Verdict footage, Reeder noticed something he should have seen a long time ago: *The holdup man up front with the AK-47 didn't flinch when Venter was shot!*

The other intruder *knew* that kill was coming. Was Granger the AK-47 wielder? No, the Verdict guy looked beefier than Granger, and maybe shorter.

Neither holdup man at the Verdict, despite the apparel, despite the weaponry, seemed part of the Granger crew. They had to be ringers, meant to fool investigators into wrongly identifying the out-of-state tavern robbers.

When the two pretenders ran out, the vehicle they climbed into had a waiting driver. He might or might not be Tom Marvin. Yet another question, but at least it made Marvin a potential source of further information.

Reeder moved on to the Gutierrez crime scene. The Remington 870 was no help at all. Both he and Gabe had owned that model shotgun at one time or another, along with ten million other gun owners. The slug, however, held a certain significance: Brenneke was an uncommon brand, sold mostly to hunters and law enforcement. Its atypical weight-forward design allowed for a flatter, more powerful trajectory . . . and maximum penetration. Wilhelm Brenneke, a hunter himself, had wanted to kill humanely, if such an oxymoron was possible, and designed his slug to kill, not wound. Most law enforcement people knew about Brennekes, as did avid hunters. The general public? Not so much.

That was consistent with someone on the task force being involved—someone in law enforcement. Beyond the team, the only real possibilities were CSI Darrell Grogan or that young detective at the Gutierrez crime scene, McCrosky. Both knew of Reeder's involvement, though not before he showed up at the Gutierrez home.

But how could they know what progress the team might be making? They seemed long shots at best.

No, somebody on the team had to be tied to the conspiracy and perhaps had been one of the pretenders at the Verdict who took Justice Venter down. After all, cops could be as coldly effective with deadly weapons as any criminal.

He studied crime scene photos of Butch Brooks dead on the bed, having shot at Sloan, who'd returned fire. Butch lay there with staring idiot eyes, brain spatter on the headboard, gun in his right hand.

*And Reeder knew.*

He felt the blood drain from his face, and then came the nausea. He'd been running on pure adrenaline since the kidnapper called and now felt physical exhaustion overtake him like instant flu. He barely made it to the bathroom to puke up what little he had in him, then retched and retched until he was crying.

The tears lasted not very long. The whiteness that had overtaken his face gave way to red. Rage flowed through him like savage fuel, but by the time he was back on his feet, he was under control. Breathing evenly, steadily. Amy needed him to be strong. He would be strong.

He staggered just a little, but his stride was back by the time he returned to the home office. He sat back down. He looked at the photo again, close and hard, giving any other explanation a chance to explain itself. But he knew it wouldn't. He should have seen this long ago. It was as obvious as the Venter footage, wasn't it?

But the footage he replayed now was from his memory:

*Sloan yelled, "Federal agents!" and Reeder took off down the hall, halfway there when a shot came, followed by a second.*

Reeder had, like everyone else on the scene, accepted what he saw. Now the gun lying on Brooks's right side—*in the wrong hand*—seemed to glow and throb.

Brooks—the left-handed wheelman, never a gunman, no violent crime on his rap sheet. Two shots had been fired, sounding identical, but since the gun in Sloan's hand was a Glock and the one in the dead suspect's hand was, too, what was suspicious about it?

*The gun that killed Venter was in that house, in that room, because Sloan planted it there.*

Sloan killed Brooks from the door, went to the bed, pulled the murder weapon from concealment, and fired back toward the door, possibly with the gun in Butch's dead hand to create powder burns. Precious seconds were available to wipe his prints and put the gun in Brooks's hand on the bed. No fingerprints on the shells in the clip, or even the ejected one on the floor. A hell of a frame. Bold, audacious even, expert. Of course Sloan had kept the street-savvy Patti Rogers away from the raid, bringing along Reeder instead, away from the field for several years, likely gun-shy from getting shot last time out.

That had helped.

Nicky Blount said the killer had blue eyes. So did Sloan. The shooter was right-handed. So was Sloan. Circumstantial evidence was raining down on Reeder. Sloan had a Remington 870 about the vintage of the one that gunned down Justice Gutierrez. Was the next perfect frame coming, any moment now, with Reeder fitted for it?

The why of it was obvious—Sloan's daughter, Kathy, had died under a back-alley abortionist's blade. All Gabe's conservative beliefs must have burned to sudden ashes. The repeal of Roe v. Wade, thanks to the Supreme Court, had paved the way for Kathy's death. So had Gabe's beliefs, but a father could hardly blame himself, right? And Gabe had continued to wear his conservative views as a disguise, and Reeder had not discerned a single warning sign indicating his best friend capable of changing from bereaved father to cold assassin.

So much for the people reader.

But was there anything here that wasn't circumstantial? Was there enough, say, to take to AD Fisk? Or was a frame sliding into place that he couldn't crawl out of?

His cell phone vibrated, and he checked it: Bobby Landon's phone was calling.

*"You've done well. Stay out of it now. Head down. Continue that course, and Ames will be back soon, safe and sound."*

The caller clicked off.

And any lingering, last shred of doubt disintegrated. Under that mechanized, disguised voice was Gabriel Sloan. *Ames,* he'd said. A nickname few on Earth but her godfather called her by.

Was it a good thing for Amy, that Sloan was part of the conspiracy? Reeder could not imagine his friend harming her, or putting him through the same kind of parental hell Gabe himself had suffered. But Sloan might be a cog in this, the way to get at Reeder through Amy, and the wheel could still roll over her.

*Who were the other conspirators?* The flunkies, of course, but they were pawns. The AK-47 gunman at the Verdict was another, and possibly the driver of the getaway SUV. Of course, the latter might have been Brooks, part of why Sloan had killed him.

Was it someone above Sloan who had managed to make him SAIC in charge of the task force investigating his own crimes? Or had Sloan himself maneuvered that? Certainly Gabe had recruited Reeder to keep an eye on his old pal, after "Peep" had analyzed the Verdict footage.

So was anyone else on the task force aligned with Sloan?

The most obvious possibility would be Sloan's longtime partner, Rogers, but if Reeder's people-reading skills were working at all, she was no part of this. Obviously, she wasn't the other gunman at the Verdict—she didn't have the size. She might have been the getaway driver—Miggie had combed traffic cameras for the driver, but without any luck. Probably Brooks behind the wheel, but didn't *have* to be.

The only other task force member he trusted at all was Carl Bishop; but the DC detective didn't have the resources.

He had advised Rogers to trust her instincts, hadn't he? He decided to trust his. He got a cell from a desk drawer.

"Patti, it's me."

"Joe. Good to hear from you."

*Something off about it.*

Too loud, for one thing. As if for someone else's benefit. Should he hang up?

Instead he said, "I know who the Judas on the team is."

". . . Really?"

Her voice had lowered—she seemed to be talking to just him now, but something was *still* off.

He said, "Not good news."

She said nothing for long enough a time to make him think maybe she'd set the phone down. *Why hadn't she asked who the Judas was?*

Finally, she said, "Why would that not be good news?"

Okay, she was stalling. They were tracing the call.

He clicked off.

What exactly was going on, he had no idea; but no way was it good, especially considering what he now knew. He yanked the battery out of his phone, killing the GPS, then dropped the cell on the floor and rolled a leg of his chair crunchingly over it.

From another desk drawer he withdrew his SIG Sauer and stuck it in the back of his pants. He went to his bedroom and got on a gray sports coat and threw it on over the polo he was wearing, covering the gun in his waistband.

From a nightstand drawer he took one thousand dollars in twenties and fifties—his emergency stash—before going downstairs and out the front door and down to the sidewalk. Casual, just another guy out for a late-afternoon stroll. In the distance, sirens were coming for him.

He rounded the corner, then peeked around to see the red-and-blue-trimmed white police cars rolling up along with the FBI SWAT team van. In a few eyeblinks, vehicles blocked the street in front of his house. He walked quickly away.

He hailed the first taxi and said, "The Navy Yard."

M Street was plenty far from where they would be searching for him. He knew there'd be a BOLO, a "be on the lookout" alert. He wondered what Sloan had cooked up for him to deserve that. Judging by the fuss outside his town house, he must at least be a murderer.

The cabbie dropped him a few blocks shy of the Navy Yard, where Reeder crossed to the north side and walked east. Just off M Street, on Tenth, was a guy who traded supplies and no questions for cash.

Walking just fast enough not to attract attention, he made good time to Tenth before turning north. On the west side of the street stood a lone building, two-story brick, housing a tailor and a pawn-shop on street level. On the north side, fire-escape-style stairs rose to the second floor, where a locked steel door with an eyehole awaited.

Reeder looked up at the security camera as he knocked.

Silence.

He didn't knock again, but kept staring at the camera.

Finally, a voice from a speaker reminiscent of a carryout window's said, "We don't got any."

"I need a phone."

"Try Radio Shack."

"DeMarcus, I need a special phone."

"Cops lookin' for you, man. All over the scanner. Don't need that grief."

"Then sell me what *I* need and I'll be on my way."

The door opened a crack enough to see DeMarcus Shannon, an African American of at least thirty who looked twenty. His head was bald and his build slender. His burgundy Redskins T-shirt and navy Georgetown basketball shorts clashed like the Crips and the Bloods.

"Get the fuck outta here."

"No."

"Maybe I should just call the cops myself. What I hear on the scanner, man, mus' be a big-ass reward."

"Complete with questions and media. I did you a favor once. Actually, twice."

"Shit. Yeah. Okay. Two C's."

Reeder handed him two crisp hundreds and the door closed. Within thirty seconds, it cracked open, not as wide, and DeMarcus passed across a cell phone.

"Now get the fuck gone."

"How clean?"

"You can use it leas' twice."

"For two C's? Throw in another."

DeMarcus made a face, sighed, and seemed about to protest when a siren blared a few blocks away, a regular occurrence around here, but disconcerting in these circumstances.

"Shit," the seller said, and practically threw a second phone at Reeder before the door slammed shut.

Going down the stairs, Reeder punched in a number.

She answered on the third ring: "Rogers."

"Sloan killed Venter."

"Funny—he said the same thing about you."

On the move now, Reeder was walking along Tenth, away from M Street, head tucked slightly.

He said, "I was wondering why the cops were after me. Gabe murdered Brooks, planted the murder gun."

She said nothing.

"Tell me, Patti. Would the evidence against me be purely circumstantial, by any chance? It would have to be, since I'm innocent."

"Why don't you come in," she said stiffly, "and we'll talk about it."

"Forget the trace, Patti. It's a burn phone."

"Joe, if you're innocent, come on in. We'll get it straightened out."

"The boss of the task force—my best friend—is framing me for the murders of two justices. He at the very least aided in the kidnapping of my daughter. And you suggest I come in, on his turf, and talk about it?"

"Joe, you're talking crazy."

"Will you do me this favor?" He stopped and tucked into the recession of a doorway. "Will you hear me out?"

". . . All right. Okay. Yes."

He laid it all out, quickly but in detail: everything he had figured out about the Venter, Gutierrez, and Brooks killings.

"Joe, all of that's circumstantial."

"Like what Sloan has on me," Reeder reminded her. "And I can't prove any of it. The kidnapper, on the phone, called my daughter *Ames,* Patti. That's a nickname only Gabe uses anymore."

"Joe . . ."

"He has my daughter. My God, would I use my *daughter* as a pawn in this game? You know, I almost didn't call you. You were his partner. You could be with him in it."

"Then why did you call?"

"Because I get paid to read people. I did a lousy job where Gabe Sloan is concerned. But you—I have you nailed, Patti. I know exactly what you are."

"What's that?"

"*My* partner now."

"What . . . what do you expect from me?"

"You have to choose. Choose between us."

"And I'll pick you over a man I've worked with for six years?"

"Trust your instincts and that brain of yours. Think about the things I've just told you. Look at the circumstantial evidence he's lined up against me."

"There's . . . another killing you haven't mentioned."

"I don't know of any."

"Granger. In his jail cell."

"Who saw him last?"

"Other than guards and inmates, you."

"Who found him?"

"Eaton."

He laughed harshly. "You should give that some thought, too."

". . . And when I have?"

"Meet me at the grave of Edward Washburn Whitaker."

"Edward who?"

"Look it up. Come alone, if you believe me. If you bring the cavalry, I'll understand. Eight p.m."

He clicked off, walked to the next corner, where he tossed the cell down the sewer.

"Trials by the adversarial contest must, in time,
go the way of the ancient trial by battle and blood."

*Warren E. Burger,*
*Fifteenth Chief Justice*
*of the Supreme Court of the United States of America, 1969–1986.*
*Section 5, Lot 7015-2, Grid W-36,*
*Arlington National Cemetery.*

# TWENTY

Patti Rogers had worked with Gabriel Sloan for over five years, and partners in law enforcement, like combat soldiers, grew to have a bond not unlike marriage. She had been teamed with Reeder only a few days, during which time he'd often been remote, and she had at times been filled with doubt about his fitness in the field.

But she had also seen Reeder analyze a crime scene, with a sideways take uniquely his own, and was suitably impressed. Her temporary partner had advised her to follow her instincts, and right now those instincts told her Reeder was right—that Sloan was their Judas made a terrible kind of sense.

Spending working day upon working day with Gabe meant she'd had closer access to the man in recent years than anyone else in the Bureau. And she had, accordingly, noticed changes in him that others may have missed. He'd become less talkative since his daughter's death, and his affable surface seemed something he had to work at.

With a loss such as Gabe had suffered—his marriage had come apart, as well—all that strained behavior was no surprise. In particular he'd seemed distracted, if never quite morose, and she'd tried to give him plenty of space.

Now she found herself looking at Gabe through Reeder's eyes. Had what she'd noticed been something more than grief? Had Sloan been plotting his supreme revenge? All those times in the office or the car, when he seemed only partly with her, had he been planning murder as a means of reconfiguring the high court itself?

From the sidewalk outside Reeder's town house, Rogers and Sloan observed the SWAT team sweeping into the place, the red front door off its hinges. She could only wonder if she'd soon be entering the domain of a manipulative madman.

*Or was she standing next to one?*

Sloan looked toward the broken door, shifting his weight from foot to foot.

"Come on, come on," he muttered.

He might have been anxious for his friend inside, hoping Reeder would surrender so they could take him safely into custody and, please, God, clear the man's name.

*Or he might have been hoping Reeder was in there ready to shoot it out and get taken down, taking to the grave any knowledge of the SAIC's role in the conspiracy.*

The SWAT team came out of the house, and their leader shook his head. "No sign of him—or the daughter!"

"Damn it," Sloan said. He was already striding toward the busted-open front door.

Rogers, working to keep up, said, "Kidnap team is on it. They'll find her, Gabe."

Sloan said nothing, moving inside, and Rogers followed him into the masculine living room with its easy chairs and wall-mounted television. Frowningly taking things in, Sloan wandered toward the dining room. Seeing no reason to follow, Rogers reversed course and went up to the second floor.

In Reeder's home office, her eyes were drawn to the cell phone crushed on the floor. She glanced at the battery on the desk. Reeder knew she was having him traced and had bolted.

He'd left in such a hurry that he hadn't even bothered to turn off his computer.

*Or had he* left *it on—for her to see something?*

She moved the mouse, and the image of Butch Brooks on his bed jumped at her—haloed by the blood-and-brain-spattered headboard, gun that killed Henry Venter in his right hand.

Reeder seemed to whisper in her ear: *Glock's the murder gun, yet Brooks is strictly a wheelman—never a shooter—and left-handed.*

That, according to Reeder, meant Sloan planted the weapon. And it explained why Sloan had left Rogers behind, taking instead Reeder, rusty after years away from the field.

"Somebody must've warned Peep," Sloan said from behind her.

She flinched at that, but turned and covered with an embarrassed smile. "I'm afraid *I* did."

He frowned. "Oh?"

She nodded down at the crushed cell phone. "Must've figured out I was stalling to get the call traced."

"Don't sweat it. Not his first day at the rodeo." He met her eyes. "But not mine, either, Patti. We'll find him."

His eyes lingered on her, and she was just getting uncomfortable when he gestured toward the monitor.

Too casual, he asked, "Why was Peep looking at this crime scene photo, d'you think?"

*And she knew Reeder was right.*

"No idea," she said, too quickly.

*Did Sloan know she knew?*

What now? A game of pretend till one of them made a real slip? A shoot-out in this enclosed space, with the survivor left in one hell of a spot?

Sloan's expression was friendly, but his eyes were cold blue marbles. "What do you think his next move'll be, Patti?"

"I have no way of knowing."

He scratched his head. "Well, I can tell you what it *would* have been, before we got on to him."

"Which is?"

With a matter-of-fact shrug, he said, "Take out Chief Justice Jackson. If he's crazy enough, he may still try."

"Why on earth would he do that?"

Sloan shrugged. "Reeder as much as told us. You were there in the Oval Office, Patti, when he laid the motive out for the Venter and Gutierrez killings."

Nodding, she said, "Change the balance of the Court, yeah. But we found two *more* remote-control kill devices."

"Peep himself said those weren't legitimate attempts."

"Legit or not, Gabe, it made security even tighter around *all* the justices—particularly Van Steenhuyse, Sorenson, Jackson, all the conservatives."

He waved that off. "With Reeder on the task force, working from the inside? Tighter security wouldn't mean shit. Anyway, the point of the devices was to keep the investigation ongoing."

"Why would he want that?"

Sloan cocked his head, which made his smile slant. "Because his job was done. The two conservative justices were dead, certain to be replaced by liberals. Now all he had to do was keep the spotlight on preventing the next kill . . . while he hid in plain sight and the other conspirators faded away."

She was shaking her head. "But now it's not so certain those conservatives will be replaced by liberals. That's the news cycle right now—that the President may appoint a centrist."

"Right. You heard Peep say to Harrison that appointing a more centrist justice, a swing vote, might avoid political blowback."

She shook her head again. "But why even *make* that suggestion to Harrison? With his mission over, the Court's balance changed, the ongoing investigation a sham . . . all he had to do was walk away!"

Sloan's grin was as casual as his eyes were hard. "What better camouflage than Reeder suggesting to the President that a centrist be nominated? Of course, to make sure his scheme worked, he'd have to kill a *third* justice now."

Reeder had made a horrible kind of sense . . . but now so did Sloan. After their years as partners, did Gabe deserve the benefit of the doubt?

There was one way to know . . .

"Let me tell you," she said, jerking a thumb toward the monitor, "what I've taken away from studying this crime scene photo."

"Please."

They both turned to it.

She said, "It's that if *you* hadn't killed him, Butch Brooks might've led us to the conspirators."

His frown was nasty. "Now *you're* second-guessing *me*? What would you do, Rogers, if a slimeball took a shot at *you*?"

She held up a single surrender palm. "Same damn thing. Absolutely. Still, it's unfortunate, isn't it? Brooks and Granger both dead, and Marvin clamming up . . . Of course, who *wouldn't* shut up, in his place?"

"It *is* unfortunate," he admitted. "A bad break. But it is what it is. The only angle I had from the doorway was a head shot."

She sighed, nodded. "I can see that."

He seemed to have nothing else to say. She sure didn't.

Finally he twitched a lame grin and said, "Why don't you go home, Patti, and catch a nap or something? I need you at the Chief Justice's tonight."

"Oh, really? Okay. Sure. Time?"

"Be there at nine o'clock. Jackson and his wife are going out for supper, and I'll be along with a security team to babysit. We'll be back around then or a little later. I want you around for extra firepower in case Reeder is crazy enough to make his play after they get home."

She nodded, started out, then turned. "You want me to drop you at the Hoover Building?"

"No, thanks. I'll catch a ride back. See you at nine."

She'd been dismissed, and that was just fine with her.

In the unmarked Ford, she sat and in her head replayed her conversation with the SAIC several times. Much of what Sloan had said, attributing the Judas role to Reeder, could be read as his own veiled confession. And telling her to meet him at the Chief Justice's residence could be seen as an invitation to bring Reeder in—for an arrest, or a showdown.

She got out her cell, tried the number of Reeder's burn phone, went straight to voice mail. No surprise.

Briefly she considered going to Assistant Director Fisk. But Fisk was the one who'd appointed Gabe Sloan head of the task force, which made her a conspiracy suspect, too.

And the idea of going home and trying to catch a nap, as Sloan suggested, was almost funny.

Instead she headed to Arlington National Cemetery, way early for her meeting with Reeder. Her phone's search engine gave her the location of Edward Washburn Whitaker's grave—a Union brigadier general in the Civil War who'd received the Medal of Honor. A little of his bravery might come in handy about now.

A light, cool wind caught tendrils of her hair and wisped them around. The breeze conspired with a slice of moon and some fast-floating clouds to make the graveyard suitably ghostly. She was shivering a little—maybe more than the temperature called for.

She'd wanted to get there before Reeder. For once, she wanted the upper hand.

But of course, she didn't get it: Barely after six, and already Reeder was waiting for her. He wore black slacks and a black turtleneck with a gray suit jacket. No gun bulge showed, but she knew he'd be armed and ready.

Approaching, she said, "How'd you know I would come alone?"

He shook his head. "I *hoped* you'd come alone."

"I never took you for somebody who leaves much to chance."

"I don't. But I trust my read on people. Even if I did get Gabe Sloan wrong."

Her hair danced in the breeze, tickling her face. "We're *both* taking a hell of a risk. I'm almost positive Sloan knows that *I* know he's the Judas."

"So he might track you by GPS."

"Right. But I don't think so. He's up to something else."

She told him about Sloan having her meet him at nine o'clock at Justice Jackson's residence.

"Don't sweat the GPS," Reeder said. "If you wanted to find me, Patti, and I wasn't at my office or home, where would you check?"

"Here. Arlington."

"And you don't think Gabe knows that? You've known me how many days—he's known me how many years?"

"He'd know."

"Right." He glanced around. "And the police at Arlington are federal. Gabe could've made a call and had me picked up anytime. I've been strolling around here for a couple of hours. Nobody's come near me."

"So he *does* want a showdown."

Reeder grunted something not quite a laugh. "He sure as hell doesn't want me arrested before he can do something about the problem I've become."

She nodded. "Then let's walk into a goddamn DC police station and get your friend Bishop's help. Get your accusations out on the table before Sloan can do anything about it."

His expression was calm, but his eyes were as cold as Sloan's had been. "Tell me. Why didn't you go to Fisk about this? . . . That's what I figured. We don't know *who's* part of the conspiracy, other than it involves law enforcement. No, Patti, we need to take Gabe up on his invitation."

She knew he was right, but hearing it was still like a slap. "Isn't that suicide?"

"Didn't Granger die of 'suicide' in police custody?"

"That doesn't mean you should walk into a trap."

"I *have* to walk into that trap, just like Gabe has to set it. He needs me there when Justice Jackson is murdered, so the frame will fit."

*When Justice Jackson is murdered*—chill words made colder by the breeze.

She said, "If Gabe has a time frame, if he feels this is all about to fall apart on him? *Don't* go."

The wind ruffled Reeder's short white hair. The coldness left his eyes, replaced by moisture. "Patti . . . what else can I do? He has my daughter."

"He also has the federal government behind him."

A nod. "For now. But probably not much longer. Tonight he won't want a huge contingent around. He's been very crafty all through this, running the task force just a little shittily—we were always just a step behind, weren't we? That'll happen when the bad guy is in charge."

"I'm coming with you," she said, stepping forward, fists at her side. "Goddamnit, don't try to stop me."

He gazed at her with something like warmth. "Why, Patti—I wouldn't think of leaving you behind."

". . . No?"

"No. Gabe sent you here with his invitation. If I show up, alone or otherwise, he'll know for sure you delivered it—and that you're on to him. If we don't take him down tonight, Patti . . . tomorrow we'll be as dead as Lee Harvey Oswald, not to mention Jack Ruby."

She swallowed, worked to slow her spinning head. "Maybe we can get some help. There's Bishop and Pellin, friends of yours. Jess Cribbs is a friend of mine."

"But not as good a friend as Gabe Sloan was to me."

That said it all.

"So," she said, trying to sound strong but her voice cracking, "just the two of us, then."

"Just the two of us, partner."

She smiled a little, brushing breeze-driven hair from her face. "What do you have in mind?"

He told her.

"People are very quick to ridicule others for showing fear.
But we rarely know the secret springboards behind human action.
The man who shows great fear today
may be tomorrow's hero.
Who are we to judge?"

*Audie Murphy,*
*most decorated soldier of World War II,*
*Congressional Medal of Honor winner.*
*Section 46, Lot 366-11, Grid O/P-22.5,*
*Arlington National Cemetery.*

# TWENTY-ONE

The gentle breezy evening presented a quiet calm, but Reeder's midsection was tight, a cage for butterflies. Patti Rogers had parked the car behind the nearby elementary school, and the pair hiked through the woods, much as Tom Marvin must have a few nights before. Both agents wore black—turtlenecks, jeans, sneakers.

Reeder had the SIG Sauer in hand, and Rogers carried a Remington 870 shotgun—for the sake of irony, the same model that had killed Justice Gutierrez, but of a more recent vintage. They assumed Sloan, and God knew who else, would be waiting for them at the Justice's mansion-like residence.

They could communicate when separated—Rogers had brought along two walkie-talkies with headsets, tuned to a little-used channel. In the silence of the evening, however, even whispering seemed risky.

They moved slowly, carefully, as soundlessly as possible while picking their way through the woods by the less-than-half-a-moon and some stingy starlight. A twig broken underfoot might initiate a firefight that could see them gunned down before getting anywhere near the Chief Justice, who—like Reeder and probably Rogers—was scheduled to die tonight.

No way to know how many co-conspirators awaited them, or good guys, either, but he and Rogers were surely outnumbered. Reeder was knowingly walking into a frame for the murders of three

Supreme Court justices, designed by a man who knew him well, and who Reeder suspected was at the top of the conspiracy.

*But what other choice did he have?*

If he and Rogers failed tonight, another justice would die, and Amy? Her usefulness to the conspiracy would be over, her chances for survival negligible.

They squatted in the trees behind Jackson's house, near the bottom of the backyard's gentle slope, where not long ago he had broken Tom Marvin's leg with a baton. Bright lights, armed guards, and leashed dogs on patrol might have awaited them, the big brick home a veritable fortress. But what met them was a darkness-shrouded house with no one in back of it.

Typical night sounds kept them company—crickets, a querying owl, fingers of breeze rustling the trees. From the house, nothing at all; the place was as silent as Arlington at midnight.

A horseshoe of woods bordered the near-mansion all the way to the street, with more woods across the way. Reeder pointed to the left and Rogers nodded. Staying within the trees, she moved off in that direction. Within three minutes, she would come up parallel with that side of the house.

He waited. Sloan may well have predicted this approach, and might have a team of accomplices primed to come up through the woods behind Reeder and Rogers. But no sounds indicated that, the crickets and owls and tree rustle unperturbed.

As Reeder saw it, Sloan had only two options.

First, drown the Jackson residence in security, arranging an army to cut Reeder down, with Sloan somehow making Jackson a friendly-fire casualty.

Second, and more likely—minimize tonight's security at the Jacksons', filling the roles with fellow conspirators and/or cannon fodder, a small company of players so that Sloan might more easily stage-manage the Chief Justice's tragic demise.

Judging by the low-key—hell, nonexistent—nature of security in back of the Jackson residence, Sloan was taking the second option.

"*Set,*" Rogers whispered in his ear.

If she'd seen anything, she'd have reported it.

Reeder moved to the right, staying within the trees as Rogers had, coming up alongside the house and finally positioning himself near where the woods gave way to the street. When Chief Justice Jackson and his wife returned from dining out, Reeder would be close by, or as close as he dared.

He needed the confrontation to go down outside—inside the house, Sloan would have a distinct advantage. Reeder had never set foot in there, and the SAIC would know the layout intimately.

But Reeder also wanted to avoid putting the Justice and Mrs. Jackson at risk.

Standard operating procedure would be to whisk the Chief and his wife inside, with some of the security contingent lingering outside, making sure no surprise was coming up behind them, securing the site. If that was the case tonight, Sloan would likely be outside, however briefly, with the Jacksons safely in.

And that was exactly where Reeder wanted his old friend.

No movement in front of the house, either—no standing watch or walking patrol. *How many were inside?* he wondered. Sloan had accompanied the Justice and his wife, with several other agents, probably Secret Service.

The front door opened and a figure stepped onto the portico-covered porch, its amber overhead light glowing: Jessica Cribbs in black, a bulletproof vest discernible over her dark blouse and above dark slacks. She slowly scanned from far left to far right and then back again.

Finally, into a lapel mic, she said, *"Clear,"* then slipped back inside, leaving the door ajar.

That indicated the Jacksons were due any moment.

So there was one agent inside, anyway. Likely more. Her partner, Walt Eaton, maybe. *Did Cribbs's being here make her a Sloan accomplice?* Not necessarily. And Rogers trusted Cribbs, which carried a certain weight.

Still, the smaller the contingent Sloan had assembled tonight, the more likely it consisted of conspirators.

Reeder hunkered at the edge of the trees near the front lawn, waiting, SIG Sauer in hand. His eyes traveled across to the woods that edged the opposite side of the yard, knowing Rogers was there, glad he couldn't make her. The driveway to the attached garage was on her side, but a good chunk of yard separated her from it.

Within a minute, a Lincoln limo rolled into the driveway to a smooth stop. Simultaneously, Cribbs emerged from the house and quickly went to the vehicle.

Reeder poised himself like a track runner waiting for the starting gun.

The driver's side door opened, the dome light revealing Cribbs's partner, Homeland Security Agent Eaton, behind the wheel.

*Not in the house, then,* Reeder thought.

The beefy Eaton got out, opened the back door on his side for Mrs. Jackson, a petite woman perhaps in her sixties, in an evening dress of various shades of blue. Cribbs helped her out, Eaton shut the door, then he and his partner ushered the woman swiftly up the connecting sidewalk to the porch.

Sending Mrs. Jackson in first was probably the Chief Justice's idea—the CJ was the potential target here, after all, so getting her quickly out of any potential line of fire made sense.

But, damnit, Reeder had hoped *both* Jacksons would be inside before he had to act . . .

Sloan got out on the passenger side, providing a view of not much more than his blond head. Secret Service Agent Alan Stein from the task force emerged from the driver's side rear, swiveling his head in an immediate threat-level assessment.

Once the front door of the house had closed behind Eaton, Sloan said, "Your wife is inside, sir." Stein opened the rear driver's side door and Chief Justice Jackson stepped out, followed by Secret Service Agent Ho, sliding over.

Stein, still close to the vehicle, was looking across the vast lawn toward the woods where Reeder crouched, not seeing him. On his feet now, Ho was sweeping his eyes up and down the deserted street. That left Sloan, behind them, to cover the woods on the side where Rogers hid.

But that wasn't what Sloan was doing.

*He was bringing a silenced Glock out from under his shoulder.*

At once, Reeder knew what Sloan intended. The SAIC expected Reeder to break cover and run toward the vehicle, but if he did, the two Secret Service agents would turn their attention his way, to disastrous results.

So, still within the trees, Reeder yelled, *"Behind you! Look out!"*

But even with Reeder not visible, Stein and Ho—their unbuttoned suit coats flapping—swung their attention toward the trees from where he'd called, the latter grabbing an automatic from a hip holster, the former bringing up an MP4 machine gun to bear down on this possible new threat.

Behind them, Sloan's pistol coughed, and Stein's head cracked open like a bloody egg. The agent went limp and fell in a pile.

Reeder flew from the woods and, staying low, weaving, made for the vehicle even as Sloan's pistol coughed a second time, and Ho took the shot in the back of the head and a gob of brain, blood, and bone burst out his torn-open forehead and plopped somewhere, like a flung mud ball, and the muscular agent belly-flopped on the pavement, leaving behind a sparkling crimson mist.

Running across that wide lawn, Reeder glanced occasionally at that front door, where Eaton and Cribbs had gone in. The silenced shots and his shouts might not have alerted them. Even so, the agents would presumably stay put anyway, Mrs. Jackson's safety their priority.

But if either agent emerged to see Reeder sprinting across the grass with a pistol in hand, toward a scene of carnage, Stein and Ho littering the lawn like busted garden gnomes, he might well get caught in a cross fire.

One small blessing was that the Chief Justice had the sense to hit the deck, his tall frame flat on the pavement, as if in imitation of the late Ho.

With Jackson out of her line of fire, that freed Rogers up to let go with her shotgun, her blast narrowly missing Sloan, taking out the limo's front passenger window in a brittle spray of safety glass.

Sloan swung around toward Rogers and the woods and his silenced pistol coughed two more times, fairly blindly, and Rogers fired again, thwacking into the front right fender.

Sloan returned fire as he came around the back of the limo, to the driver's side, then fired toward the moving Reeder, again rather blindly, but the bullets were enough to encourage Reeder to follow the Chief Justice's example and hit the deck, grass cool on his face but in no way soothing.

Turning back toward the woods, Sloan emptied his clip in the general direction of Rogers's gunfire, ejected the clip, slammed in a new one, and fired one in Reeder's direction, a little divot flying up, too close.

Sloan reached down for the Justice, grabbed him by the arm, jerked him to his feet, and got behind the man. The Justice was tall, making a damn good human shield.

"Stand up and be counted, Peep!" Sloan called. His voice had a manic edge Reeder had never heard before.

*Was Rogers maneuvering around to get a better shot? Christ, he hoped so . . .*

"I'm comfy right here, Gabe," Reeder said, close enough not to need to yell.

*Those shotgun blasts should have alerted them in the house—where were Eaton and Cribbs?*

*Or were they Sloan's?*

"Get on your feet, Peep. Come closer. You have a right to a ringside seat. You'll be taking the credit, after all."

He risked looking up a little. Sloan's eyes were wide and crazed, but then so were Chief Justice Jackson's, shaking in his gray Brooks Brothers like a skeleton doing a dance.

"Really, Gabe? You *really* think these atrocities honor Kathy's memory?"

"Don't waste your time, Peep. I'm way past sentiment. Get up and come over, or I'll just shoot the Justice now. Time's limited. Even out here in the boonies, *somebody* may have heard that shotgun. *You're back there, aren't you, Patti? Let me have it with that baby, why don't you? Of course,* Jackson *will get it as bad as me!"*

Sloan was right. No matter what position Rogers maneuvered herself into, Jackson would almost certainly be collateral damage.

*Where were Eaton and Cribbs?* And would they ride to his rescue, or ambush his ass?

Reeder got to his feet but kept the SIG Sauer trained. He had a decent shot at Sloan's head, mostly exposed next to Jackson's. Getting closer was not a bad idea. A head shot would take Gabe out, shutting off his motor reflexes like a switch. No danger of Jackson dying, despite the silenced pistol in his neck.

"Yes, yes, Peep, come on over . . . good. Good. No, let's hold it right there. A little respectful distance will do us both some good."

"I agree," Reeder said, weapon still aimed at Sloan. "I don't want you anywhere near my gun. Killing the Chief Justice with your own piece wouldn't do—you need me to give up mine so you can shoot me, and then the Chief Justice, with it."

Sloan gave the Justice a nudge in the neck with the silenced pistol. "Oh, this *is* your gun, Peep. Seems you bought it from a guy I know who could use a friend in the Bureau about now."

The Justice looked faint, like he might collapse, the dignity of his bench worlds away.

"Gabe . . . I understand. I really do. If something happened to Amy, I'd go as crazy as you losing Kathy. We really *were* friends, right? So how could you *do* this? Oh, I don't mean killing right-wing bastards like Jackson here."

The hostage's wide eyes tightened. *This* was the man pleading his case?

Reeder continued: "But taking Amy. *Kidnapping* her. How the hell could you stoop that fucking low? After everything, after all these years?"

Sloan's eyes glittered with moisture. And insanity. "How could *you?* How could you love your daughter so little that you didn't back off when I told you to? What the hell kind of man, what the hell kind of *father,* are you, Peep?"

"Tell me you won't hurt Amy."

"That I will give you, Peep. I promise that when you are dead and this quivering piece of shit here is likewise, she will go free."

*A head shot and the Justice would be saved.*

But killing Sloan might cost Amy's life.

Sloan did have affection for Amy, and the man was, after all, motivated by good things that got twisted into something foul. But with Sloan gone, would the others working with him see Amy as anything but a loose end that needed clipping?

*Where was Rogers?*

*Where were Eaton and Cribbs?*

*And where were the fucking cops?*

As if in answer to that last question, a distant siren teased him.

"Gabe, you can see we've got a standoff here. Let's take it down a couple of notches, and you can tell me where Amy is and explain to the world how the tragedy that befell your daughter inspired your righteous actions. That you were a patriot in this."

"I *am* a patriot . . ."

"You are. You think I don't share your views. But I do. *I* was the bleeding-heart liberal all these years, remember. You've done a real service, exposing what Jackson and these other fascist justices did to our country."

Jackson gaped at Reeder while Sloan said, "You are goddamned right I did."

"So let Amy go. Let me go. Let me go to Amy. And tell the world your story. But not the story of a madman. The story of a patriot."

Sloan swallowed, eyes still glittering. "I'm not that easily manipulated, old friend. Goddamn you, anyway."

The siren seemed not so distant now.

"You ruined things from the start," Sloan continued, "analyzing that damn security footage. And, Jesus, did you *have* to talk Harrison out of appointing liberal replacements?"

"That's what you get, Gabe, not bringing me in at the start of your coup."

Sloan almost yelled in Jackson's ear: "You are going to *die* because of *this* do-gooder, Your Honor! Because he's the one who made a third justice death mandatory. Must be done, to make sure what I've accomplished was for a reason."

Jackson found the nerve to growl, "A *reason?*"

"A reason! I'm fixing what you fucking broke, you dithering piece of shit. My daughter didn't *have* to die. She wouldn't have, before you came along. And now a new, more liberal Court will reestablish Roe v. Wade. And all the girls like Kathy, like Amy, will be safe from the interference of old white men like you."

Reeder said, "You almost certainly have already made that happen. You've said I'm your best friend. Do you really want to murder me, or frame me into lethal injection? Do you want to put Amy through that? Haven't you done enough to her already? Put the gun down, Gabe. It's over. Hear those sirens? Your window has closed. Let's stop this right here."

Rustling trees announced Rogers finally emerging from the woods, coming around the front end of the limo; but she had no shotgun in her grasp. She did have a gun—a Glock . . .

. . . at her temple.

Courtesy of a glowering Walt Eaton.

"We're not stopping *anything*," Eaton said. "I have too much riding on this."

Rogers gave Reeder a look that mingled apology and fear.

This left Reeder facing two gunmen, each with a human shield, one right in front of him, the other to his left. Chances were, if he killed one, the other would kill him, and Rogers. And the Chief Justice.

And what would happen to Amy?

*Help was coming. Should he just wait it out? Stall some more?*

"Put the gun on the ground, Peep," Sloan said, aware of the sirens nearing, and a new sound: a helicopter.

Reeder shot Sloan in the head and blood spatter kissed the Justice's cheek. Eaton, horrified and amazed, swung his gun away from Rogers's temple and toward Reeder, but a second head shot ended that ambition, Rogers lurching from Eaton's grasp as he fell like a bag of cement from a high window.

Sloan, a hole in his forehead, eyes wide with surprise, slid down to sit slumped against the limo like a kid in the corner taking a time-out. The Chief Justice moved away and stood slouching, with a hand on his forehead as if taking his own temperature. He seemed to be trying not to throw up.

Rogers rushed to Reeder, who said, "Go inside and make sure Mrs. Jackson is all right."

With a nod, she went off to do that.

Reeder approached the Chief Justice. "Are you all right, sir? My apologies for some of my remarks."

Jackson's face was the color of wet newspaper. "My God . . . we survived it. Thanks to you, we survived it. You handled him . . . handled him *very* well, Mr. Reeder. Was he *really* your friend?"

"Apparently not," Reeder said.

Soon Rogers came running back, and she was holding off tears. "Jess Cribbs is in there with her head caved in. Fucking Eaton must have pistol-whipped her. I don't get a pulse. Mrs. Jackson was locked in a closet. She's okay. I've called 911, but . . ."

She trailed off because the sirens were on them, the flashing lights, too, as well as the churning blades of a chopper.

"Oh, Joe," Rogers said, clutching his arm. "You took such a terrible risk."

"You were safe. The Justice, too. A head shot stops all motor skills."

"No, I don't mean that. I mean . . . *Amy.* With Sloan dead, how do we find Amy?"

"I think I know where she is," he said. "But even if I'm wrong, she'll be fine."

"She will?"

He nodded. "One thing Gabe Sloan wouldn't do is hurt his goddaughter."

"You're sure of that?"

"Of course," he said. "I'm the people reader, remember? Goddamnit, I *hope* I am . . ."

He sat suddenly, almost collapsing, onto the sloping lawn. He began to cry, a sobbing man in the company of so many littered corpses.

Rogers leaned down and put a hand on his shoulder. "No time for self-pity, Joe."

The lights of the helicopter were strobing the area as it set down on the street. She was having to talk over its churning blades.

"If you know where your daughter is," Rogers yelled at him, "I think our ride is here."

"Our most basic common link
is that we all inhabit this planet.
We all breathe the same air.
We all cherish our children's future.
And we are all mortal."

*John Fitzgerald Kennedy,*
*Thirty-Fifth President of the United States of America,*
*former senator and representative*
*from the Commonwealth of Massachusetts.*
*Section 45, Grid U-35,*
*Arlington National Cemetery.*

# TWENTY-TWO

The chopper had barely touched down when its back door whammed open and three Kevlar-clad agents clambered out, pistols at the ready. They closed in on the two subjects standing near four fallen, in the apparent aftermath of a shooting. Uniformed police from patrol cars went to Justice Jackson, who hugged his arms to himself as if chilled, down where the driveway met the street.

Reeder and Rogers had their hands up, though the latter held her FBI ID wallet open in her right hand.

"Special Agent Rogers!" she called, working to get over the copter noise.

The front passenger-side door of the helicopter swung open, and Assistant Director Fisk stepped out and down, her perfect dark hair barely impacted by the slowing blades, though her gray pantsuit flapped like a flag.

Fisk came over, weaving her way through and around the bodies.

"Jesus God," she muttered, eyeing the dead. Then louder: "What the hell's going on here?"

Though Reeder was in something like shock in the aftermath of the shooting, he remained driven by the need to get to his daughter. He took a step forward to meet Fisk, and the Kevlar-vested agents moved with him.

Rogers, in better shape to do the briefing, cut in front of Reeder, holding him back like a crossing guard. She filled Fisk in quickly but thoroughly, the AD wearing an astounded expression but asking no questions.

That expression may be what prompted Chief Justice Jackson to interrupt, pointing to the dead Sloan, saying, "That man confessed to killing Henry and Rodolfo." Then he pointed to Reeder. "*That* man saved my life."

Fisk swung to the agents who still had the drop on Reeder: "*Lower those weapons!* Mr. Reeder, we all owe you a debt of thanks."

"I'll collect right now," he said. "I need to get to my daughter."

Rogers touched Reeder's arm and said, "Let me . . ."

In a swift but businesslike fashion, she filled Fisk in on that aspect.

Then Fisk asked Reeder, "Will your daughter be in a hostage situation?"

His breathing was almost back to normal. "Doubtful. Sloan was her godfather. I don't think he would hurt Amy. My opinion is that he and Eaton were the key conspirators, with few, if any, confederates at large."

"But Sloan *did* kidnap her," Fisk said.

"Yes, though I imagine he did so under false pretenses, not force."

Fisk thought for a moment. "I'm sending one of my SWAT agents with you. You need to leave the weapon you used in this firefight here at the crime scene, Mr. Reeder, but we'll fix you up with another sidearm. Agent Rogers, do you have a sidearm?"

"Not presently."

"Go get yourself one, and Mr. Reeder."

"Yes, Director."

Rogers went off to do that, and Fisk gave Reeder a tight smile and stuck out her hand, which he shook.

"Go get your daughter, Mr. Reeder. And by the way . . ."

"Yes."

"Thank you for your service to our country . . . even if the President you saved *was* a jackass."

She grinned at him, and the surprise of it was enough to get a smile out of him, as well.

Within scant minutes, Reeder, Rogers, and a Kevlar-vested agent boarded the Sikorsky 60.

Fisk leaned in to tell the pilot to fire up the engine and to "take Mr. Reeder here where he wants to go. But keep me informed."

The pilot nodded while Fisk returned to personally supervising the crime scene, which was already turning into a carnival of lights, bodies live and dead, and technology.

Reeder was in the front rider's seat with Rogers right behind him and the SWAT agent next to her. Rogers and Reeder had both been on copters before and quickly got with the program, closing their doors and donning headsets, the latter making in-flight conversation possible.

The fortyish pilot, who in his time had seen everything twice, asked, "Where to?"

He might have been a cabdriver.

Reeder said, "Shenandoah Mountain ridge."

"Maybe a little more specific, Mr. Reeder?"

"US Highway Thirty-Three, Rawley Springs. Emergency situation."

"Understood."

The pilot eased back on the stick and the chopper slowly lifted. When they were above the electrical wires and the treetops, the seasoned flier hit the throttle, hurtling the aircraft through the night sky, southwest bound.

"ETA?" Reeder asked him.

"How long's it take you by car?"

"Three hours. A little more."

"We'll be there under two."

Reeder's stomach did a flip, and it had nothing to do with fear of flying. "Can you make it an hour?"

"In daylight, no wind, maybe. But at night?"

"My daughter's been kidnapped. We're headed to where I think she's being kept."

The pilot said nothing but goosed the throttle and the air speed gauge went from 170 knots to north of two hundred. They were already out of the DC metro area, the ribbon of headlights that was I-95 disappearing as the chopper turned farther west.

Rogers's voice came through the headset: "What's our destination?"

Reeder said, "Sloan has a rustic cabin in the mountains off US Highway Thirty-Three. Been in his family for generations."

"I heard you two talking about it. No cell service, no TV?"

"Right. I'm betting that's where Sloan put her."

"Put her . . . how?"

"Amy and Gabe were close—he knew how down I am about her and that Landon kid. I figure he showed up on her doorstep and gave her a birthday present—weekend at the cabin with Bobby. Maybe even said it was my idea, that I'd come to my senses."

"Would Amy have driven there herself?"

"She doesn't have a car, and neither does the Landon kid."

"Gabe drove her."

"No task force business last night. Yes. He drove her."

How sure of himself he sounded.

*Tell that to his stomach . . .*

They flew through a darkness only occasionally leavened by the lights of some hamlet. He seemed to exist in an enclosed limbo where dashboard glow was his only reality, where his confidence that he was right, and his hope for Amy's welfare, could not burn bright enough to light the way through all this goddamned darkness.

An eternity passed, and the pilot said, "Should be close to where you want to be."

Reeder's heart raced as he looked into nothing. Then the pilot toggled a switch and, from the underside of the chopper, a flood-lamp spilled light, illuminating a two-lane road.

The pilot said, "Highway Thirty-Three."

Straining against his seat belt, Reeder searched for any recognizable landmark. Not a lot in the way of towns or businesses out this way.

The pilot said, "Rawley Springs, up ahead."

Reeder pointed out at the darkness and said, "Just outside of town, highway curves left, but a dirt road veers off right."

"That's the way to the cabin?"

"That's the way."

They flew over the unincorporated little town, likely waking up more than a few residents.

When the chopper found the dirt road, the pilot followed it through a wooded area and up a mountainous ridge.

Perhaps ten minutes later Reeder pointed. *"There."*

The thickness of trees left the pilot little room for error as they followed the dirt road into a small clearing, where Sloan's cabin sat on a flat spot near the top of the ridge.

"Can you land there?" Reeder asked.

"Tight," the pilot said.

"Try that." Reeder pointed out a spot beside the cabin about where Sloan usually parked his car—just big enough for the Sikorsky. Maybe.

As the chopper descended, the spotlight turned night to noon around the rustic two-story cabin. The front door flew open and a figure emerged—Bobby Landon in a pair of boxer shorts, shielding his eyes with a raised forearm, not just from the brightness but dust the rotors were kicking up.

*Okay, the kid was all right, but where was Amy?*

"That's a friendly," Reeder told their FBI chaperone via headset mic. "I see no sign of vehicles. Patti, I think they're alone . . . but stay frosty."

"Copy that," she said.

The helicopter touched down and settled, and as the pilot cut the engine, Reeder jerked off the headset, released his seat belt, and threw open his door. Behind him, Rogers did the same.

When the trio stepped down, both Rogers and the SWAT guy had their handguns poised, but Reeder didn't bother. Everything was all right. It had to be.

*But where was Amy?*

And then there she was, belting up a shorty robe, her hair tousled, no makeup, irritation clenching her pretty features, rushing out barefoot.

"*Daddy!*" she blurted.

Then reeled back as she saw Rogers and the other armed agent approaching, though her father was in the lead, patting the air gently with his palms.

"Everything's okay, sweetie . . . Are you alone up here?"

"Just Bobby and me . . . Goddamnit, Daddy, isn't this a little *extreme,* even for *you?*"

And he went to her laughing, crying, taking her into his arms, holding her close, and she squirmed at first, but then, for all her confused irritation, she was hugging him back.

Rogers edged up to him. "I'll get word to your ex-wife! And I'll fill Bobby in. Let's take it inside."

Reeder nodded to his partner gratefully and, with his arm around his daughter, walked the girl inside Gabriel Sloan's cabin. Sidearm holstered, the SWAT guy and a confused, rattled Bobby were bringing up the rear.

In the hours and days to come, with Rogers helming the task force, Reeder would learn that Sloan and Eaton were indeed the chief conspirators. That former Fairfax County Deputy Eaton had recruited Granger, Brooks, and Marvin and funded their robberies, by way of creating fall guys. That Eaton's motivation was money and career advancement, and that he'd murdered Granger. That Sloan had indeed given Amy a "birthday present" of a weekend away at his cabin.

And of course Reeder would have to tell his daughter the awful truth about her godfather.

But for now, nothing else mattered but Amy.

# SUPREME THANKS

My co-plotter/researcher, Matt Clemens, and I wish to cite the following books: *The Supreme Court Explained* by Ellen Greenberg, Norton Publishing, 1997; *The Complete Idiot's Guide to the Supreme Court* by Lita Epstein, Alpha, 2004; and *Images of America: Arlington National Cemetery* by George W. Dodge, Arcadia Publishing, 2006.

Thanks to Chris Kauffman (ret.), Van Buren County Sheriff's Office, for weapon information; and to mystery writers Alan S. Orloff and Eleanor Jones for geographical material concerning the DC metro area.

Special thanks to Aimee Hix, our go-to person for all things DC.

Also, thanks to agent Dominick Abel; Jacque Ben-Zekry of the Amazon Author Team; and Thomas & Mercer editor Alan Turkus.

# ABOUT THE AUTHOR

Photograph by John Deason

MAX ALLAN COLLINS has earned an unprecedented nineteen Private Eye Writers of America "Shamus" nominations, winning for his Nathan Heller novels *True Detective* (1983) and *Stolen Away* (1991), receiving the PWA life achievement award, the Eye, in 2007. In 2012, his Nathan Heller saga was honored with the PWA Hammer Award for making a major contribution to the private eye genre.

His graphic novel *Road to Perdition* (1998) is the basis of the Academy Award–winning Tom Hanks film, followed by two acclaimed prose sequels and several graphic novels. He has created a number of innovative suspense series, including Mallory, Quarry, Eliot Ness, and the "Disaster" series. He is completing a number of Mike Hammer novels begun by the late Mickey Spillane; his audio novel *The New Adventures of Mike Hammer: The Little Death* won a 2011 Audie.

His many comics credits include the syndicated strip *Dick Tracy;* his own *Ms. Tree; Batman;* and *CSI: Crime Scene Investigation,* based on the TV series for which he wrote ten bestselling novels. His tie-in books have appeared on the *USA Today* bestseller list nine times and the *New York Times* three. With frequent collaborator Matthew Clemens, he wrote the Thriller Award–nominated *You Can't Stop Me* and its sequel *No One Will Hear You*. His movie novels include *Saving Private Ryan, Air Force One,* and *American Gangster* (IAMTW Best Novel "Scribe" Award, 2008).

An independent filmmaker in the Midwest, Collins has written and directed four features, including the Lifetime movie *Mommy* (1996), and he scripted *The Expert,* a 1995 HBO World Premiere, and *The Last Lullaby* (2008), based on his novel *The Last Quarry.* His documentary *Mike Hammer's Mickey Spillane* (1998/2011) appears on the Criterion Collection DVD and Blu-ray of *Kiss Me Deadly.*

His play *Eliot Ness: An Untouchable Life* was nominated for an Edgar Award in 2004 by the Mystery Writers of America; a film version, written and directed by Collins, was released on DVD and appeared on PBS stations in 2009.

His other credits include film criticism, short fiction, songwriting, trading-card sets, and video games. His coffee-table book, *The History of Mystery,* was nominated for every major mystery award, and his *Men's Adventure Magazines* (with George Hagenauer) won the Anthony Award.

Collins lives in Muscatine, Iowa, with his wife, writer Barbara Collins; as "Barbara Allan," they have collaborated on nine novels, including the successful Trash 'n' Treasures mysteries, their *Antiques Flee Market* (2008) winning the *Romantic Times* Best Humorous Mystery Novel Award in 2009. Their son, Nathan, is a Japanese-to-English translator, working on video games, manga, and novels.